For the Love of My Enemy

For the Love of My Enemy

M. E. Blaustone

Two Sisters Press

Copyright 2024 by M. E. Blaustone

All Rights Reserved

Published by Golden Bridges Publishing, LLC, Pittsburgh, PA.
www.goldenbridgespublishing.com

ISBN (hardcover): 979-8-9907356-1-3
ISBN (softcover): 979-8-9891040-9-3
ISBN (EBook): 979-8-9907356-0-6
Printed in the United States

Library of Congress Control Number: 2024938876

To Christopher, the love of my life

CONTENTS

CONTENTS

Author's Note

Acknowledgments

My head literally swims when I think of the many people who inspired and encouraged me to write *For the Love of My Enemy*. Seriously, it makes me dizzy. And so, I will, to the best of my ability, attempt to do justice to the following.

First out of the box, I'd like to thank my friend and mentor, Francine Rivers. Francine didn't know me when I first reached out to her five years ago to ask if she would meet up with me so that I could ask her some questions about writing novels. Graciously, she did just that. She sat with me for hours on different occasions in a coffee shop, telling me her stories and then listening to me ramble on about mine. She was the second person to read for me (after my husband, Chris). Then email after email...she was there for me. Her encouraging words and belief that I actually could write was everything I needed to take my first baby steps. She will forever be one of my all-time favorite authors and favorite humans on the planet.

I wouldn't have been able to even begin writing this novel without Steven Lehman and the Windsor Historical Society. From my very first meeting with Steve, he became a tremendous resource of historical information on Camp Windsor, as well as the town of Windsor. I'm truly grateful for his kindness and support. If I could choose one word to describe the Windsor Historical Society and what it's like to walk through the museum doors, the first word that comes to mind is magical.

To everyone who read for me, however I referred to you. Whether the Alphas or Betas... You know who you are. You are the ones who faithfully, patiently, and graciously read through my unedited manuscript.

You gave me your unfettered critique and advice. You didn't hold back. Thank you, from the bottom of my heart. You are precious to me.

To Chantelle Bogue, who designed the gorgeous, ethereal bicycle graphic for my book cover. Chantelle, you are a goddess of design. Whenever I would sit at my computer to write, I would look at that picture and be transported back in time. It became my muse, and I would think to myself, *Adina rode that bicycle... I'm just sure of it.*

Lastly, to my husband, Christopher...the man I call The Love of My Life. He's my loudest cheerleader, and my biggest fan. My rock. Thank you, my Love, for allowing me to read to you late at night. The story came to life as I did. This one is definitely for you.

Author's Note

From 1942 through 1945, more than 425,000 Axis prisoners were shipped to the United States. They were detained in 686 camps located across the US. One hundred seventy-five branch camps served 511 smaller area camps. Most were located in the South and Southwest, with some in the Great Plains and Midwest.

Publisher's Note

Many of the German POWs, like some you'll meet in this story, vehemently opposed Hitler and the Nazi regime and were conscripted into the German military. Those who tried to resist or claim conscientious objector status were sent to military prisons or concentration camps for the crime of "pacifism." While the evil of the Nazis should never be understated or excused, we feel it is also important to remember that fascist leaders target *anyone* who disagrees with them, even if that person looks like one of their own. As the world is racked by war yet again, we urge readers to use discernment and not judge an individual solely by the government under which they happened to be born.

The following story is a work of fiction. Though Camp Windsor was a real place, names, characters, and incidents are products of the author's imagination, and are not to be construed as real. Any resemblance to actual events, organizations, or persons living or dead, is entirely coincidental.

1

Going Home, October 2011

Death was the last thing on Adina Ableman's mind.

It was true, she was dying. Her doctor confirmed it, and her body screamed of it every waking moment of every day. But she refused to give the idea of it any thought. Not today. The eighty-five-year-old woman sat quietly with her eyes closed in the back seat of a Ford Expedition. Her daughter, Talia, or Tali as Adina lovingly called her, sat next to her, nervously looking out the window. Highway 101 sped by in a blur of rain mixed with color and fog.

Adina woke the morning of their departure in pain. This wasn't anything new for her. She had been diagnosed with cancer many years prior. First in her breast in her late fifties. She conquered that battle, only to have to fight it again when it came back with a vengeance in her colon. She was then seventy-nine years old. Two surgeries and two rounds of chemotherapy gave her three more years. She wasn't completely cancer free, but with the aid of medication, she was well enough for a temporary truce. Yet cancer isn't fair. It doesn't play by the rules.

Six months ago, Adina's oncologist met with her to inform her that her war was over. She would need to surrender this one. Nothing more could be done for her, and there was no more mercy to be had.

Talia pleaded with her mother to cancel the trip. Adina would have none of it.

Their flight from Pittsburgh to Oakland had been delayed several hours due to bad weather. It was the end of October, and the East Coast was already experiencing its share of early winter. The two spent several hours waiting in the airport for the weather to clear. The physical toll this took on Adina was evident, yet she never complained.

After twenty hours of waiting and air travel, they finally arrived in the Bay Area.

Fifty-nine years had passed since Adina last saw her hometown of Windsor, California. When she married her husband, Joseph Ableman, in 1949, she didn't intend on leaving the only home she'd ever known. She figured that she and Joe would put down their own roots in the small community. But in 1950, the opportunity of a high-paying job and a new life in Pennsylvania presented itself. With Joe having family in Pittsburgh, he strongly felt it was an opportunity they couldn't pass up. Adina wasn't so sure that she believed the same, but she believed in Joseph. He was her rock, her stability in more ways than one. Because of her trust and growing love for him, they made the move to the other side of the United States. Sadly, Adina's father, Henry, died of a massive heart attack just two years later. She made one last trip back to Windsor in 1952 to bury her father and close his affairs. There was nothing left for her in the small town after that. She hadn't been back since.

Adina wished she and Talia were traveling under better circumstances, such as visiting friends who were still living. She wished her body were whole and in less pain, at least for her daughter's sake.

Adina never talked much about her upbringing, though there were times when she'd speak of the lovely landscape of Sonoma County. The vineyard-covered hills and valleys, prune farms, and the Pacific Ocean, or "the coast," as she referred to it. She reminisced about the colors of the vineyard leaves in autumn, and how the hills seemed to roll in fiery tones of red, brown, and gold. The colors shined so bright in the sunlight it would hurt her eyes to look at them, yet they were just too beautiful to look away.

She remembered the unique smells of the area: eucalyptus, bay leaf, and summer jasmine, as well as cedar and oak trees. And the smell of the Pacific Ocean—how it would drift over the western hillsides when the offshore breezes blew. Certain fragrances would trigger specific memories for Adina. When Joseph was still alive, he and Tali found amusement in Adina's ability to remember an event in detail, simply by taking in a sudden aroma. Bread baking in an oven, for instance. Or the burning of autumn leaves. Now and again, Adina would inhale, and she would remember.

There were those memories she spoke of openly, such as the death of her mother, Luisa, when Adina was twelve years old. Adina remembered her as the most beautiful angel of a woman she had ever seen, with a heart to match. It was obvious why her father fell madly in love with Luisa. She had a rare beauty that some described as exotic. Dark, wavy hair the color of molasses. Adina's hair, now thin and silvery gray, was once the same delicious color. Her mother's eyes, as Adina recalled them, were a sunny brown. They would sparkle like the sun shining off the river on a summer day. Adina's eyes were a perfect combination of her mother's brown and her father's blue. Some people called them hazel blue and some hazel green, depending on the weather, or the clothing she wore that day.

Luisa carried herself in such a way that she often appeared taller than her five-foot-five stature and slight frame. She was bold, confident, and respected. Yet it wasn't only her mother's outward beauty that distinguished her. Luisa Robbins was a genuinely good soul. She tirelessly gave of herself to anyone, at any time. Whether it was her deep, selfless love and care for Adina and Henry or tending to Henry's weekly patients, she was always the servant. Luisa had been Henry's righthand nurse for many years, working alongside him since the day they were first married. Even after they moved to the United States from Lithuania, she continued to be the one and only nurse in their small-town practice. And though her life and light were extinguished when Adina was very young, Adina would forever miss her.

Grief-stricken after the death of his wife, Dr. Henry Robbins poured himself into his work. He didn't have the time or the energy to be emotionally available for Adina during her tender teenage years. She had to grow up faster than any twelve-year-old should ever have to, and she did it alone, without any brothers or sisters, and without her dear, sweet mother.

It was then that Adina decided to become a nurse. She was young and didn't quite see herself as the selfless giver her mother had been. It could have been that becoming a nurse was some selfish way of hanging onto her memory—a tangible connection of sorts to the great beyond. Nonetheless, she resolved to study hard to earn her nursing certificate. She would work to make her mother proud. Making her father proud would be a task that would prove to be much more difficult. At sixteen years old, Adina graduated high school and then was accepted into the Santa Rosa School of Nursing. The demand for nurses in the United States was high during the war—"that godforsaken war," she called it. Medical professionals enlisted in droves to help the effort overseas. Because of this, many nursing schools lowered their requirements to become a licensed nurse. Adina achieved her certificate just before her eighteenth birthday. She then stepped into her mother's role of nursing alongside her father.

It was that war that now brought Adina and her daughter back to the small town of Windsor, more than sixty years later.

The SUV continued down Highway 101, and Talia's eyebrows creased as she watched her mother resting.

"What is it, Tali? Why are you looking at me?" Adina said without opening her eyes.

"Geez, Mom. How'd you know I was looking at you?"

Adina chuckled. She turned her head to her daughter and opened her eyes. Neither age nor fatigue could obscure the beauty of her eyes. "Talia, I know you. I know you hated the idea of coming here. I know you're worried about me."

Tali laid her hand on Adina's knee. "You're right. I am worried about you. You're much too fragile for a trip like this. Your doctors told you not to overexert yourself. No unnecessary risks, remember? What in the world could be important enough to fly across the US on a moment's notice?"

Three months ago, the Windsor Historical Society sent Adina a handwritten letter saying they'd received an important piece of history that she might be connected to. The director of the historical society wasn't clear as to what the item was, only that the name Adina Luisa Robbins was written inside it. He also said it may have something to do with Camp Windsor. Adina hadn't shared this with Talia.

"Mom, please," Talia said, grabbing hold of Adina's hand. "I'm trying to understand the urgency of this trip. I've taken time off work, set my life aside, even ignored common sense to get you on a plane." Tears pooled in her eyes. "Your body's failing. You're weak. I'm afraid this trip may be the death of you, and I'm the one who agreed to it. Just the thought that I could lose precious time with you because we took this risk... It makes me sick to my stomach." She squeezed her mother's hand, her eyes tenderly pleading. "Please, Mama. I need you to be honest with me. No more hiding."

She called her "Mama." Adina knew her daughter only did that when she felt lost or afraid. She took hold of Talia's hand. Her own fingers were aged and crooked, much smaller than Talia's. The skin on top was mottled and thin as tissue paper. She looked up into Tali's eyes. Eyes that looked more like her husband Joseph's, filled with so much love and concern. So much questioning. Not unlike her own eyes, once, desperately seeking truth.

"Forgive me," Adina said.

Tali raised her head, her eyes wide.

"I'm so sorry," Adina whispered. "I never meant to hide from you. Truly, I never thought I was. I may have been quiet about things, but I never thought of it as hiding."

She struggled for words. How would she be able to tell her daughter the story of who she was back then? Especially after she had buried it so deep for so long. She thought she'd forgotten. The camp. The ache deep within her heart.

"Your father wasn't the first—" She paused and for a moment seemed to look through her daughter and to the memories she knew she needed to face. Reaching up, she gently cupped Tali's cheek. Oh, how she loved her, and she knew she needed to tell her everything. She had buried the memory of that life and felt for sure that digging it up would disturb the preciousness of what once was. Like breaking the lock on a treasure chest filled with a love so pure, so true. Once opened, its contents would vaporize and float away. Yet it was that treasured love that brought her here, back to her once beloved hometown.

"I had another love before your father."

Tali's eyebrows raised.

"I thought I'd forgotten," Adina continued. "I tried to forget. But how does one forget their first love?" She stared out the window through streaking beads of rain to the rolling green hills beyond. "I could never forget."

2

June 1944

The early morning sunrise projected a cinema of pink and purple clouds pillowed above the eastern hillside. A thick coastal fog had rolled in the night before, leaving a layer of mist on everything that had all but burned off in the warmth of the morning sun.

Adina Robbins ran out the back door and down the porch steps. She buttoned up a light sweater and grabbed her bicycle as two P-51 Mustangs roared overhead. She was used to it. The United States Army had taken over the local Santa Rosa airport two years ago. Then last year, the Air Corps came in and turned it into a training site for fighter squadrons. Planes were a constant feature in the blue skies above Windsor.

"Adina Luisa," her father called out. He stood in the front entrance of the clinic that sat at the corner of their property on Redwood Road. "I have one more delivery for you to take." He held out a small, brown paper sack.

She glanced at her wristwatch, the one that once belonged to her mother. It was a quarter past seven in the morning. She wanted to get to the Groceteria before it was too late.

"Take this," he said, handing her the bag. "Mrs. Walters telephoned as soon as I walked through the door this morning. She's out of her ferrous sulfate." Dr. Henry Robbins stood there looking as though he'd been up and working for hours. He wore a stark white lab coat with two fountain pens neatly tucked in the upper left pocket and a wound-up stethoscope protruding from the hip pocket. Under the lab coat, he wore his usual gray wool slacks, starched-collar white shirt, and bow tie. He had a thinning shock of black hair flecked with silver, which he Bryled and combed straight back. A thick, matching mustache above his lip connected to a well-groomed, graying beard. Round-rimmed wire glasses sat on a pronounced, bulb-tipped nose. "Take it to her first thing, Adina."

Adina rolled her eyes, strapping the bag down on the storage rack behind the bicycle seat. Her front basket was already crammed full. The day-to-day tasks of working in a small-town doctor's office weren't exactly her idea of excitement. Taking temperatures, giving vitamin B injections, and helping to set the occasional broken bone didn't quite live up to a young girl's dream of adventure. And then with the endless medicine deliveries. More than anything else, Adina wanted to serve in the Women's Army Nursing Corps. Now *there* was adventure.

"Papa, what do you suppose you would do if you didn't have me around?"

Papa's left eyebrow raised to its usual position of questioning. "What exactly is that supposed to mean?"

She weighed her words. Why was it that her tongue knotted whenever he questioned her? Her answers were never perfect and never enough, but the words flew from her mouth with swift ease. "Even Jeanie Mae is joining the WAC, and her parents are allowing her to do it. At least she'll contribute to this godforsaken war...even if I can't."

There, she said it. She waited, jutting her eyes to the side, anticipating his response.

"I suggest you take a room at Jeanie Mae O'Brien's home," he said, his Lithuanian accent still thick after all these years in America. "I'm sure her mother and father would be delighted to board you. Maybe then you'd be able to take up your cause."

Papa was adept at putting Adina in her place, but he wasn't a very good communicator—unless he was answering a medical question. When Adina was studying for her nursing exams, she was sure to do it when Papa was nearby and she could engage him in an in-depth conversation on a medical subject, such as the skeletal structure of the hand. She learned early on that if she purposely pronounced a term wrong, saying something like "metacarpalaries" instead of "metacarpals," Papa would interject, "No, no, no. That is not correct. The correct pronunciation of the word is—" He would then sit next to her, sketch a diagram of the hand, labeling all its bones, and talk her through the correct pronunciation of each one. It wasn't much, but for Adina, it was everything.

"Papa, would it be all right if I dropped the meds off to Mrs. Walters later? I wanted to stop at the Groceteria before—"

"Do not argue with me, Adina. First thing, yes?" He retrieved a clean handkerchief from his pocket and wiped a smudge from his glasses. "And do not forget, I have a very important meeting later this afternoon. I might be home later than what is usual."

She huffed and hopped on the bicycle, riding down the dirt drive.

"Adina Luisa, you heard me?" he called out.

"I heard!" she yelled back and stepped up her pace.

———————————

Adina pedaled down Redwood Road toward town. She loved early morning rides, with the smell of wet earth and the feel of damp, cold air blowing in her face. She tipped her head back and breathed in deep, closing her eyes every now and then. She breathed in the stillness, the quiet. So quiet, all she could hear was the sound of her bicycle tires spraying mist off the dew-laced road.

It was a wonder how a bicycle could become a trusted old friend. Adina's Elgin had been in the family since before she was born. Her mother used the same bike on her home nursing route. After Mama's death, Adina gave the bike a fresh coat of navy-blue paint and replaced the well-used wicker basket with a newer one. She also attached a battery-operated headlight for riding at night. A nurse never knew when she'd be called out on an emergency in the dark of night. Being prepared was an absolute must. Adina hadn't gone on many night calls—or *any* night calls, for that matter—but she added the headlight, nonetheless.

It was hard to believe the world was still at war on such a bright, beautiful summer morning as today. Yet Adina was still here in her protected, quaint hamlet of a town in Northern California. She wanted to be over there—wherever "over there" might be—in the thick of it, serving in some capacity for the greater good. She'd considered enlisting last year when she first got her nursing certificate. She and her best friend, Jeanie Mae, had been talking about it ever since the US entered the war. The two of them envisioned it in detail. Jeanie would entertain the troops, and Adina would tend to the wounded and dying soldiers. But Adina's father would have none of that kind of talk in his house. He insisted he needed her here, nursing alongside him at the clinic.

"It is for our town, Adina," he told her. "You must think of the great need here at home. There are plenty of nurses risking their lives overseas. Adding one more nurse over there won't make any difference to the effort." Papa wasn't known for tactful communication, at least not since Mama died seven years ago. The loss of her tore a deep hole in him. Anything resembling joy fell into its depths, and he lost interest in most of the things he once loved.

Adina spent most of the first year after her mother's death fighting for Papa's attention. At age thirteen, she came to understand and accept that her father would not be what she needed him to be. With her mother gone, she would need to buck up, grow up, and begin to make decisions on her own.

Pouring herself into the lives of others through nursing became a type of sanctuary for her. She lived for it. Thrived in it. Not only did it fulfill a deep need for her to connect with others, but it also enabled her to be the giver her mother once was. And it allowed her to spend time with Papa. When she nursed alongside him, they were working toward a common goal. They operated on the same level. He respected her. Depended on her. He needed her. Adina craved this and fed on it as often as she could.

But the war had brought different types of challenges to the home front. Adina and Papa were more than busy attending to the medical needs of the town: illnesses, aches and pains, regular checkups and medications, and pregnant wives left behind. None of these things ceased just because a war was happening across the seas. One thing was for certain: anxiety and depression were on the rise. Broken hearts, mostly, and death. It was a medically proven fact that a person could die of a broken heart. That was the worst sickness of all.

Still, the town of Windsor soldiered on, its residents resilient and determined to see the war through. Some of them had already made it through the Great War by the skin of their teeth. Papa was one such person, though as a little girl, Adina didn't remember seeing any of the negative effects of war on him. Not the kind she'd heard about, shell shock and the like. She'd heard stories of men who had returned home completely changed. It was as though their normal reasoning had been ripped out of them and replaced with unending anxiety and fear. She'd heard tales of men thrashing and screaming in their beds at night, running from invisible enemies. Some would walk around during the day like dead men, yet still alive, trapped in a shell of who they once were.

But not Adina's father. Her early childhood memories of Papa were nothing but joy. He loved to laugh, to experience life. When he wasn't working at the clinic or making his rounds through the town, he was at home treasuring every moment with her and her mother. In Adina's memory, they were an inseparable trio. Nothing could break them apart.

Yet death has a way of butting in where it's not wanted, especially when one isn't looking. It barges in to take what it wants at will. It wasn't a war that emptied Papa of who he once was. It was a broken heart. Luisa Robbins got sick and died. As far as Papa was concerned, Mama took his heart with her when she left, leaving in its place a cold, empty sadness. From that time forward, he went through each day broken, working tirelessly from sunrise to sunset. Work became his life —the very air he breathed, day in and day out.

Though working alongside her father proved difficult at times, Adina was grateful for the opportunity to do so. Papa was a brilliant doctor and highly respected in the community. Adina had learned so much from working by his side. She watched his every move, followed his lead. She listened intently as he gave instructions to his patients, marking his words in her mind so she could imitate his ways when she was out on her visits, nursing alone, as she was today, and every day.

Into Town

Redwood Road curved and stretched its way toward town. Adina followed through with Mrs. Walter's "first thing" delivery at her father's request and now made her way downtown to the Groceteria. The trousers she chose to wear today were giving her grief, catching in the bike chain.

Should've tucked them into my socks, she thought.

She paired them with a white-collared cotton blouse, the one she usually wore with her skirt and white stockings, but the stockings were out of the question today. She only owned three pairs. One had a small hole that raced up the back of her leg no matter how many times she patched it. Another, she saved specifically for work. That pair was in pretty good shape but hadn't been rinsed out in a couple days. When it came down to it, she was just too tired at night, and reading a good book was much more inviting. As for the third pair, they were in fine form. But with nylon being in short supply, she didn't want to risk snagging them. A girl needed at least one decent pair of stockings ready for a night on the town. But then again, who was she kidding? She couldn't remember the last time she had a night on the town.

Her wavy auburn hair was pulled back into a loose ponytail, and a red wool beret sat on top. At five foot two, she was almost as tall as her mother had been. Adina favored her mother in more ways than just her petite size. Her thick, wavy hair and the sparkle in her eyes, as well as the freckles on her nose and cheeks. "For a moment, I thought I was looking at your mother," Carl Sanderson, the owner of the Windsor Groceteria, once said to her. To which her simple reply was, "Thank you."

The small town of Windsor was just waking up on this unseasonably cool June morning. Newspapers lay in driveways and on porches. For the last two weeks, their headlines had declared the valiant successes of the Allies' landing and advancements at Normandy. D-Day, they had called it. Finally, a slight ray of hope that this long, bloody war could be winding down. Yet the listings of the dead continued to flood in. There was no escaping it.

Adina rode past homes and businesses as she neared the main street. Banners with stars hung in front windows, and ribbons were tied on trees in honor of loved ones still serving. Town residents were out and about, sweeping front porches or picking up newspapers. She passed them by to the occasional tune of, "Good morning, Adi," or, "Hello there, Nurse Robbins."

She in turn called out in acknowledgement to each one personally. "Well, hello there, Mr. Murray. You're looking fit and chipper today." A turn of the head, a wave of the hand. "Good morning, Mrs. Quinn. That baby will be here any day now."

Adina had lived in the small town for as long as she could remember. She loved her hometown, and it loved her back, even if she did feel trapped. If she did ever make it into the Army Nursing Corps and overseas, she knew for certain that when her service was over, she'd come back home to Windsor.

A full day lay ahead of her as she rode past the Texaco station and the post office. Home visits would fill the morning hours. On some days after lunch, she would head back to the clinic to assist her father with patient after patient who walked into the small clinic sitting at the front of the Robbins' property. Papa and Mama set up the practice twenty-five years ago, working hard to earn the trust and respect of the community, and providing medical care to anyone who needed it. Even in the heat of the Depression, when folks couldn't pay for a doctor,

Papa treated them, Mama tended to them. The town had been grateful ever since.

Adina pulled up to the small town market and leaned her bicycle against the side of the red brick building. Showing up early at Carl Sanderson's Groceteria for a fresh-baked pastry was a hard and fast ritual for her. Carl's wife, Gracie, was known all over town for her delicious, home-baked pastries. Sugar rationing limited Mrs. Sanderson's confections, but if there were pastries today, they'd be sitting in a glass case at the front counter. Adina had been thinking of them since she first woke up this morning.

Tinkling bells rang out as she walked through the front entrance. A sweet aroma greeted her, along with the soft sounds of Les Brown and His Band of Renown from the Philco behind the counter.

"Morning, Adina," Carl Sanderson called out. He was standing in front of a fastidiously stacked display of vegetable soup cans. Right next to it stood a cardboard cutout of a woman ladling steamy hot vegetable soup into cups. The bold print next to the woman's perfectly coiffed blond hair read, "*Wouldn't I be silly to make it myself?*"

Sanderson stepped back to admire his work. "Ain't she a beauty?" he said, eyes beaming.

Adina wasn't sure if he was referring to the pretty woman or the stacked cans. She stepped closer to the display, tilted her head, and folded her arms. She didn't want the man to think she didn't care.

"Yep, she's a beauty," she said.

Satisfied, he turned to Adina. "You're out at the crack again, Adina. Seeing some patients this morning?" He walked behind the front counter. "Bet you'll be wanting one of these fresh, warm pastries." He tempted her by lifting the lid on the glass case.

"You know me well, Mr. Sanderson." She hovered over the sugary confections, breathing in their delicious aroma. "Any blackberry today?"

"You're in luck. They're all blackberry. The wife canned a bumper crop of those berries last summer. Got 'em coming out of our ears."

She flashed a smile at Carl. "Well, guess I'm just lucky today," she said.

He placed the pastry in a brown paper sack and handed it to her. She couldn't wait and immediately pulled it out, sinking her teeth into the berries surrounded by flaky pastry and powdered sugar.

The sound of the front entrance bells drew her attention. Adina lit up as she saw Jeanie Mae O'Brien walk in. Jeanie was what the boys would call a head turner. She wore her loosely curled, shoulder-length blond hair in victory rolls, the sides neatly pinned at the base of her neck. She only recently started wearing it that way, saying it made her look more mature. She had all the curves in all the right places and was a talented fashion plate. She could pull a used skirt and blouse out of a charity grab bag, add a scarf and hat, and look like she stepped off a page of *Look* magazine.

Adina met Jeanie in grade school, and the girls became fast friends. Not having any siblings made it easy for Adina to attach herself to Jeanie Mae. They grew up together, an inseparable pair. Day in and day out, they walked to school together and ate lunch together. They shared clothes, as well as all their secrets. They laughed and cried together. To each other they were Jee Mae and Adi Lou, bosom buddies through and through.

Jeanie caught sight of Adina and threw her arm up in a wave. "Hey there, buddy," she yelled. She was wearing a white summer dress with a matching jacket. She held her wide-brimmed hat to her head with her white-gloved hand as she excitedly ran to Adina. Jeanie always had some big news or juicy gossip to spill. She pulled Adina into a big hug, like she hadn't seen her in years, though they had just seen each other the day before yesterday.

"Oh, Adi, am I glad to see you." She gave Adina a kiss on the cheek, leaving a red stain behind. "Oops. Sorry, sweetie, I left some lips on you." Taking off her glove, she licked her thumb and attempted to wipe away the stain.

"Stop that, Jee," Adina said, brushing Jeanie's hand to the side. "What on earth are you so excited about?"

Jeanie looped her arm through Adina's. "Come, let's go outside. I need to talk to you about something."

Adina pursed her lips. "All right, but I don't have much time. I have an appointment at the Quinns'. I'm already late."

The two walked arm in arm toward the exit.

"Thanks again for the pastry, Mr. Sanderson," Adina called out.

Once outside, Jeanie Mae tugged at Adina's arm, practically dragging her along the walkway.

"Hurry up, over here," she said, pulling Adina toward her bicycle. Adina was getting annoyed with her friend's antics. Jeanie always had something up her sleeve.

"For crying out loud, Jee. You're crazy." Adina placed the bagged pastry in her bicycle basket. With her hands on her hips, she looked at her friend. "Okay, who is it this time? Let me guess. It's that sailor you met in the city last weekend. Frankie, Freddie, or whatever his name is."

Jeanie rolled her eyes. "It's Felix, and he's old news." She moved in closer to Adina, taking hold of both her hands. Her eyes were wide and alive, filled with urgency.

Adina could see that this wasn't one of Jeanie's typical GI-on-leave scenarios.

"I'm doing it," Jeanie said. "I'm joining up. The recruiter will be in town again next week." She searched Adina's eyes.

Both girls dreamed of joining the Women's Army Corps since the start of the war, but Adina always thought of it as a teenage romantic fantasy. It would never come true—at least not for her.

"The WACs are calling, Adina. I need to respond." Jeanie Mae tugged Adina's arms. "Come on, Adi. We can't do this anymore—just sit around this town waiting for something to happen. There's a war going on. Our boys are dying. Women are dying, too, you know that, right? I mean sure, we've had some victories here and there, but there's so much more to be done."

Adina held onto Jeanie's hands. She loved her friend. She couldn't imagine being separated from her one true cohort. They were closer than blood-related sisters.

Wow, Jee. Are you sure? I mean, this is for real. You're really going to do this?"

Jeanie Mae's eyes widened. Her face lit up, determined. "You're going to do it with me, Adi. We need to do this together, just like we planned." She squinted, waiting for Adina to respond. "You need to do this, Adi Lou, you know you do. You can't just stay in this dumpy town nursing the old folks and pregnant women who were left behind. There's a world of hurt out there that's in need of your service. It's time to go...before it's over. When it's all said and done, don't you want to be able to say you did something?"

Adina stood speechless. Of course, she wanted to make a difference. If joining the WACs and leaving town would make it happen, she'd do it right now. She just wasn't sure that it would. Maybe she was too afraid to leave. Besides, her father would fight it, that was for certain. Would she have the guts to fight back? Would it be worth it?

Jeanie Mae was different. Jeanie Mae was *brave*. When they were kids, she climbed the highest trees and ran the fastest. She wasn't afraid of spiders or rats, not even ghosts. She never let anything stand in her way. When an older boy at school had bullied Adina to tears, it was Jeanie who kicked him in the shins and said if he didn't leave Adina alone, she'd have her big brother, Jimmy, beat the tar out of him. Jimmy was now on a battleship fighting somewhere in the South Pacific.

Adina tilted her head back and shut her eyes. "Jee, you know I can't go with you. My father would never allow it." She opened her eyes to see her friend's smile collapse. "Besides, there aren't enough nurses here as it is. They're all overseas." She looked down. "I'm his only assistant, Jeanie. I can't go with you. Not now."

Jeanie's eyes narrowed. She dropped Adina's hands. "What are you talking about? I can't believe what I'm hearing. You're a full-grown woman, Adina. An adult. You know what that means, don't you? It means you can do whatever you want." She jutted her face close to Adina's. "That's what happens when you grow up. You know that, right?" She took a step back, shaking her head. "I swear, Adina. You'd allow your father to control you until his dying day, and that's a fact."

Jeanie's words were a fist to Adina's gut. Jeanie was right, and it made Adina boil inside. She'd been battling her father's control for years. The last thing she needed was her best friend reminding her of it.

"I'm not allowing my father to do anything, Jeanie, and I resent you saying so." Adina tried hard to sound confident, even though her heart wasn't convinced. "I know I can make my own decisions. I've been doing it ever since my mother died. But this is different. I can't just leave my father without a nurse. There's way too much need in this town. He asked me to stay with him, and I told him I would." She turned to her bike, adjusting the supplies in the basket. "I don't have any problem with going with you to sign up, but I'll be the one to make that decision, not my father."

Jeanie grabbed hold of Adina's arm. "Then do it," she said, eyes brightening once again. "Or at least promise me you'll seriously think about it. You've got a whole week to decide."

Adina slung her medical bag strap over her head and across her chest. She grinned at Jeanie, wondering what she would do without her best friend. "All right, Jee. I promise I will seriously think about it. There. Are you happy?"

Jeanie squealed, pulling Adina into her arms.

"Oh, Adi Lou, you're a peach. An absolute peach. Think hard on it. I just couldn't bear to go without you."

Adina kissed her friend on the cheek. Already late for her first visit, she started to push off on her bicycle.

"Hey Adi," Jeanie called out. "Why don't you stop by my place when you're done with your day? I hear there's a fresh shipment of killers at the new prisoner camp."

Adina knew the look in Jeanie's eyes all too well. It used to get them in trouble when they were kids. And even as a full-grown woman, Jeanie couldn't resist acting like a kid. Adina loved that about her.

"Come on, scaredy cat. Let's go spy them out," Jeanie said.

Adina sighed. "Oh, all right," she said, rolling her eyes. "I'll try to finish up around two. Sound good?"

Jeanie radiated. "That's swell, sugar. See you then."

3 |

The O'Brien Home

With the last delivery of the day completed, Adina checked her schedule book to be sure she hadn't missed anything important. Satisfied, she set out for the O'Brien property. Dazzling June sunlight shone bright, warming everything and everyone it touched. Cotton dresses and short-sleeved shirts were the order of the afternoon. Perspiration beaded on Adina's forehead as she rode down Main Street.

The O'Briens lived a half mile west of downtown, and only blocks from the road leading to the front entrance of the prisoner camp. The camp's site had housed migrant workers until it closed in 1940. The US military came in and leased the property for housing prisoners of war just this year. They called it Camp Windsor.

Adina was familiar with the abandoned migrant workers' camp. She passed the entrance whenever she rode to Jeanie's house, but she had no idea what changes had been made to fit it for German prisoners. How very strange that her government would bring Nazi prisoners to her safe and quiet town. Killers, in her opinion. All of them. She really had no desire to see them or to have anything to do with them. But in the spirit of adventure, she would go and spy them out, if only to satisfy Jeanie Mae's curiosity.

She made a right turn down the narrow dirt road that led to her friend's house, an old Victorian situated back off the main road. Adina knew this ride like the back of her hand. Old oaks and big-leaf maples lined the way. An old, elegant Pistache tree sat right in the middle of the O'Brien front lawn. As children, Adina and Jeanie would climb its red-leafed branches and sit in the tree for hours. One hot summer night, they convinced Jeanie's parents to let them sleep up in the thick branches of the tree. Blankets and pillows in tow, the girls succeeded in settling themselves about halfway up, only to make their way back down when Adina almost fell out. They instead bedded themselves on the cool grass under the canopy of the majestic tree and a sky full of stars. Adina couldn't remember ever having a better night's sleep.

She leaned her bike against the tree and walked up the porch steps of the beautiful house. Jeanie's family had lived in Sonoma County for more than fifty years. Her father worked in the wine industry and was well known throughout the county. Money had never been an issue for the O'Brien family.

Adina knocked on the front door and waited. No response. Apparently, Mr. and Mrs. O'Brien were not at home. Pressing her ear to the door, she heard the faint sound of radio music. She rang the front bell and pounded on the door again.

"The door's open, Adi. I'm upstairs," Jeanie yelled from inside.

Adina slowly opened the door and stepped inside. The music grew a bit louder. It was coming from upstairs. The house was otherwise quiet. She laid her medical bag on the floor at the base of the stairs and went up.

Jeanie's bedroom was the last door on the right side of a long hallway, the one bedroom at the very front of the house. When Jeanie was fifteen years old, she begged her parents to let her switch her bedroom at the back end of the house to the guest room at the front. She cited the stifling heat in the summertime due to the west-facing windows as her reason for wanting to make the switch. The truth was that right next to the front bedroom's window, overlooking the front yard, grew one of the big-leaf maples, its branches reaching just above the window frame. It was so close that on windy nights, the branches would eerily scrape against the window glass and wooden frame. Equally, and more fitting for Jeanie's purposes, it was close enough for her to make middle-of-the-night escapes and reentries when the opportunity knocked.

As Adina neared Jeanie's bedroom, the music became more distinguishable. The Mills Brothers were singing "Paper Doll." Jeanie stood in her open closet, throwing dress after dress onto her bed. Stockings, shoes, and brassieres covered the floor. Jeanie danced a swing step and sang along. She caught sight of Adina and sauntered over to her, singing and kicking scattered items of clothing out of the way to clear a path. She grabbed Adina by the hand, swung her around, and took the lead. "Come on, Adi Lou. You've been practicing, haven't you?"

Adina fell right into step with Jeanie. Step, step, triple-step. Step, step, triple-step. "Practicing with who? My father keeps me so busy, there's no time for dancing."

"Well, you've been practicing with someone 'cause you're cookin', honey." Jeanie spun Adina around under her arm, cradling her into a backward dip for the finale. "And that's how we do it," she said, breathless. She walked over to the bed, a little jig left in her step, and continued sorting clothing.

Adina picked a shirt up off the floor and laid it on the bed. "What on earth are you doing?" she asked. "Looks like a bomb went off in here."

"Trying to decide what to take with me, obviously. Don't think they'll let me take much though." She tossed a pile onto the floor. "A couple of shirts, skirts, stockings. An evening gown. Ya think they'll let me take an evening gown, Adi?"

"One at the very least," Adina said.

Jeanie stood in front of a full-length mirror, holding a yellow chiffon party dress up to her shoulders. "A girl's just gotta have at least one evening dress for the officers' balls, right?" She posed, bending at the hip.

Adina sat amused, watching her friend. She admired Jeanie—her looks, her spunk, her drive to always be pushing ahead of everyone else. All the qualities Adina aspired to achieve, yet always seemed just out of reach. Jeanie didn't care much about what people thought about her. If she wanted something, it was only a matter of reaching out and grabbing it. As a child, Jeanie would *tell* her parents what she was going to do, rather than *ask* to do it. They might have objected here and there, but more often than not, they bent in agreement to Jeanie Mae's wishes. Now here stood Jeanie, a week away from enlisting, yet already packing her bags to leave.

Adina, on the other hand, was dragging her feet. A battle raged inside her. She wanted to go with Jeanie, truly she did. This could very well be her opportunity to escape the restraints of the town, as well as her father. She wouldn't even need to tell him. She, too, could pack her bags, enlist with Jeanie next week, and leave without a word. But who was she kidding? She wasn't going anywhere. Adina stood and walked over to the open window. Looking out, she breathed in the soft scent of jasmine and allowed the breeze to cool her.

Jeanie dropped the dresses in a heap on the floor and walked up behind her. "Hey, sugar," she said, placing her hands on Adina's shoulders. "I need a break. Whatta you say we take a little walk—see if we can get a peek at those Nazi killers."

For the life of her, Adina couldn't understand Jeanie's fascination with the camp or its prisoners. To her it felt like spying on animals in a zoo.

"And what makes you think we'll be able to get anywhere near that camp?" Adina asked. "It's guarded, you know. Lookout towers, barbed-wire fencing—the works."

Jeanie smirked. "I have my ways." She reached into her dresser drawer, taking out a small pair of binoculars. "We might need these," she said with a wink and ran out of the bedroom. Adina followed close behind.

The Encounter

Jeanie Mae bounded down the porch steps and into the front yard. She headed in the opposite direction of the driveway, toward the wooded fields.

"Have I told you you're crazy yet?" Adina teased. Bending down, she snatched up a wild white daisy. Twisting its stem, she brushed its petals across her fingertips.

"You tell me every single day," Jeanie said.

"Why are you going this way?" Adina asked, quickening her step to keep up. "The main road is in the other direction."

"You don't expect us to just waltz up to the front gate, do you? I'm taking us around the back side where we'll have plenty of tree cover. They'll never see us coming."

Jeanie walked with purpose, cutting across the thick green grass of the side yard and just past an old shed which housed a few garden tools, as well as Jeanie's brother's 1923 Indian Scout motorcycle. He bought the bike used and dilapidated just before the war began. He had pounded out the dents, fixed the engine, and put a fresh coat of red paint on it when he was called up to service. He never even had a chance to show it off around town.

Just ahead lay a dirt path leading to a grove of oak trees at the back of the O'Brien property. As children, the two girls loved frolicking in the wooded grove. They called it their enchanted forest. Though they never strayed far from the property line, the grove became their childhood fantasy land and a cool escape on summer days.

Afternoon sunlight filtered through the trees as they entered the wooded trail. Spindly oak limbs arched overhead, so many in spots that only fragments of sky remained above. The air was rich with the fragrance of earth and leaves. Adina took a deep breath of it as a way of solidifying this moment with her best friend before Jeanie left.

Adina giggled, breaking the silence. "Remember the time we planned to run away together and join that circus—the one that came to Santa Rosa? We were what, nine years old? You wanted to swing from that trapeze, and I wanted to train a poodle to jump up into my arms, just like the clown did. The day the circus was leaving, we both packed our suitcases and planned to meet downtown at the market."

Jeanie threw back her head and laughed. "We would have made it, too, if you hadn't gotten caught before you reached the end of your drive. Boy, was your mother mad."

Adina's heart ached at the mention of her mother. "I know," she said, eyes distant in the memory. "Mama rarely got angry. She was scared. For Pete's sake, I left the house at ten at night. It was dark outside. What were we thinking?" She grabbed hold of Jeanie's hand. "You know the craziest thing, Jee? Days later, I was at your house with you, up in your bedroom. I saw your suitcase still sitting on the floor, stuffed full. That silly pink ballerina tutu was sticking out of it. You were determined to join the circus the next time it came to town. No matter what it took, you were gonna fly on that trapeze. You wanted to be ready to go, remember?"

Jeanie turned her face toward her, a bit of mischief in her smile. "You'll come with me this time, Adi," she said. Pulling her hand away, she ran down the trail, the wind carrying her laughter through the trees.

Adina ran after her, ducking under low branches and jumping over tree roots. She relished the feeling—free like a child. She didn't pay attention to where they were going. She just ran, heart pounding, trying her best to keep up with her friend. The farther Jeanie sprinted into the trees, the more disoriented Adina became.

Adina lost sight of Jeanie as she made a sharp right turn around the trees. How far back were they going? "Jee, wait up!" she yelled. She slowed as she approached a clearing.

"Shhh." Jeanie crouched on her heels behind a large, bent oak tree. "It's right in front of you."

Adina heard voices—men's voices. She stood still and listened, peering around the thick trunk of a tree. A short distance beyond the tree was a line of barbed-wire fencing stretching a perimeter she couldn't see the end of. One guard tower stood maybe five or so feet off the ground. She could also see canvas tents, too many to count from where she stood.

Cautiously, she backstepped out of the clearing and into the covering of the trees, settling herself next to Jeanie. "You ran too fast, Jee. I couldn't keep up," she whispered.

Jeanie peered through the binoculars, pointing her finger in the direction of the voices.

A group of men dressed in dark gray uniforms stood in a dirt clearing behind the tents. Some of their uniforms looked haphazard and mismatched. All of them had the letters "PW" sizably stamped in white on their shirts and trousers. Clouds of dust and dirt puffed around their feet as they kicked a red ball back and forth, laughing and bantering in German.

Adina's eyes darted, taking in the scene. Were these men the prisoners? The Nazi killers? These were the beasts that killed America's sons and daughters, as well as her own friends? The ones who murdered entire races? How could that be when they were here, laughing and playing around like children?

Is this how our military treats murderers? she thought.

Eyes narrowing, she turned and looked at Jeanie.

"I know," Jeanie whispered. "They brought the bastards here and gave them a party. If it were up to me, I would've lined them up and shot them in cold blood, same as they've done to our boys."

Jeanie was right, wasn't she? They deserved to be shot for their crimes, not treated to a game of kickball. Adina squinted, straining to get a closer look at their faces. She snatched the binoculars out of Jeanie's hand and pressed them to her eyes. She found herself speechless. Some of these men looked more like boys she would've gone to school with, her friends who even now were fighting over seas. The faces of the men she watched contained no malice, no hate. These were not the faces of killers.

Adina stood. She had to get a better look.

"Adi, what do you think you're doing?" Jeanie said. "Come back here."

Adina ignored Jeanie, her friend's pleas seeming to fade as she stepped forward into the clearing. "I just need a closer look—a better look at their faces."

Slowly, Adina stepped into the clearing, leaving herself in plain view. Just then, something hit her hard on her thigh. "Ouch!" she yelled, rubbing her leg. She looked down to see what hit her. The red ball—the one the men were kicking around. She looked back at Jeanie who sat gaping, eyes like saucers.

"Guten Tag, Fräulein."

She snapped her head toward the voice. One of the prisoners was calling out to her. Another, a hefty man, whistled and laughed. He said something else in German that she couldn't understand, making a gesture with his hands, mimicking the curves of a woman's body. The other men whistled and catcalled. The one who had called out to her gave the fat one a stern look and a hard shove. "Halt die Klappe, Dummkopf," He pushed the fat one out of his way and walked slowly toward the barbed-wire fencing. His eyes were set on Adina.

Jeanie May stood from her hiding place.

"Adina, run!" she yelled.

Adina didn't move.

"Adina Luisa Robbins, you need to run...now!" Jeanie pleaded.

Adina stood like a statue, eyes fixed on the young man standing just ahead of her.

"Fine," Jeanie said in frustration. "It's your funeral." She took off, running back into the woods.

"Hallo?" the prisoner said, smiling as he neared the fence line.

Adina didn't answer, much too taken by the young man's appearance. He had thick, rusty hair, cut close on the sides. Scattered waves lay on top with loose strands hanging over his forehead. A damp curl fell into his eyes—eyes that lit up sky blue with his smile.

"Ball?" He pointed to the red ball lying at Adina's feet.

She felt dizzy and a bit paralyzed. She side-eyed the ball at her feet, then looked back at the young man. "That?" she said, pointing to the ball.

The young man laughed. The sound of it made Adina's heart race. She giggled, placing her fingers over her lips.

"Ja, or um, yes, that," he repeated, folding his arms. He tilted his head, looking at her curiously, the smile never leaving his lips.

Adina bent down guardedly and picked up the ball. She could hear the other men laughing, some calling to the prisoner in front of her. Slowly, she walked toward the fence. The space between them seemed to tunnel in front of her. Her legs felt like rubber. What was she thinking? Jeanie Mae ran away. Jeanie, the fearless one. But Adina stayed.

After what felt like a lifetime, she reached the fence line where the prisoner stood on the other side. A gust of wind blew strands of hair into her eyes. Flustered, she swept them back, tucking them behind her ear. She saw that her hands were filthy and wondered if her face looked the same. How could it not when she had just charged full speed down a wooded trail and hidden in the dirt and weeds behind a tree?

The prisoner lifted his hands for the ball, his eyes not leaving hers.

Adina looked at the barbed fencing separating them. She wouldn't be able to push the ball through without damaging it.

He lifted his hands again, pointing to the top of the fence.

Adina stepped closer. The top wire was level with the top of her head. The prisoner held his hands over the tips of the barbs. She stretched her arms up, and for a moment, their eyes locked. Carefully, she lifted the ball over the fence and into his waiting hands.

He raised the ball over his head like a trophy. The other prisoners whistled and cheered as though some great feat had just been accomplished.

"Danke," he said. "I'm Daniel." He waited, the eager smile lighting up his face.

Adina stood breathless, entranced by what she was seeing and feeling. *He's a killer*, she thought. *Why aren't I running away?*

"Your name?" he asked.

She looked toward the guard tower. Oddly, there wasn't anyone in it. She could hear the other prisoners calling to Daniel, beckoning him back to finish their game.

Slowly, she stepped back. "What am I doing here?" she whispered to herself. Then, to Daniel, "I shouldn't be here." She turned back toward the trail.

"Wait!" he called. "Tell me your name!"

She took one last look at him over her shoulder. Even from a distance his smile beamed. She waved to him one last time and took off back down the trail.

4

Happy Birthday Adina, 1938

Luisa Robbins lay in her bed. The same bed she shared with her husband. The place where they enjoyed Sunday afternoon naps and long, intimate conversations. The same bed where they offered the preciousness of their love to each other over and over—too many times to count.

She slept fitfully, her labored breathing staggered and shallow. How long had she been asleep? There was no way for her to know. Luisa's life had been confined to her bed for days now—maybe it was weeks.

A cool October breeze blew through the open window, gently brushing across her face and left arm. Her thick lashes fluttered. Faded brown eyes struggled to focus, scanning the room to see what it was that had pulled her out of sleep.

With some effort, she lifted her head to look out the window. How she longed to rise from her sick bed, if only to climb out that window and into the glorious day. Just one more chance to take a long walk into town with her beloved Henry or to chase sweet Adina in the cool grass. To allow her eyes to see the magnificent reds and golds of autumn, and to breathe deeply the sweet fall air. But she wouldn't be doing any of those things. Cancer had made that decision eight months ago. Luisa Robbins was dying. Radiotherapy treatments helped somewhat in the beginning, possibly giving her a little more time. But the rapid deterioration of her bones and organ tissues warranted the doctors to halt the treatments—Henry's being the loudest voice against them. He couldn't bear to see his sweet Luisa in such pain. He was a doctor, and a good one at that. Yet he couldn't heal the love of his life. She was his light, his very soul, and he was losing her.

Today was their daughter Adina's twelfth birthday. Yet there would be no party. No party dress, cake, or friends. Henry had told Adina it would be wrong to celebrate with Mama so sick. Instead, Adina sat in the living room on the overstuffed floral sofa, reading a book. *Little Women*, to be exact. It was her absolute favorite book, and she'd read it three times since the age of ten. She loved the story and imagined herself diving through the pages of the book and joining the lives of the March sisters. Adina had no siblings, and Papa's attention was less and less on her since Mama got sick. Some days he barely noticed her or even spoke to her, unless it was to order her to help him with Mama or to tell her she was making too much noise. He wasn't always like this. Adina could remember all too well how she and her father shared so much together, so much love and laughter. But ever since Mama got sick, Adina felt as though she didn't know him anymore, adding to the overwhelming heartache of watching her mother slip away.

Papa was rarely away from Mama's bedside. He tended to her day and night. Like clockwork, he administered her medications. He fed her meals, though she stopped taking food two days ago. He bathed her and helped her when she needed to use the bedpan. Some nights, he would read to her. Others, he would just sit with her, quietly holding her hand, watching her sleep. For Papa, there were no other patients who needed him more than his Luisa. Nothing else mattered.

Adina sat cross-legged, elbow resting on the back of the sofa, her head in her hand. She had given up on reading and was staring dreamily out the front window. It was a clear, cool Saturday, and she was stuck here at home. On her birthday, no less. Papa had demanded she stick close to home when she wasn't in school, including on the weekends. He needed her to be available to help him with Mama's care, especially if someone in town had a medical emergency and he needed to leave. She felt trapped, like a prisoner in her own home.

The pendulum swinging in the grandfather clock ticked out a hypnotic pulse that grated on Adina's nerves. She wanted to open the door of the clock and make it stop. Instead, leaving her open book on the sofa, she walked over to the front window. She could see Mama's beautiful rock and flower garden at the base of the front porch. Over the years, Mama collected rocks of all shapes and sizes. They were found on day trips to the coast or on family hikes in the hills. She would bring them home, wash them, and place them in her garden. Some were stacked three and four high on top of one another. Smaller ones were laid out in a variety of designs, shapes like hearts and circles with colorful flowers exploding from their centers. A magnificent spectrum of botanical color wound its way in and around the rock designs— daffodils, orange poppies, and gladiolas. It was the place of Mama's memories. The flowers were dry and dying away now. Mama hadn't been able to work in her garden for quite some time, and Papa was too busy taking care of Mama. The seasons were changing.

The bedroom door at the end of the hallway opened, then quietly latched shut. Papa walked into the living room.

"Adina, I will be working in my study and must not be disturbed. Please listen for your mother."

Adina knew all too well that she was not to disturb her papa when he was in his study with the door closed. Papa's study was his bastion, his sanctuary. Its adornments consisted of dark leather furniture with brass upholstery pins on the arms and legs—legs that sank into a rich, burgundy oriental rug. In the far corner of the room was an ornately carved dark-wood cabinet. Adina didn't know what was in the cabinet because its doors were always locked tight. In the center of the room sat a large mahogany desk. Adina remembered barely being able to see over it when she was little. She saw that desk as the place where her father would sit smoking his cherry-tobacco-stuffed pipe, while he pondered all things medical.

Matching mahogany bookshelves lined the room from floor to ceiling. Each shelf contained physician reference books and encyclopedias, but medical volumes weren't the only books on the shelves. An entire section was dedicated to beautiful leather-bound copies of the works of Shakespeare, Keats, Walt Whitman, and the like. But the book that intrigued Adina the most was one on the life of the great Harry Houdini. Magic fascinated Papa. Now and again, he loved to learn a good magic trick. He could be consumed with his work and duties throughout the day. Then, with childlike excitement, he would present a new magic trick to Luisa and Adina. A sleight of the hand, a flourish, and a final bow. The two adoring ladies in his life would applaud with enthusiastic exuberance every time. For some reason, Adina couldn't remember the last magic trick he performed for them.

She continued staring out the window, not realizing Papa was still in the room.

"Adina Luisa," he repeated, his voice stern.

Startled, she spun around. "Sorry, Papa." She glanced down at the floor. "Is Mama all right? Does she need anything?"

"It has been a struggle for her, but she is finally asleep." His eyebrows knit, connecting in the middle as he looked at her over the rim of his glasses. There wasn't so much as a curve of a smile on his lips, not even for his daughter's birthday. "I will be in my study and must not be disturbed. You understand this, yes?"

Adina shrank. He always seemed disappointed in her these days. "Yes, Papa," she answered. "I understand."

Her heart ached as she watched him turn to leave. She wanted to burst into tears, but by force of will, she didn't. When she heard him close the door to his study, she felt her heart closing up more and more and fought against it, pushing the sad, angry thoughts away. Yet hope felt desperately out of reach. Staring out the window, she felt as though the living room walls were closing in on her. She glanced back at her open book lying on the sofa. The thought of picking it up where she'd left off made her even more restless. Besides, with every turn of the page, she knew exactly where the story was going.

She walked to the entrance of the kitchen but wasn't a bit hungry. Defeated, she relegated herself back to the sofa and picked up the book. As she did, a faint sound came from the direction of the hallway. Listening intently, she heard it again.

It was Mama.

Mama

Adina stood quietly, resting her ear on the outside of her mother and father's bedroom door. She listened. There was only quiet. She turned the knob, pushing the door open. It creaked, and she stopped. She could see her mother lying motionless on the bed with her back to the door.

The smell of urine and antiseptic hung heavy in the air. It was the smell of sickness and death, and it overwhelmed Adina. She was grateful for the open window and the breeze that blew through it. Tentatively, she walked around the foot of the bed and was surprised to see that her mother's eyes were open.

"Mama?" She waited at the foot of the bed for a response.

Mama's eyes stared dreamily out the window, and Adina moved closer into her mother's line of sight. At last, Mama's eyes brightened.

"Adina, my sweet girl," she said, her voice weak and hushed. With a shaking hand, she gently patted the bed. "Come, sit next to me."

Adina sat down close to her mother on the wrinkled white sheets. She laid her arm across her waist and leaned into her. Mama moaned.

"I'm sorry. Did I hurt you, Mama?"

"No, no, my love. It's all right." Mama struggled to adjust her position. "Come, snuggle closer to me, mano meilė." She laid her cool hand on Adina, gently tugging her close. She gazed lovingly into her daughter's eyes, her own pooling with tears.

"Why are you crying, Mama? Have I done something wrong? Papa told me not to make any noise. Did I wake you?"

Mama reached for Adina's cheek. Adina closed her eyes, savoring the touch of her mama's gentle fingers.

"No, my sweet. You didn't wake me. It's quite difficult to sleep these days." Mama winced. "I am sad because today is your birthday. You are twelve years old this very day."

Adina took hold of her mother's hand. "Please don't worry about me, Mama. I don't need anything today. I just want to sit here with you."

"No, Dukra. A twelve-year-old young lady deserves a wonderful party to celebrate. When I was growing up in Lithuania, a young girl became a woman at twelve."

Adina found this odd. She still felt like a child. "I don't want to be a woman yet." She squeezed Mama's hand, as she always did when she was afraid.

Mama's eyes deepened.

Adina didn't like that her mother looked at her that way. It made her uncomfortable. She wanted Mama to look at her and smile—the same smile that made her eyes light up like the sun. But no sun shone in them. Mama's eyes were cloudy now, their light fading away.

"My love," Mama said, tenderly stroking Adina's cheek. "You will be a woman someday. Much sooner than you think. I fear much sooner than you would want." Tears spilled from her eyes. "There is so much you will learn. So much about who you are, my darling girl," she said through slow breaths.

Adina frowned. She didn't want to know anything right now. All she wanted was for her mother to stay with her, always.

"Your papa loves you so very much," Mama whispered. "Someday, you will understand why he made his decisions. He did it for us. You must love him. Care for him, Adina Luisa."

Adina's eyes narrowed. She looked at her mother, questioning, wanting desperately to understand what she was trying to communicate. What decisions?

Mama's eyes widened. "Have I ever told you how we named you when you were born? Adina. It means 'gentle.' You came to your papa and me on an autumn day." She lifted a shaking finger, pointing to the open window. "Just like the wind, blowing softly through that window. There you were, my sweet, gentle Adina." Again, her eyes closed.

Adina gently laid her head on her mother's breast, quietly listening to her heartbeat. "I love you Mama," she whispered.

Luisa rested her hand on Adina's head. "I love you, too, my sweet. Papa loves you. Someday, you will understand. You must forgive—"

Adina lay still, listening until Mama's breathing became slow and steady. Sitting up, she looked at her mother's face. Even in her illness, Mama was so beautiful. Adina carefully lifted herself from the bed, so as not to wake her, and quietly stepped out of the bedroom. As she closed the door, the words her mother spoke pricked at her. What decisions was she talking about? Forgive? For what? She had to speak to Papa now. Her impatience would not let her wait. She walked down the hallway and stood at the door of her father's study.

The Secret

Adina lifted her hand to knock on the door of her father's study but pulled back as she heard faint, muffled sounds on the other side. She tilted her ear closer, yet still couldn't make out what she was hearing. Was it singing? Melodic tones traveling up and down, repeating. Maybe Papa was listening to the radio.

She hesitated. Papa might be angry with her for disturbing him, whatever it was he was doing. But her curiosity regarding what Mama had just said was greater than her fear.

With an even rotation, she gently turned the door handle and slowly pushed the door open. The room was a shroud of darkness. All the window blinds were drawn shut. At the corner of Papa's desk sat a single brass lamp with an opaque emerald glass shade. Its eerie green glow did nothing to help Adina see.

Still, the melodies continued. It sounded like Papa's voice. Where was he? Her eyes strained to look for him as she stepped farther in. She scanned the room from the far right, past the bookshelves and his desk to the other side. There he was, standing in front of the carved wood cabinet, its doors, usually locked shut, were now wide open. A single lit candle sat on the cabinet shelf. Papa's head and shoulders were covered with a white linen cloth—a veil of some kind. He swayed back and forth to the words he sang.

Adina stood still, stifling her very breath so as not to alarm her father. What was it he was singing? She had never heard this language before.

"Baruch ata Adonai, Eloheinu Melech ha-olam...Baruch ata Adonai."

He repeated the phrase, still swaying to its melody.

Adina stood mesmerized and drawn in by the scene. The air in the room felt different, almost otherworldly. Was he praying? She wanted to see more and to hear more clearly the words her father sang. Step by step, she moved closer, as though compelled by some unseen force.

Suddenly, her knee bumped something in the darkness. There was a crash and the sound of breaking glass. She stopped, paralyzed and shocked by the noise and the sharp pain in her knee.

The singing cut off and the room flooded with light as Papa flipped the light switch, revealing an overturned plant stand and shattered vase. Adina squinted her eyes.

"Adina Luisa!" he yelled, his eyes blazing. "What are you doing here?"

"Papa, I...I'm sorry. I didn't mean to—" She squinted, adjusting her eyes to the light.

"Get out!" he roared, pointing his finger toward the door.

"Papa, I'm sorry. I only wanted to ask you a question."

Papa's eyes narrowed. "You did not knock? Were you spying on me?" His voice rose, and his hands were shaking.

"No, Papa, no. I would never do that. It's just, I was with Mama and she had said something."

He turned his back to her. "You are a disobedient child."

"Papa, please don't be angry with me. I never meant to disobey you. I can work to pay for the vase if you like." Tears streamed down her face, frightened and confused by her father's rage. She had never seen him this angry before, ever.

Papa kept his back turned. "Leave this room immediately, Adina."

She stood stunned and crying.

"Leave me!" he roared.

"Yes, Papa," she said, choking back her tears.

Adina stood outside the closed door of her father's study, sobbing and shaking. Her thoughts raced. What was her father trying to hide? Why was his head covered? What was it he was chanting? Or was he praying? None of it made any sense to her. Mama would know. Mama would have the answers.

Without hesitation, Adina ran down the hallway to her mother's bedroom, through the door, and straight to Mama's bedside.

"Mama, I did something I wasn't supposed to do. I went into Papa's study without his permission. I didn't knock. He's so angry with me."

Mama lay still, eyes open and fixed on the open window.

"Why would he do that, Mama? You said I needed to forgive him."

Her mother didn't respond.

Adina took hold of Mama's hand. It was cold. She ran her fingers up her mother's arm and shook her shoulder. "Mama? Wake up, Mama."

Panic seized Adina's heart. Taking her mother's face into her hands, she sobbed, "No, no... Please don't go. I need you, Mama. Please don't leave me." She laid her head on her mother's breast and wept.

Adina didn't hear her father walk into the room. He came to the side of the bed where his wife and daughter lay. Gently, he placed two fingers on Luisa's wrist. He then bent down, placing his cheek next to her mouth and nose. There was no breath. With his hand, he gently closed Luisa's beautiful brown eyes and then fell to his knees. Chest heaving, Henry Robbins wept deep, soulful cries.

"Luisa...mano miela. My sweet love."

Henry's Memories

Henry reached out to stroke his daughter's hair, desperately trying to comfort her. "Adina, please don't cry, child."

She sobbed into her mother's breast, unresponsive to his plea.

"Dukra...please, my child." He tugged on her arms, trying to lift her off his wife's lifeless body.

"No, I don't want you," she cried out. She recoiled from his touch, shutting down her tears, and shutting him out. Adina looked at her beautiful mother one last time. Tenderly, she touched her brow and gently kissed her cheek. Without so much as a glance toward her father, Adina walked out of the bedroom, closing the door behind her.

Henry sat down on the bed next to his wife. She was gone. He was alone. He looked out the open window. A deluge of memories and regret flooded his mind. *Hero.* That's what he was called as he returned home from the Great War. The word meant nothing to him He came home alive, nothing more. He was a medic. He saved lives. It was his duty to do so. *What were we fighting for? A free and independent Lithuania, was it not? We all fought for Lithuania.* These were the questions that haunted him. No number of medals or accolades could make up for the lives he'd lost—the ones he couldn't save. Henry believed the true heroes were the ones who died on the battlefield, the ones who didn't come home. Those were the ones who deserved the medals, not him.

"Forgive me, my love. What have I done?" He spoke aloud—to the red and gold trees outside the bedroom window, to the air, and to his sweet Luisa. Her lovely face filled his head. Memories of their wedding day, after his return from the war, and their first home. They shared a deep love, unfettered, that transcended every area of their lives. As husband and wife, they worked side by side during the day. At night, lying awake in each other's arms, they would dream of the years to come, of children, grandchildren, and growing old together. She was his escape from the nightmarish memories of war and the hate that surrounded them. She was his home.

"I only wanted to protect you and our child and to give you a better life," he said, now holding her hand in his. The battle in his mind continued to rage, tears streaming down his face, as he told himself, and her, that it was all for the best. Lithuania, the home where they were both born and raised, had changed. With each passing year he felt less safe, less free. The hatred toward his people grew at an alarming rate, along with his own fear of it. When Adina was born, he knew what needed to be done. He moved them out of their homeland. He changed their name.

And he turned his back on his faith and his people.

"We must do this, Luisa," he'd told her. "It is for our safety. Our freedom."

But Luisa knew the reality of what this would mean. She would have to deny who she was. She would no longer be a Jew, nor would her child. She would be reckoned dead by her remaining family members. Her mother, father, and grandmother were still alive, as well as her oldest brother. The very idea was unthinkable to her. She begged Henry for a different solution.

"Please, my love," she said. "Do not make us do this. We will find a way to be safe and to live. Do not make me say goodbye to my family in this way."

Henry remembered the look in her eyes. The pleading haunted him. But he would not heed her. He would not listen. He had seen enough of the death and hate that the war brought. The pogroms of years past had brought death to family and friends. He wouldn't allow it, not again. He had made up his mind. They would say a forever goodbye to their family, and they would leave.

Luisa agreed and supported him in all of it. She trusted him. She loved him.

In 1927, Henrikas and Luisa Rabinovitz became Henry and Luisa Robbins. Henry escorted his wife and daughter into a new world. It would be a new life, free from fear. Free, because nobody would know the truth. Henrikas Rabinovitz no longer existed. He would do everything in his power to make sure that Luisa and Adina would be loved and cared for. They would be safe.

"I did it for us, my love. I would do it again," he whispered.

Henry lay down on the bed next to his wife. He cradled her head with his hand and closed his eyes.

5

We Will Treat the Germans, 1944

Adina turned onto the drive and looked at her watch. It was later than she thought, yet Papa's Olds wasn't parked in front. She felt relief as her head reeled from the excitement of her encounter with the German prisoner.

Inside the kitchen, she washed her hands and began rummaging through the refrigerator. She pulled out the leftover meatloaf she and her father had been eating off of for the last two nights, as well as two carrots, and set them on the counter. She turned on the gas oven. As she cut up the carrots, she couldn't get the young prisoner out of her head. He had said his name was Daniel, and like an idiot, she said nothing. It felt like a dream.

Throwing the carrots into a pot with a little water, she placed them on the stove to steam and heard car tires crunching on the gravel drive outside. Her father was home. Pushing down the nervous feeling in her stomach, she put the meatloaf in a casserole dish and popped it into the oven. *Pull it together*, she thought.

Papa came up the back porch steps, stomped the dust off his shoes, and opened the door.

"Adina Luisa, you are home?" he called out.

"I'm making supper, Papa," she answered, nervously stirring carrots.

"Very good," he said, walking into the kitchen. "I have something important to speak with you about."

Adina stopped stirring and looked wide-eyed at her father, her heart pounding wildly. Did he know where she and Jeanie went this afternoon? How would he?

The carrots began to sizzle and smoke.

"What is the matter with you, Adina? Pay attention to what you are doing."

She turned off the gas and set the pot to the side of the stove. "Oops, guess I had the heat a little too high." She took a deep breath. "What is it? What's so important?"

Henry removed his hat, placed it on the kitchen table, and sat in a chair. He folded his hands and with serious eyes, looked at his daughter.

"I just had a meeting with Lieutenant Major Williams. He oversees operations at the prisoner camp here in town."

Adina's stomach sank.

"He has informed me that they do not have an onsite medic to treat the prisoners. He has requested my services to oversee their medical care."

Her mouth fell open. She couldn't believe what she was hearing.

"Adina, why are you looking at me that way? Are you listening to what I am saying? This is a very serious matter. I will need your help."

She sat in the chair next to him. "I'm sorry, Papa. I heard what you said. I'm just a little confused. This is something that you actually want to do? You want to doctor German prisoners? You...treat Nazis?" She picked at her fingernails.

"Nonsense," he responded. "Major Williams specifically requested me. There are nearly two hundred prisoners at the camp. I will need you to assist me." He scratched his head. "What is your concern with this, Adina?"

She searched his eyes. "They're Germans, Papa. Murderers. You've read the newspapers. You've seen the newsreels. I find it hard to believe that you— What I mean is, I find it hard to believe that you would even consider this." As she heard her own words, Adina battled with her feelings. Her encounter with the prisoner intrigued her. But to actually treat them and care for them... She never expected this.

Papa pursed his lips, shaking his head. "They are human beings, are they not? They have the right to decent medical care, same as any other."

Adina pushed back from the table and stood. "You of all people should—"

"Enough, Adina," he said, hands fisted on the table. "They are prisoners and the responsibility of the United States military." He pushed back his chair and stood, hat in hand. "It's all arranged. We start next week. Monday morning with physicals." He turned from the table and left the kitchen.

Adina stood, dumbfounded by the news. They would be treating and caring for the German prisoners at Camp Windsor. Un-admittingly so, Papa was a Jew. Those prisoners were Nazis. Yet he seemed perfectly fine with it. She knew one thing for certain... Jeanie Mae would never believe this.

6

First Day at Camp, July 1944

Monday morning started early, filled with nervous anticipation. The unexpected encounter with the prisoners last week had left Adina feeling unsettled. What would she do if one of them recognized her today? Especially the one who introduced himself. Daniel.

With today being their first visit to the camp, Papa insisted Adina wear her full nursing uniform. She stayed up extra late rinsing her white stockings, ironing her button-up blue blouse, and mending a tear in her white pinafore dress. Slacks were unacceptable. She even polished her white pumps, a task she didn't worry about for daily home visits. White pumps made no sense for country bike rides. Everything would need to be in order. She neatly pinned back the sides of her hair so that it tumbled down the back of her neck in shiny, loose waves. She crowned the look off with a white nurse's cap, securely pinning it to the top of her head. Then, standing in front of the full-length mirror, she swiped a touch of red lipstick onto her lips, blotting with a tissue. Finally, she pinned her Santa Rosa School of Nursing pin to the front of her pinafore. She didn't want anyone to think she was an amateur.

"Adina," Papa called from the kitchen. "Come and eat some breakfast. We have a full day today."

"I'm coming, Papa," she yelled, winding her mother's wristwatch as she left her bedroom.

Henry didn't bother to look up from his newspaper as she entered the kitchen.

"What's up with our boys today?" she asked, buttering an already toasted piece of bread she found waiting for her on the counter. It helped to know her father was thinking about her this morning. She poured herself a cup of coffee and sat at the table.

Papa drained the last bits of coffee from his cup and folded the newspaper.

"It appears the Russians are advancing on the Germans. A bit of good news for a change. Even if they are Russians." He peered over the rim of his glasses at her. "What is that on your lips?"

She took a tentative sip of coffee. "It's lipstick, Papa. Is it forbidden to look nice?"

"We are working today, Adina, not attending a party." He pushed himself from the table. "Please hurry and meet me in the clinic. I'd like to brief you on what our day at the camp will entail. This is a very important assignment. You understand this, yes? I would like you to be keenly aware of what is expected of you."

"Of course, Papa. I'll come out to the clinic as soon as I finish my coffee."

Adina watched her father walk out the back door, scorning his insistence on treating her like a child. Did he really think she didn't understand the importance of the assignment? Of course she was aware of what would be expected of her. Her thoughts argued with her as though Papa were still standing in front of her. She brushed off her defeated feelings, gathered her things, and went to the clinic.

Papa was at the supply cabinet loading up his black leather medical bag when Adina walked in. He'd carried that same bag for as long as she could remember. Like an extra appendage, the bag went with him everywhere. Henry Robbins was a dedicated physician, always ready for any medical emergency. He trained Adina to do the same.

"You have been given a gift, Adina Luisa," he said to her the day she received her nursing certificate. "You must strive to make your mother proud."

"What would you like me to do, Papa?" she asked now. Her own medical kit was packed and strapped to her shoulder.

"We will need to keep accurate records for each prisoner. Bring a new record book, medical forms, as well as a clipboard. You will be able to compile the records into chart files after the visits." He set his medical bag on the examination table. "I want you to watch and follow my lead today. These are German prisoners of war. They are under the strict care and supervision of our government."

She stepped closer. "I understand completely, Papa. As you know, I've been nursing on my own for over a year now. I am quite capable of handling things at the prisoner camp." The old familiar feelings of frustration crept up inside her, yet she wasn't about to let them get the better of her. "But of course, I will, as you said, follow your lead."

Papa snapped the medical bag shut. "Very good." He placed his hat on his head, snatched up the bag, and walked toward the door. "Please collect the record book and forms and meet me in the car."

She heard the clinic door open.

"Don't waste time, Adina. I don't wish to be late for our first visit."

7

Camp

Adina stared out the window, fidgeting, as the Oldsmobile crept through town. The short drive had been quiet apart from Papa re-emphasizing the need for Adina to only do as he instructed her.

"I don't know how many men we will be screening today. Most of them have only just arrived at the camp and may need more attention. You will assist with vitals and charting to begin with."

Adina's one-word responses seemed to satisfy him, and so she quietly took in the beauty of the drive. The curve of the tree-lined road, the speckled sunlight casting through the leaves and into the car windows.

Soon, the Camp Windsor sign came into view. The tents behind the barbed-wire fence were now clearly visible—canvas-sided with pitched roofs, rows and rows of them. Servicemen in uniform, along with prisoners like the ones she saw the other day, mulled about. Eyes wide, Adina straightened and sat forward.

Papa brought the car to a stop at the gate entrance where a young man in uniform stood at attention. Papa rolled down his window as the guard approached.

"Hello, sir," the young man said. "Are you lost, or do you have business here today?"

Papa cleared his throat. "I'm Dr. Henry Robbins. This is my daughter, Nurse Adina Robbins. I have been asked by Major Williams to begin prisoner medical care today."

The guard walked back to the fence, removed a clipboard hanging from it, and flipped through its pages. Satisfied with what he saw, he walked back to the car.

"You're all clear, Dr. Robbins. You can pull your car right over there to the administration office. Welcome to Camp Windsor." With a set of keys, he unlocked the gate and rolled it open, allowing the Oldsmobile to pass through.

A smile curved on Adina's lips. Her heart raced as Papa drove through the narrow entrance, then a short distance to where he parked. The sign in front of them read "Administration." Papa turned off the engine, opened his door, and got out.

"Adina, you're sitting like a bump on a log. Please get your things. We don't want to keep Major Williams waiting," he said, shutting the door.

Adina did as her father asked. Getting out of the car, she smoothed the wrinkles from her pinafore and casually gazed around, feeling as though she had stepped into another world—a world surrounded by barbed-wire fencing, where men lived in tents under close supervision. Yet these weren't ordinary men. Or were they? Some stood in groups, bantering back and forth, smoking cigarettes. Others exercised in an open area. Another prisoner was sitting in a chair in front of one of the tents while another gave him a haircut. All of them wore the letters PW on the side of their dungarees and the backs of their shirts.

"Adina Luisa," Papa called, standing at the entrance of the office.

The small building was modestly furnished. A desk sat at the front, and two sets of wooden file cabinets were positioned along the back wall. A round clock and a framed map of the campground were the only adornments on the slat-wood walls.

The front desk telephone rang out, startling both Adina and Papa. It rang and rang until finally, a young private burst through the front door to answer it.

"Private Jenkins here," he said, panting as though he'd just run a marathon. "Yes sir, I believe I'm looking at them right now, sir."

Awkwardly, he looked at Adina and Papa. "Yes sir, I'm sorry, sir. I'll bring them over right away." The private fumbled to put down the receiver. "You must be Dr. Robbins. I'm Private Jenkins." He held his hand out to Papa but couldn't take his eyes off Adina.

"Yes," Papa said, taking his hand. "I'm Dr. Henry Robbins. This is my daughter, Adina. She will be my assistant on our visits here at the camp." Papa stood stiff shouldered, eyeing the young man over his glasses. "You can refer to her as Nurse Robbins, if you don't mind."

Jenkins removed his cap. "I'm pleased to meet you, Miss, or um...Nurse Robbins." He reached for Adina's hand, his goofy smile adding to his awkward behavior.

Stifling a laugh, she held out her hand to him. "Hello there. It's very nice to meet you as well. Do you have a first name, or should we just call you Private Jenkins?"

"It's Harold, but the boys call me Hardy, ma'am."

Papa raised an eyebrow. "I believe we had an appointment to meet with Major Williams at nine a.m., yes?"

"Oh, yes, sir," Jenkins said. "The major's waiting for you in the mess tent. If you'll just follow me, I'll take you right to him." He adjusted his cap and held the door open for Adina and Papa. "Is that a foreign accent I'm hearing, Dr. Robbins? Where might you be from?"

"I was born in Lithuania, but I've lived in the United States for many years." Papa's tone clearly communicated his impatience.

Jenkins abruptly stopped at the open door. He turned to face Papa and removed his cap, holding it to his chest with both hands. "Gosh, I'm sorry, sir," he said with a slight stammer. "What the Krauts did to your people in forty-one is unforgivable."

Papa stiffened, keeping his eyes forward. "I appreciate your concern, Private Jenkins. But as I said before, I've lived in this country for many years. The United States is my home. I have no family in Lithuania anymore." He pushed past Jenkins and walked out the door.

Adina mouthed an apology to Private Jenkins as she passed by.

Outside, the camp hummed, alive with activity. Adina bobbed her head, looking and listening, taking in as much as she could on the short walk to the mess tent. The sounds of Benny Goodman emanated from what she thought was the latrine tent. A group of prisoners gathered just outside. One stood dripping wet with only a towel wrapped around the lower half of his body. He sang along with the music, his thick German accent ringing clear. The others joked and laughed. Someone whistled at Adina. "Howdy, Fräulein," another called out.

Heat rose to Adina's face. She smiled and lifted her hand in a half wave. Papa shot the men a sharp glare, which only encouraged them.

"Hey!" Jenkins yelled. "Behave yourselves, or it'll be extra kitchen police duty for all of you. And you!" He pointed to the wet one. "Put some clothes on. There's a lady on the grounds."

Adina realized that she was, indeed, the only lady on the grounds. There was no need to draw any more attention to that reality.

The three continued on. To the left were six rows of tents, each row about eight tents deep. An infirmary and a canteen tent sat separate from the rest.

They arrived at the mess tent and went inside. The open space was filled with rows of tables and chairs. A gentleman in uniform sat intently studying documents laid out on the table in front of him. Adina assumed him to be Lieutenant Major Williams. He looked up as the three entered.

"Good morning, Dr. Robbins." He stood, stepping forward to greet them. His uniform was simple—khaki slacks with the usual issued button-up shirt, rank insignia at the collar and on his cap. He had a Clark Gable-trimmed mustache and close-cut graying hair that poked out from beneath the cap. A pair of black, thick-rimmed glasses sat on his nose. The eyes behind them were dark yet kind, cradled in deep-set lines that looked like they could tell their own stories of battle, if asked. "My apologies for any confusion at the front office," he said. "Jenkins was supposed to meet you at the gate. No matter now. Why don't you set your things up at this table here."

Papa set his medical bag on the table, then reached out to shake the major's hand. "We are happy to help in any way that we can, Major Williams. I'd like you to meet my daughter, Adina. She will assist me today."

Major Williams straightened at the sight of Adina. He removed his cap, wiped his right hand on his slacks, then reached out to shake her hand. "I'm very pleased to meet you, Miss Robbins," he said, grinning.

Adina shook his hand, yet she couldn't resist staring at the man's head. There was more skin on top than there was hair. She hoped her distraction wasn't obvious. "It's very nice to meet you as well, Major Williams. Please, call me Adina."

"Adina it is, then," he said, quickly turning his attention back to Papa. "Let's get started, shall we? You can use this table here to set things up however you like. We've set up this privacy screen over here." He motioned to a makeshift screen made of wooden poles and bed sheets. "The men can use that if you need them to, you know, remove some clothes, or what have you."

Adina got right to work moving chairs out of the way to create a temporary triage station with one of the tables, placing one chair on either side. She then set the patient information forms from the clinic in a neat stack on the table, along with two fountain pens. From her kit, she removed a clean white towel and laid it out, along with her stethoscope, blood pressure cuff, and thermometer, arranging them neatly on the towel.

"We are hearing good reports of troop advancements in Europe. Is that not correct, Major?" Papa asked while his hands rummaged through his black leather bag.

"Yes, yes," Major Williams responded. "It's a damn bloody mess, though. We've lost so many of our boys. But they've taken the beaches and are moving forward." He glanced out the open tent entrance. "I suppose it's good to be here at home and not over there, that's for certain." The look in his eyes seemed to tell a different story. "You ever fight in a war, Doc?"

The question seemed to catch Papa by surprise. He looked up from his bag. "Why, yes," he said, hesitating. "I served in the Great War." He continued to busy himself, rearranging some items he'd laid out on the table.

"Boy oh boy, I surely didn't think we'd be doing this again so soon. How 'bout you, Doc?"

Adina could tell by the irritated look in Papa's eyes that the very last thing he wanted to do was to engage in a discussion over the how and whys of the first world war. Her own attempts to ask him questions on the subject would render a swift change of subject, or even a complete shutdown of the conversation. As a field medic, Papa would have seen things that no human should ever have to see. Gunshot wounds to the face and head. Arms and legs blown clean off, never to be found again. And the blinding, blistering gas, its victim foaming at the mouth, suffocating. Of course there were the lesser culprits: disease, cold, and hunger. He had to have witnessed enough horror and death on the battlefield to last him a lifetime, twelve times over. And when it was all said and done, his people were still blamed and hated, more than before that Great War.

Papa peered over the rims of his glasses at the major. "Major Williams, what do you have planned for the men today? Just how many would you like us to see?"

Williams cleared his throat. "Well, as we spoke of at our meeting, you won't be able to see all of the men in one day. Half of them will be working in the fields today. You gotta believe those vineyard owners love having PWs close by. They're eating up the free labor. And that's a good thing. Keeps the farmers happy and keeps the prisoners busy." He paused, tugging his bottom lip forward. "Do you think you can get through fifty or so by the end of the day?"

Adina's head snapped toward her father. "Holy cow, fifty?" she said, eyes wide.

"Adina, please," Papa said, shooting her a look she understood all too well. "Fifty will not be a problem at all, Major. We may even be able to see a few more, depending on how the day progresses. Please, we will need about fifteen more minutes, and then you may start sending the men in."

Major Williams handed a clipboard to Papa. "Here's a list of all the prisoners we have to date. I'll leave Private Jenkins here with you. Be sure to let him know when you're ready for the men, as well as if you need anything at all."

Papa flipped through the papers on the clipboard. Adina glanced over his shoulder to see page after page of handwritten names. Most were Germans. "Very good, then, Major. Thank you," he said, continuing to look over the names.

The major adjusted his cap and turned to walk away. He stopped short, turning back toward Papa. "Dr. Robbins, I certainly hope I didn't offend you just then with my questions about the war. I apologize if I did. You'd think I would have learned by now to leave the past behind."

Papa pursed his lips, forcing the slightest curve of a smile. "Not to worry, Major. Please don't give it another thought."

Williams waited as though he thought Papa might say something else. He then glanced over at Adina, who smiled apologetically back at him. "Oh, and by the way," he said, "chow time is at twelve thirty. We'd be happy to serve you some lunch." He walked out of the tent, leaving a deafening silence behind, as well as Private Jenkins, who paced and fidgeted.

"Adina," Papa said, breaking the silence. "I would like you to triage the men as they enter. Be sure to start a clean chart for each one. I trust that you brought plenty of forms from the clinic, yes?" He handed her the clipboard with the listed names. "You may keep track by marking the names off of the list." He scratched his head. "Though I very much doubt all of these men speak English. I speak enough German to help, if necessary."

Adina perked up. "Oh, they speak English pretty well—" She caught her mistake, but not before Papa's eyebrows shot up.

"How on earth would you know this, Adina Luisa?"

She cut her eyes to the side, scrambling for an answer, all the while remembering the young prisoner at the back fence. "I, um…You remember, Papa, one of them said, 'Howdy Fräulein,' when we were walking past on our way to the mess tent?" She smiled. "Howdy? That's English, right?"

"She's right, Doc," Jenkins interjected. "You'd be amazed how well some of these Krauts speak English." The private looked proud of himself and his response. Relieved, Adina thanked Jenkins with a timid grin.

Papa grunted and focused his attention on pulling supplies from his medical bag.

Adina breathed a sigh and stepped closer to him. "More than fifty men today, Papa?" she whispered. "What are we trying to accomplish here?"

"We will assess fifty men today, Adina. And if we are able and we have the time, we will assess more." His eyes narrowed. "This is not a problem for me, and I would hope it is not a problem for you."

She despised the thick tension that lingered between them. Like a fortified wall, ever present, keeping him from her, and vice versa.

"Not a problem at all," she lied. Everything was a problem when it came to her father. Every battle she encountered with him pushed her closer and closer to saying yes to Jeanie Mae and signing up with the WACs on Wednesday. *He doesn't need me*, she thought as she arranged and rearranged the instruments on the table. *Jeanie's right. I'd allow him to control me until his dying day.* She stacked the forms again, setting the pens parallel neatly beside.

"If you are ready at your station, Adina, please let Private, um—" He tapped his temple.

"Jenkins, Papa."

"Yes, yes. Please inform Private Jenkins we are ready to begin."

Adina walked over to the tent entrance where Jenkins was standing at ease, hands clasped behind his back. He straightened, smiling at her approach. With a nod, he left the tent. She walked back to her station and took a seat. Folding her hands in front of her, she waited. She looked at her father. He busied himself, not even so much as a glance in her direction. Her heart ached with love for him.

The voices of the approaching men grew louder, and the anticipation grew.

"All right, men," Private Jenkins bellowed as he entered the tent, a boisterous line of men following behind. "Line up along the tent wall." He stepped aside, motioning to the men with his hand. "Settle down, men, settle down." Jenkins, who until now appeared the befuddled buffoon, now worked hard at appearing in charge in front of the prisoners. "This here is Dr. Robbins and his daughter, Nurse Robbins."

A couple men snickered, gawking and whispering. Jenkins looked right at them. "I want you to be respectful and wait until you are called. Is that understood?"

"Yes sir!" one of them shouted, exaggerating a hand salute.

"Watch it, mister," Jenkins responded, "or it's double KP duty for you." He turned toward Papa. "Welp, they're all yours, Doc."

Papa looked at Adina and nodded.

Adina caught eye with the prisoner standing at the front of the lineup. She motioned with her hand for him to take a seat. "Good morning. Name, please."

The young man didn't appear much older than her. His boyish face flushed red, accentuating his tired, watery eyes. "Frederick Becker," he said. Removing a soiled handkerchief from his pants pocket, he blotted his forehead and blew his nose.

Adina ran her finger down the lengthy list of handwritten names. "Ah, yes. Here you are. Frederick Becker, twenty-one years old. Is that correct?"

The young man nodded.

"How are you today, Frederick? Have you been ill? Any aches, pains, fever?"

He reached for his throat. "My, umm—"

"Your throat? Is it sore?" she asked.

"Yes, my throat. It feels, um...hot?" He placed his hand to his head. "And my head aches very badly."

Adina, now in her element, had an actual patient to attend to. She went right to work. "Oh, I see," she said, reaching for the thermometer. "Let's just place this right under your tongue. While that cooks, I'll get your blood pressure." At her approach, Frederick flashed a smile with the thermometer clenched between his teeth. "Mouth closed please," she said, wrapping the blood pressure cuff around his arm. She couldn't help but stare at his face as she worked. *So young,* she thought. *So far away from home, wherever that may be.* She removed the thermometer. "It looks like you've got a fever, Frederick."

"Freddie," he said, patting his chest.

"Freddie it is. Your blood pressure is elevated, which makes a lot of sense since you do have a fever. I think you may have the flu." She jotted notes on the patient form.

"Flu?" he questioned.

She looked up from the chart. "A virus. You're sick. Do you understand, sick?"

He looked at her, half smiling and dazed. Adina gathered that it was more due to his illness than from a lack of understanding English.

"I'm going to ask you to step right over there," she said, motioning to her father. "Dr. Robbins will take a look at you. We'll see what we can do to get you feeling better."

"Ah, danke, Fräulein," he said.

She quickly finished charting her findings on her very first patient information form for Camp Windsor and handed it to her father. "Only forty-nine more to go," she said.

The morning continued much the same. One by one, the men would step forward. Some young, some as old as Papa. Most of them were in good health but some were not. Adina spoke with two other men who had the same symptoms as Freddie Becker. She saw another prisoner with a gunshot wound that went clean through his left shoulder. The bandage appeared to have not been changed in days. She assumed he was a new arrival. Another young man had a broken arm that had been splinted in a field hospital prior to him arriving at the camp. It seemed to be healing nicely. Like clockwork, Adina triaged the men, noting their charts, then sending them to Papa, who gave them his expert evaluation and care. By chow time, Adina had lost count of how many men she had assessed.

Lunch was served at the tables right alongside their makeshift clinic. Adina and Papa filed through the same chow line as the prisoners. They were served a hot meal of hearty meat hash with gravy, mixed vegetables, and fresh-baked bread. To Adina, the entire spread looked more plentiful than the meals she and Papa had been eating since war rationing began. The site of it caused her stomach to growl, having only nibbled a half piece of toast before they left the house this morning. Sitting alongside Papa and the other prisoners, she devoured every delicious bite while listening to the sounds of conversation—German and English mingling together. The tinkling of silverware, the comforting smell of a hot meal, and the occasional rise of laughter all added to the intrigue of this unusual place. Still, there was no sign of the prisoner she'd met at the back fence.

As lunch ended, the men efficiently bused their tables, setting their chairs back in place. One prisoner walked over to Adina and Papa and removed their plates from the table.

"Allow me, Fräulein," he said, addressing Adina and nodding to her father.

Taken aback and blushing, Adina thanked him. With a wink and a quick bow, the young man turned and walked away.

Papa cleared his throat and left the table, making his way back to his workstation.

The men were already lining themselves up along the tent wall, anxiously awaiting Adina's return. At the front of the line stood a rather large man. He had a thick head of dishwater-gray hair. A bushy mustache of the same color hung over the top of his upper lip, with the tip of a chewed, soggy brown cigar poking out from under the smoke-stained hairs. His dungarees, too big even for his extra-large size, hung low on his ample waist. His shirt looked about a size too small. He joked with the prisoner standing next to him in a thick German accent that settled into a sort of growl at the back of his throat. When he laughed, his entire body seemed to laugh right along with him.

Once Adina had situated herself at the table, she lifted her head, calling, "Next." She gaped at his approach, recognizing him as the fat catcaller from the backside of the camp last week. Her heart pounded. She looked up and down the lineup of men, wondering if she would see any other familiar faces.

"Howdy, Fräulein," he said, as he took a seat in the chair across from her. He smiled, revealing that some of his teeth were missing. The ones he did have were smoke-stained and desperately in need of care. He didn't say anything else to her, other than the thick-accented cowboy greeting. Adina wondered if he recognized her.

"Name, please," she said. She kept her head down, pretending to search the list of names on the clipboard.

"Günter Schmelz-Heimer. The comrades call me Heimee. That's H-e-i-m-e-e. Two e's if you please, Fräulein." He found his rhyme amusing, heaving a deep, guttural laugh through his teeth, so as not to lose his cigar.

Adina couldn't help herself and laughed out loud as well, drawing a glance from Papa. She straightened and continued searching the list for his name. "Ah yes, here you are. Günter Schmelz-Heimer. You're fifty-four years old, correct?"

He chuckled. "If you ask my wife, then yes." He glanced right and left out the sides of his eyes, then motioned for Adina to lean in closer. "But," he said, his voice hushed, "if you ask meine Hure, she would tell you I am a spry forty-five." He paused, holding his position, waiting for her response. When she only eyed him skeptically, he again burst out laughing. "Nein, nein, Fräulein. I only joke with you. There is no strumpet for me. Truly, I tell you. I love my wife, my Gertrude." His fat fingers fumbled inside his pocket until he retrieved a small, tattered photograph and handed it to Adina. The woman in the faded print was not large like her husband. Quite the contrary. She had a petite frame and wore a pinafore dress with a full skirt. Soft, fair curls hung over her shoulders. The black-and-white photograph had been touched up with color, giving her lips and cheeks a rosy hue, as well as a bright blue tint to her eyes.

"She's lovely," Adina said. "Did you add the color yourself?"

"No, not me. Danny did that for me. I described my beautiful Gertie to him. He used his pencils to bring her to life."

Adina wondered about that name. *Danny? Short for Daniel?* "Danny? Is he your bunk mate?" she asked.

"Ja, he is, Fräulein. You met him the other day. Remember?"

Her heart dropped to the pit of her stomach. He did recognize her. She looked over at her father, hoping he hadn't heard what Heimee just said. She was relieved to see Papa engrossed in noting the patient chart in front of him.

Heimee's lips curved up and around his cigar. "Danny hasn't stopped talking about you, Fräulein." He laughed out loud and sputtered a cough.

Papa glanced over his glasses in Adina's direction, and she quickly changed the subject.

"Let's get your blood pressure, Heimee. Tell me more about your wife. Gertrude, you said?" She stretched the cuff around his plump arm.

"My Gertie, ja. Even after birthing four daughters, she is still the most beautiful."

"Four daughters?" She removed the cuff. "Tell me about them. What are their ages?"

His face lit up at the question. "Let me see now. Two years is a long time to be away from home. I've missed a few birthday celebrations." He scratched the side of his stubbly cheek. "There's Amelia, named for my Mutter. She would be fourteen. She wishes to be a doctor someday. Ada just turned twelve last month. That one still loves to dig in the mud more than to play with the dolls." He chuckled. "I tell Gertie to let her be. What harm could it do if she wants to play in the dirt? And then there is Andrea. She is eight—no, nine years. Sweet, gentle Andrea. He then paused, a distant look in his eyes. "And lastly, mein schatzi, Adelaide. She is six years old."

Adina glanced up from her charting. "You must miss them terribly."

He straightened, tucking the photograph back into his front pocket. "Ja, ja. But what can I do? I am here, they are there."

She felt an overwhelming sympathy for him. This oversized oaf of a man was more like a teddy bear than a killer. How difficult it must be for his daughters to not have their father for two years. She had only ever thought of American soldiers making that kind of sacrifice, not the enemy.

Adina finished up her notes and handed him his chart. "All right then, Günter. You're all set. You can take this over to Dr. Robbins."

"Danke, Fräulein. And don't forget, the name's Heimee." He stood. "I'll be sure to tell Danny Boy you said hello." He chuckled as he walked away.

Throughout the rest of the afternoon, Adina found her heart warm to each prisoner who sat across the table from her. Of course, some were much quieter than Heimee, some even a bit withdrawn. Yet each prisoner revealed aspects of their lives that characterized them as genuine human beings. They were soldiers, fighting under the Nazi regime, criminals to be sure. But they were also men with lives before the war. Lawyers, shopkeepers, teachers, farmers, even a mail carrier. And they were husbands and fathers. She wondered if they joined the fight under force or from shear fear of the cruel leader they served under. The prisoners she spoke with today never wanted a war in the first place and wished it to end quickly so they could all go home—with one exception.

The day was winding down when the tall prisoner approached Adina's table. He appeared kempt in his prison-issued shirt buttoned to the collar and neatly tucked into his trousers. His face was clean shaven, showcasing a sharp, set jaw and chiseled cheekbones. His Aryan blond hair was crewcut short and precisely trimmed around his ears. He sat in the chair across from Adina and raised his square chin a bit higher, so as to look down his nose at her. At the sight of him, the slightest tinge of intimidation came over her, yet she poised herself, looking directly in his glassy blue eyes.

"Name, please," she said.

"Klaus Schneider." His voice, thickly accented, had a slight upward inflection.

"Yes, Klaus Schneider. Here you are." She checked his name off her list. "You are thirty-two years old, correct?"

"You are correct, Fräulein."

"And how are you feeling today, Klaus?" she asked, fountain pen in hand, ready to take notes.

"You may address me as Herr Schneider, Fräulein. That is, unless you would like to address me as Oberscharführer Schneider, which is my rightful rank." He smirked. "I believe that is the equivalent of—how do you say it? Ah yes, a 'sergeant' in your American army."

Adina narrowed her eyes, never breaking away from his gaze. "We won't be addressing you that way here, Herr Schneider. You forget, you're not fighting a war anymore. You are a prisoner of the United States." Until this point, Adina's day had gone smoothly. The prisoners had kindly received Papa and her, thankful for the medical care afforded them. And now, was this how their first day at Camp Windsor would end? With a sanctimonious, holier-than-thou Nazi? He was the epitome of all she had imagined the Germans to be.

"I'll need to take your temperature and blood pressure, Herr Schneider." She refused to give him the courtesy of a kind smile and instead shoved her chair back, snatched up the thermometer and pressure cuff, and walked to the other side of the table. "Open your mouth, please," she said, shaking down the thermometer.

"You are disgusted with me, Fräulein?" His tone dripped with sarcasm. "But why would you be? Do you deny me the right to fight for the cause I believe in? To serve under the leadership of our beloved

Führer? To fight for the common good of the Fatherland?" The smirk seemed to be a permanent feature on his lips.

Adina's jaw ached. She had been clenching her teeth from the moment this man sat down, and now her blood boiled. Setting the thermometer down, she leaned in close to Schneider's face and lowered her voice "And what exactly *is* the common good, Klaus?"

His eyes fixed on her, the smirk becoming a sinister grin. "Why, a united and strong Germany, free, and cleansed of all undesirables, of course." His stare lingered.

The heartless response infuriated her, and Adina regretted asking the question. She carelessly inserted the thermometer in his mouth, clinking the glass on his teeth. "Under your tongue, please. And keep your mouth shut, Herr Schneider," she said, her anger surging. She finished with his blood pressure, removed the thermometer, and sat down, feverishly scribbling notes in a chart.

"Have I offended you, Fräulein? Did I say something you do not agree with?"

She glared at him. His feigned smile and sarcasm made her ill. Try as she might to remain cool, calm, and courteous, it wasn't working. She was failing with this one.

Just then, Schneider's expression changed. His mouth fell open, and his eyebrows raised. "Aha, I see," he said, wagging his pointer finger at her. "You wouldn't happen to be Juden...would you, Fräulein?"

She wanted to scream. Instead, shoving her chair back, she stood and handed the uncompleted patient form to him. "You may take this to Dr. Robbins now, *Mister* Schneider."

"Do forgive me, Fräulein. Believe me, I do understand." His feigned apology sounded more like a mockery. "You see, I would be offended, too, had someone assumed the same about me." He clicked his heels, giving a half bow. "Good day, Fräulein."

Adina seethed. Turning her back to Papa's workstation, she folded her arms, allowing her anger to steadily brew inside her. She was sure her face was a contorted mess and didn't want her father to question it.

Yet she herself reeled with questions. What just happened? Why would he ask her if she was Juden? A Jew? She glanced down at her wristwatch. It was almost five o'clock. The day was just about over. She squeezed her eyes shut. Tapping her toe, she tried to quell her anger, all the while gesturing with her hands, mouthing her rebuttal, as though talking to an imaginary enemy. *"Who the hell do you think you are, you no good Kraut? It's because of you that—"*

"Hallo?" A man rapped his knuckles on the table.

She jumped and whirled around. She'd been so caught up continuing to bristle the argument under her breath that she hadn't heard anyone approach. Her gaze settled on a young man, and her eyes widened. It was him. The prisoner. The one she'd met at the back fence. His ruddy hair wasn't quite as tousled as it was the other day, except for the pieces that fell forward into his blue eyes. His smile brought back the lucid feeling of that day. He was looking at her the same way now. She stared, dumbfounded.

"I am here for the medical?" he said, pulling the chair out and taking a seat across from her. "I hope I am not too late."

She struggled to compose herself, compulsively smoothing the wrinkles from the front of her pinafore. "No, um, It's quite all right. I'm sure we could... If you would just give me one minute." She sat down across from the young prisoner and fumbled for a new patient form, causing the stack to slide off the table and onto the floor. Flustered, she gathered up the papers, setting the wrinkled pile back onto the table. "Now, where is that pen?" she said, lifting every item on the table.

"Can I help?" he said, reaching toward the papers.

"No, no. It's my pen," she said. "I can't find that stupid pen."

At that, he reached under the table and retrieved the lost pen. "Is this the one, Fräulein?" He handed it to her.

She took a breath to compose herself and snatched the pen from his hand. "Yes, thank you." She was frustrated with her lack of confidence in front of him. Why did he make her feel so uncomfortable? "Name, please?" she asked a bit too loudly, avoiding his eyes.

He leaned in, trying to make eye contact. "Daniel Christensen."

Adina ran her finger down the written list of prisoner names, willing herself not to look at him. "Yes, here you are. You're twenty-four years old, correct?"

"Ja, yes, twenty-four." His voice was gentle, forgiving of her blundering behavior.

She finally looked up at him. He had an easy-going demeanor, a relaxed confidence. How could he be so calm when she herself was such a mess? Only a few minutes earlier, she had given herself over to so much anger and frustration. She berated herself for her silly, school-girl emotions and insecurities. She straightened her back and folded her hands on the table, if only to appear a little more professional.

"Very well, then," she said, making sure to look him in the eyes. "And how are we feeling today, Mr. Christensen?"

He laughed out loud. When Adina narrowed her eyes at him, he stifled his laugh and cleared his throat. "We are feeling well today," he joked. "And please, Mr. Christensen was my father. Call me Daniel."

Adina was in no mood for his antics, yet his smile continued to weaken her, melting her from the inside out. She glanced over to her father's workstation. Papa was speaking to Schneider, but the man wasn't looking at him. He was staring at Adina, watching her like a wolf stalking its prey. Papa seemed too busy to notice.

Are you all right, Fräulein?" Daniel side-eyed Schneider.

"I'm quite all right, Mr. Christensen. I'd be even better if you would leave the jokes outside." She hated her response, even as it came out of her mouth. It wasn't the prisoner sitting in front of her who made her so angry, it was the one sitting across from her father.

"I'm sorry, Fräu—" He stopped. "Please, what is your name? I asked you the other day, but you ran away so fast."

She remembered, chuckling under her breath. "Adina Robbins," she said. Could it be that the reason he made her so uncomfortable was because Heimee said she was all he talked about since that day? She was determined not to let him get to her.

"It's very nice to meet you, Adina." He reached out his hand.

Adina stared at his hand, as though she'd forgotten how to shake one.

"You shake hands in this country, ja?" he asked.

"Oh yes, of course we do." She took hold of his hand and held it, warm in hers. His grip was firm. He held her hand the same way he held her eyes. Heat rose to her face. She wondered what he saw in her. "It's getting late," she said, pulling her hand away. "Let me get your vitals and send you on over to Dr. Robbins."

She got to work asking her list of medical questions, then jotting down notes on the form. When it came time to take his temperature and blood pressure, his eyes didn't leave her face. Hard as she tried to stay focused on her tasks, she fought a losing battle. *He's a Nazi*, she thought. *A killer*. She finished up as quickly as she could and handed him the patient form. "You can take this over to Dr. Robbins now." As he took the form from her, she held onto it and studied his face. She couldn't explain it, but there was something about his eyes that intrigued her.

Definitely not the eyes of a killer.

"Danke, Adina," he said. He stood to leave, then stopped. "Adina?"

She looked up. "Yes?"

"You are mutig, Adina Robbins."

She raised an eyebrow.

"Mutig. Brave," he said, his smile igniting his blue eyes.

She watched as he made his way to Papa's workstation and wondered why he would say such a thing. Did sneaking around the backside of the prisoner camp prove she was brave, or just plain stupid? Daniel Christensen was the first prisoner she met by chance last week and the last to come through her line today. Fated bookends. What did it all mean?

8 ▌

Adina awoke the next day with a dreamy anticipation of what the days ahead would hold. The first visit to Camp Windsor was unlike anything she could have imagined. It was early in the morning, and she lay in bed quizzing her memory as the faces of the prisoners passed behind her eyes. Large one, mustache and cigar, loved to laugh—Heimee. Quiet one, red nose and bad sore throat—Freddie. Clean cut, conceited, very rude—Klaus Schneider. That one, she could forget. There were so many others to remember.

And there was Daniel.

Adina and Papa evaluated more than fifty prisoners on that first day. Apparently, her father was right again. They made an excellent team when they worked together toward a common goal. Unfortunately, that goal happened to be medicine and not family. But Adina would take whatever she could get. Today was a new day.

She got herself out of bed, quickly dressed in full uniform, and made her way to the kitchen for breakfast.

Papa sat at the kitchen table with the newspaper laid out in front of him and coffee cup in hand.

"What's on the schedule today, Papa?" Adina poured herself a cup of coffee, burning her tongue on the first bitter sip. "What time do we need to be at the camp?" she asked, sucking air in and out over her tongue.

Papa folded the newspaper, setting it aside. "Adina Luisa, are you aware that thousands of women and children have fled the city of London? Thousands, Adina, for their own safety. The city is devastated by the bombings." He removed a handkerchief from his pocket and inspected one of the lenses of his glasses. "You should be thankful, Adina. Thankful that you are safe here in America." He worked a smudge from the lens. "You are thankful, yes?"

She marveled at her father's ability to ignore and sacrifice her question on the altar of current events. Did he really think she wasn't aware of the world's turmoil? How she dreamed she could be over there to help those women and children. Yet here she sat with her father, who had the nerve to ask if she was thankful. She set her cup down, bracing her elbow on the counter. "Of course, I'm thankful, Papa. But apparently you didn't hear my question. What time do we need to be at the camp? We worked through fifty prisoners yesterday like clockwork. Will it be another full day?" She waited, eager to hear his response, sipping her coffee more cautiously.

Papa stood from the table. "I heard your question, Adina." He dabbed the corner of his mouth with a napkin and walked his dishes to the sink. "There will be no camp evaluations today."

In a single moment, her expectations for the day were dashed. "Why is that? We saw less than half the men yesterday."

"Major Williams informed me that most of the prisoners will be working in the fields today. I believe he said something about the prune farms. Not that it matters. Today you will assist me in the clinic, that is after your scheduled morning visits." He scrutinized her dress. "Obviously, you will need to change out of that dress uniform. You should have checked with me about today's schedule before you dressed, Adina."

As she watched him walk away, she drew on every ounce of her emotional strength to not burst out in anger. How was she to know they wouldn't be working at Camp Windsor today? If he had told her sooner, she wouldn't be wearing a full dress uniform. But it wasn't having to go back to her room to change her clothes that upset her. She woke this morning with an excitement she hadn't felt in a long time. The unmitigated thrill of treating the German enemy. And, of course, the possibility of seeing Daniel. Instead, today would just be another day of the mundane and monotonous.

But then she remembered that Wednesday was only one day away. With all the excitement of her first visit to the camp, she'd forgotten she was supposed to meet Jeanie Mae at the recruiter's office tomorrow with her decision. Would she be joining the WACs? Would she be serving in the war effort? Her best friend was counting on her. Adina was torn. She still had a strong desire to join up and escape the control of her father and the confines of her small town. Yet now there was an unexpected new purpose, right here at home, and it didn't fall into the day-to-day drudgery of back pain and gout. Camp Windsor was filled with energy, excitement, and purpose.

Adina didn't enjoy being cooped up in the medical clinic. So much of her time was spent charting and filing or dusting shelves and organizing instruments. Of course she assisted Papa as he stitched up a wound or set a broken bone. But the most riveting day she'd had was two weeks ago when Mrs. Hollister fainted during her examination, almost hitting her head on the instrument table before she landed on the floor. When she came to, Papa had her give a urine sample. The back counter of the exam room was set up for simple lab work. Right there he took a few drops of Mrs. Hollister's urine and mixed it in a test tube with Benedict's solution. He placed the tube in a can, then in a pan of water on a single countertop hot plate. Once heated, the urine would react with the solution and change color, ranging from light bluish-green to red. Red denoted a high sugar level, possibly signifying diabetes. Mrs. Hollister's test came out light blue: low blood sugar.

"You ate breakfast today, Mrs. Hollister?" he asked.

"Um, golly, don't know that I did," she groggily replied.

The prescribed treatment was a glass of apple juice, which Adina administered without delay. Mrs. Hollister was then sent on her way. In Adina's opinion, that was an exciting day.

With today proving the same caliber of excitement, Adina was happy that the last clinic appointment was at one p.m. The rest of her day would consist of a visit to the Quinn home for Sally's monthly pregnancy checkup, followed by two prescription deliveries. She actually looked forward to it. She'd be able to ride her bike into town and soak up the warm summer air, fragrant with star jasmine. She'd pedal and sweat out her frustrations, breathing in what felt like a bit of free air, even if it was within the limits of her small town.

9

Sally Quinn

The afternoon was especially warm, with not a single cloud in the sky. By the time Adina reached the Quinn home, her blouse was stuck to her back, wet with perspiration. She parked her bicycle at the bottom of the porch, grabbed her kit from the basket, and made her way up the porch steps. A blue star flag hung in the front window. Sally's husband, Donald, was serving in the Pacific.

Sally Quinn was twenty-one years old, just two years older than Adina. She and Donald married after Sally became pregnant with their first child, Donald Junior—DJ for short. The toddler was two years old. Donald Senior was called to serve overseas six months ago. Sally found out she was pregnant with their second child a month after he left.

Adina knocked on the front door of the small, cottage-style house. She could hear squeals and the patter of little feet on the other side. Sally opened the door.

"Hello, Adina. Come on in." Sally was petite with long blond hair she liked to wear pulled back in a ponytail. She wore a floral house dress that draped loosely over her growing belly. Little DJ waddled around in nothing but a sagging diaper.

"Phew, it's a bit warm out there today," she said. She reached down and hoisted the toddler onto her hip, grunting as she did. Her cheeks flushed. She puffed a stray wisp of hair out of her eye and wiped sweat from her forehead with the back of her hand.

"You really should be careful with lifting, Sally," Adina said, following her into the tiny living room. "The last thing you want to do is stress the baby into coming early."

"I know, I know," Sally responded, out of breath. "Not much I can do about it. It's just me and DJ around here." She sat down on the sofa and snuggled the curly-haired boy on her lap. She pecked him with kisses, pressing her nose to the side of his neck. He giggled. "There's no telling when Don will get back. I haven't had a letter in weeks."

Adina's heart ached for the young mother. She wanted to be a comfort to Sally but wasn't sure how. She didn't have any family members fighting in the war and couldn't relate to being alone and pregnant. She patted Sally's knee.

"You know how slow the military mail can be. Hopefully you'll get a letter in a few days." Adina knew she had no idea what she was talking about. She didn't want to offer false hope to Sally. Any hope would do. "Let's check you out—see how this baby's doing. You've definitely grown since my last visit."

"I feel as big as a house," Sally said. She plopped DJ down on the floor and lay on her back on the sofa. This wasn't her first baby, and she knew the steps of a routine visit well. She lifted her dress up over her ample belly and gently stroked its bare skin in a circular motion. "This little nugget has been moving constantly. Kept me up most of last night." Her eyes looked distant. "I just wish Don could be here to feel it move. We've got a strong one in there." She smiled. "He'd be so proud."

Adina placed one end of the measuring tape at the base of Sally's sternum and stretched it over her tummy to the top of her pelvic bone. She jotted the measurement in her notebook. "Yep, definitely bigger than last time," she said. She then carefully pressed and palpitated Sally's abdomen to determine the position of the baby. "Baby's turned sideways. I think I feel a foot under your right rib."

"Ya think?" Sally said sarcastically. "A foot in my rib, a knee in my side. This one does whatever it wants, whenever it wants."

Little DJ had lain down and fallen asleep on the rug, and Adina decided to take advantage of the quiet.

"Let's listen to the heart." She took the Pinard horn and placed the end on Sally's tummy, right where she assumed the baby's back to be. Leaning down, she put her ear to the flat end, closed her eyes, and listened. Adina never grew tired of hearing the tiny sounds through the horn. She described them as sounding like a swishing horse's gallop, for lack of better terms. Once she was sure she had picked up the beat, she looked at her watch and timed and counted the beats. "Good, strong heartbeat," she said. She noted the rate in her book.

"Wish I could hear it," Sally said. She pushed herself up, resting on her elbows. Her belly protruded high and straightforward, like a tabletop.

Adina tilted her head, a smile curving on her lips. "Sally, sit yourself straight up. I want to try something."

Sally scrunched up her face and grunted as she scooted herself up, legs stretched out straight in front of her on the sofa. "What are you thinking, Adina?"

"Humor me," Adina said. She felt Sally's abdomen again to be sure the baby was still in the same position. She then placed the Pinard horn right at the top of Sally's belly, just below the breastbone.

"Do you think you could bend yourself forward?" Adina asked. "Try to get your ear to the top of the horn."

Sally grinned. "It'll be like bending over a watermelon with knees, but I'll give it a shot." She bent herself forward, exhaling to alleviate the pressure building under her ribs. She squeezed her eyes shut tight. Her discomfort was obvious.

"You can stop if it's uncomfortable," Adina said. She placed her hand on Sally's back for support, gently urging her forward.

"No," Sally said. "I'm fine. Almost there."

Adina inched the horn to meet Sally's ear. Once there, the two waited in silence. Sally held herself steady, breathing slowly, in and out. Sweat beads gathered on her forehead.

"Wait," Sally said. "I think I can hear it." She laughed. "Boom, boom. Boom, boom." Tears filled her eyes. "That's my baby."

Adina laughed along with her. "It sure is. That's your baby." She gave Sally another minute to take in the sweet sounds. "Have you heard enough?"

"I could listen to it all day." Sally said and relaxed back against the arm of the sofa. "That was the most miraculous sound I've ever heard."

"It truly is a beautiful sound. There's nothing quite like it." Adina placed the Pinard, along with the rest of her instruments, back into her medical bag.

DJ began to stir on the floor. Eyes still closed, he pushed himself up onto his bottom and yawned.

"He gets bigger every month," Adina said. "Funny how that happens." She looked at the adorable, curly-haired boy and wondered if she'd ever have a family of her own. She couldn't imagine that happening anytime soon, but she definitely wanted it someday.

Sally picked up DJ, snuggling him on her shoulder while he slowly awakened. "He's growing so fast. Wish there was something I could do to slow it down until Donald gets home."

Adina slung her kit across her shoulder and walked toward the front door. "He'll be home soon, Sally. Real soon."

PW Parade

Adina left the Quinn home, reveling in the satisfaction the visit brought her. The sheer joy on Sally's face as she listened to her baby's heartbeat... Those were the visits that made the daily monotony worth it. People like Sally Quinn ignited the spark of purpose Adina craved. There truly were needs in her small town, and not just Sally. There were many more. Was she just being selfish by not wanting to see it? Selfish in wanting to run away—to get out from under Papa's thumb? What was it that was awakening her to the reality already around her?

It was after three, and the sun beat hot on Adina's face as she rode toward town. She envisioned the cool, green water of the river and how delicious it would feel to take a dip after work today. She'd ring up Jeanie Mae when she got home. It would be the perfect last summer hurrah before... She remembered, and it hit her deep in the pit of her stomach. Jeanie was waiting for Adina's answer, expecting her to say yes to leaving with her.

"I only said I would think about it," she said out loud as she pedaled.

Adina heard the roar of a truck approaching behind her, its low growl growing louder as it neared. She rode closer to the side of the road, giving it room to pass easily. Slowly the truck came alongside her. It was an army vehicle, a flat, stake-bed truck. The back of it was filled with PWs from Camp Windsor.

The driver sounded the horn and somebody whistled at her. Adina laughed and waved. She noticed that some of the men were shirtless, their faces and shoulders red from a long day of field work in the hot sun. Together, the men sang out in German. It sounded like some kind of drinking or marching tune. Adina wished she spoke better German, like her father.

"Howdy, Fraulein!" It was Heimee. He yelled and waved to her from the back of the truck.

Adina beamed a smile, ringing her bicycle bell and waving back. "Hello, Heimee!" she called out.

Just then, a second truck maneuvered around her. It, too, was filled with prisoners, boisterously belting out the same German melody as the others, though a bit out of sync. The truck slowed, coming to a stop at the corner in front of the Windsor Groceteria. Two of the men pointed at her and smiled. Another stood up from the front end of the truck bed. Stumbling over feet and legs, he made his way to the tailgate. Adina waited behind the truck until she could clearly see who the young man was.

Daniel.

He knelt at the tailgate, shirtless, sweaty, and filthy. He looked at her through the wooden stakes and smiled, eyes as blue as the first day she met him. He held up his hand and waved. She was so taken by the sight of him that she didn't wave back. The other men laughed, jeering him on. He ignored them, his eyes lingering on Adina.

The truck growled and began to pull forward, its roar startling her, waking her from her trance. Not wanting to miss her chance, she caught hold of Daniel's eyes, raised her hand high, and waved back to him, smiling brightly.

Daniel lowered his hand and held on to the stakes. He watched Adina as she rode behind. Both trucks moved farther on, driving toward the camp.

Adina stopped at the side of the road, shielding her eyes with her hand from the hot sun. She watched as the trucks drove west on the main road until she couldn't see them anymore. As she stood staring westward, excitement moved like a wave through her entire body. Why would he single her out that way? More than that, why did her heart race at the sight of him? One thing was for sure... She wouldn't be leaving Windsor.

10

The River

The Russian River rippled over pebbles and stones in ribbons of clear blue and green. Its tree- and reed-lined banks wafted the musky scent of wet earth and moss, the breeze carrying its soft scent to where Adina sat. She adored the river. Its waters overflowed with childhood memories of summers spent splashing about with Mama and Papa. And then picnics on the rocky sand, wrapped up in a towel on her father's lap. These were the memories she cherished the most—carefree days when Mama was still alive and Papa was happy.

Adina sat on a smooth boulder at the edge of the riverbank. She soaked and kicked her feet in the cooling waters, waiting for Jeanie to show. Dipping her hands in, she sloshed water up onto her thighs until it soaked the edge of her yellow gingham swim shorts. She wore a matching top piece that was tied in a knot just under her breastbone. She closed her eyes. Cradled in the harmony that surrounded her, she listened to the gentle movement of the river and waited.

Footsteps bounded on the damp sand behind her.

"Yoohoo, Adi Lou!"

Jeanie Mae sprinted past Adina, splashed through the shallow water, and dove into the deeper pool. She bobbed up out of the water, her blond curls falling wet in front of her eyes.

"What are you waiting for, silly?" she called to Adina. "The water's glorious."

Adina waded out, dove under the cool, green water, and swam to Jeanie. The two paddled and splashed one another. The sound of their squeals and laughter echoed off the banks. After their swim, they sat together on the sandy beach, drying in the warm afternoon sun.

Jeanie patted the ends of her hair with the dry end of her towel. "Are you all packed, Adi?" she asked.

Adina gazed out over the river. Sunlight danced on the ripples like a million emerald stars. She dug her fingers into the sand, hesitating to answer Jeanie's question. The last thing she wanted to do was disappoint her best friend.

"Hey, Adina. Wake up." Jeanie tapped Adina's leg with her sand-covered toes.

"Sorry, Jee. Guess I'm a bit distracted."

Jeanie stood and pulled on her skirt over her swimsuit. "That's an understatement," she said. "Well, are you?"

"Am I what?"

Jeanie stomped her foot. "Are you packed, ready to join up tomorrow? Jiminy Christmas, Adi. Where's your head today?"

Adina's stomach knotted. She stood and grabbed her dry clothes. "Oh, that. You see, Jeanie, I guess that's why I wanted you to meet me here today." She pulled on her skirt. "Sort of like our last summer hurrah, you could say."

Jeanie frowned. "I don't understand."

Adina knew she'd stalled long enough. There was no easy way to do it. She'd just have to come out and say it. "I'm not going with you, Jee. I've decided to stay here and help my father."

Jeanie stood, barefoot in the wet sand, her shoes dangling from her fingertips. The brightness in her face melted away. Silent, she turned her back to Adina and stared out across the water.

Adina walked over and stood behind her friend. "Jee, I'm so sorry. Please try to understand. I can't leave now, not with all that's happening here. My father needs—"

"I knew you would do this," Jeanie replied flatly. "I should've known you'd never leave your father. He rules you, Adina. The sad thing is you're perfectly fine with that. Go ahead then," she said, throwing her hands up in the air, "stay here. Nurse his patients, cook his meals, darn his socks—and never leave this crummy little town, for all I care."

Jeanie's words cut deep into Adina's heart. Tears stung behind her eyes, choking at the back of her throat. She never wanted to hurt her friend, not like this.

"Jeanie, it's not what you think. My father and I have been asked to give medical care to the prisoners at Camp Windsor. It will be ongoing with new men arriving regularly. It's a very important assignment that Major Williams has entrusted to us."

Jeanie whipped around, eyes glaring. "Oh, that's rich. The prisoner camp?" Her face reddened. "Nazi criminals, Adina. *Killers*, remember?" She forced her shoes onto her sandy feet. Stalking past Adina, she snapped up her towel and handbag. "That just makes it all the harder to accept—the fact that you would rather stay here in this suffocating town to take care of Nazis instead of serving the very country we're fighting for." She looked Adina square in the eyes, her own pooling with tears. "This was our dream, Adi. Yours and mine." The tears rolled down her cheeks. "How could you do this to me?"

Adina ran to her, taking hold of her hands. "Jee, please. Try to understand. I *am* serving my country. The United States military asked my father to do this. I know it's not the same. Certainly not as heroic as traveling overseas to aid the wounded in war-torn Europe. But it still serves a purpose, and a good one at that." She tugged on Jeanie's hands, leaning in to catch her eyes.

Jeanie looked at Adina, her eyes fiercely pleading, the tears still trickling down her face.

"What, Jee? Say it."

Jeanie took a deep breath and closed her eyes. "I'm scared, Adi. I don't want to go without you."

Adina threw her arms around her friend. "You're gonna be just fine, Jee. We both will. You're the brave one, remember? We'll both be making a difference. You over there, and me here." She pulled back, catching Jeanie's eyes and wiping away her tears. "I couldn't bear the thought of you leaving, knowing that you're angry with me."

Jeanie wiped her eyes. "I could never be angry with you for long, Adi Lou." She tilted her head. "Maybe for just a bit though. I think you deserve that, at the very least." She smiled through pursed lips and winked.

"Promise you'll write every day. Or at least once a week. I'll need to hear all about the dashing fighter pilots and the officers' ball," Adina said.

"Only if my busy schedule will allow it, Adina Louisa."

Jeanie kissed Adina's cheek, wiping the red stain away with her thumb.

11

Daniel

"Aufstehen, Soldat, aufstehen!"

The early morning call to rise echoed in the distance. Daniel rolled onto his side, pulling the pillow over his head. He was grateful for the pillow and grateful for the mediocre cot he slept on, which was far superior to the mud and rocks of the past six months. He had food in his belly and canvas over his head. He was no longer across the ocean on a frozen, bloody battlefield, forced to fight for a cause he didn't believe in and for a leader he could never honor. Daniel hated the Führer. Hitler's rise to power brought nothing but fear and death to Daniel's family. His brother, Max, bravely stood against it all, even when their mother begged him not to.

As he lay there, Daniel thought of his mother, her rosy cheeks and pale-blue eyes. She had golden, silver-streaked hair she wore in one long, thick braid twisted into a crown on the top of her head. Over the years, her beauty hid behind a veil of worry and fear. He pictured her hands, their skin darker than that of her face. She kept her nails clipped short and unvarnished. Prominent bluish veins snaked from her wrists to the tops of her knuckles. As a child, when he'd snuggle next to her, he'd hold her hand and run his finger down the length of the soft, blue ridges. Daniel cracked his eyes open and looked at the same raised veins on his own hands. He wondered if his mother was still alive.

At six a.m., Klaus Schneider threw back the tent flap. Sunlight and a rush of cool air streamed in. "Sechs uhr! Aufstehen, schnell!" The timbre of his voice rang out throughout the entire camp.

Camp Windsor allowed German officers, such as Klaus Schneider, to oversee the prisoner barracks. This allowed for a smoother transition for the prisoners. Instead of bowing in submission to their American captors, they followed the day-to-day orders of the leaders they were already used to, as long as that leader led in fairness and in accordance with the Geneva Convention's established rules.

Klaus Schneider's style of leadership fell desperately short of fair. He held the rank of Oberscharführer in the same regiment that Daniel, Heimee, and Freddie had served. He dealt a heavy hand of anger, rife with hostility to the men he oversaw. He thought little of punishing his men for errors made in battle, or even for falling asleep on a night watch. Making a mistake under Oberscharführer Schneider's rule could earn the offender a sharp beating or an entire night on watch in the freezing cold. He used the same iron fist at Camp Windsor. Except when he knew he was being watched by his American captors, of course. Then, Schneider was the picture of evenhanded fairness, always obedient, ever thankful to the kind Americans. But when he was alone with his men, he became the heavy-handed Oberscharführer once again, barking orders as though still on the battlefield, forgetting he was a prisoner of the United States military. Today would be no different.

Daniel ignored Schneider's orders to get up and rolled onto his back, clasping his hands behind his head. He spotted a spider on the canvas ceiling. Wiry legs carried the spider's bulbous body back and forth, as though it were frantically searching for a place to hide. Finally, it squeezed itself between the corner tent folds. Daniel remembered as a child looking forward to the daily challenge of hiding from his older brother, Max. At the end of the day, he'd squeeze into the perfect hiding place where he would wait, heart pounding in anticipation of bursting out upon his unsuspecting older brother. Once Max arrived and the long-awaited scare took place, Max would chase Daniel, always catching him to give him a much-deserved pummeling, laughing in hysterics, as brothers often do. Daniel didn't want to remember. Brushing the thoughts aside, he sat up, raking his fingers through the thick strands of his wavy hair, desperately in need of a trim. Pulling on his dungarees, he grabbed his cup and razor and made his way to the latrine.

"Guten Morgen, Danny." Heimee stood at a basin. Water dripped from his head and face, as well as the tip of the chewed cigar between his teeth. "That pig was in a good mood today, eh Danny Boy?"

Daniel rolled his eyes. "Schneider forgets his place here. He wears no eagle on his chest anymore. No stripes. He can pretend all he wants." He pushed his way past Heimee to the basin and splashed his face and neck with cool water.

Heimee blotted his soggy cigar on the side of his pant leg. "Ja, Kumpel," he said. He watched as Daniel worked the lather from the cup onto his face. "Just you be on guard, Danny. I think the pig Schneider has it out for you. He watches you behind your back. I've seen it."

Daniel didn't respond.

"You and I, we are good friends, ja, Danny? I would not want anything bad to happen to you. You understand?"

Daniel razored the soapy lather down the sides of his face in clean stripes. "I have nothing to fear, Heimee. Schneider's power is a facade. He can't hurt me anymore." He moved his mouth to the side as he talked, taking care not to cut his lip. "Besides, Herr Hitler is on the run, ja? This war will end soon. We'll all be going home." He rinsed his face. "Lend me your towel, Heimee. I left mine in the tent."

Heimee's eyes narrowed, and he tossed the towel to Daniel. "How soon you forget, Danny. You remember what that pig did to poor Freddie? Schneider tortured the little runt. He terrorized him. The boy was a coward, and Schneider made a show of him." He pinched the gnawed, brown nub out from between his teeth and spit on the ground. "He made all our lives hell. Der Arschloch."

Daniel slung the damp towel over Heimee's shoulder and looked him in the eye. "No power, mein Freund. He is a prisoner, same as you, same as me."

A half smile curved on Heimee's lips. "Ja, mein Freund, same." He tucked the cigar between his teeth. "Just be careful, Danny Boy."

The mess tent hummed with the sound of voices and the clinking of plates and silverware. A thick aroma of freshly brewed coffee and sizzling sausages welcomed the men as they entered. The first meal of the day consisted of delectable, crispy sausages, alongside steamy hot bowls of rolled oats with milk on the side. Daniel's mouth watered at the sight of the sausages, their rich scent reminding him of home. The lumpy oats he could do without. He didn't understand the idea of cooking oats until they resembled a gooey, gray mush. Back home, his mother would serve them dry with milk and fruit. The thought of spoonfuls of the sticky, hot American concoction sliding down his throat made him want to gag. But he wouldn't complain. He would eat all of it. It would fill and strengthen him, and he'd be grateful.

Daniel and Heimee were waiting in the chow line when someone shoved Daniel abruptly from behind.

"Christensen, Dummkopf!"

He turned to see Schneider standing behind him. Daniel narrowed his eyes, then turned his back. He was in no mood for Schneider's taunts today.

"Are you ignoring me, Christensen?" Schneider stepped forward, standing right at Daniel's heels. "It would not bode well for you to ignore me. Your behavior has not been—how shall I say this—exemplary since we arrived. You understand?"

Daniel whipped around, facing Schneider. "You have nothing on me, Schneider. Nothing." His eyes burned into the man.

"I wouldn't be so sure of that, Soldat Christensen. You see, I have been given the honored duty of overseeing you men on behalf of our gracious American hosts. And, from what I observed the other day—" He paused, examining his fingernails as though searching for the tiniest speck of dirt, while at the same time relishing the anxious concern in Daniel's eyes. "I'm afraid your actions were quite unbefitting a German Soldat in the service of the great Führer."

Heat rose to Daniel's face as blood pulsed through the veins in his temples. How he hated the man who stood before him. Schneider represented the express evil of the Reich, reminding Daniel of all he'd lost back home. It took every bit of his willpower not to lay him flat with one punch, right there in the breakfast line. But Daniel knew if he did, he'd end up in the brig.

"I have no idea what you're talking about." Daniel said, turning his back on Schneider again.

Heimee looked at Daniel, eyes wide, then casually moved himself forward in the line.

Instantly, Schneider was back on Daniel's heels. "Why, the other day, of course, at the medical review. Do you think I didn't see?" He lowered his voice, a sinister smirk curving on his lips. "The way you looked at the lovely young nurse. I heard the way you spoke to her."

Daniel didn't move, waves of anger rising within him.

Heimee came back to Daniel's side. "Do not listen, Danny," he whispered.

The other men, impatient with the holdup, began to walk around Daniel and Schnieder.

"Of course," Schneider continued, "one might look at a dirty strumpet in Dusseldorf in that way," his breath brushed Daniel's ear, "but not a beautiful nurse provided by our gracious American hosts."

Daniel spun back around, butting his chest against Schneider, making sure the man could see every bit of fiery hate bolting from his eyes. "You shut your filthy—"

"Is there a problem here, men?" Major Williams stood just to the side of Daniel and Schneider.

With a deep breath, Schneider steadied himself. Smiling, he brushed his hands across Daniel's shoulders, then gave him a gentle pat on his arm. "No, Major Williams. No problem at all," he said, his voice dripping with sweetness. "Soldat Christensen and I were just having a friendly chat." He looked at Daniel out the side of his eye. "Isn't that right, Danny?"

Daniel's stomach churned. He allowed himself one last hard stare at Schneider before he turned and faced the major. "Guten Morgen, Major," he said.

"Let's keep the line moving, men," Williams said. "You've got a full day ahead of you."

The sinister grin lingered on Schneider's lips. "You heard the major, Christensen. You don't want to hold up the line, do you?" He pushed himself in front of Daniel.

Heimee laid his hand on Daniel's shoulder. "Freund, you must not listen to him. He wants you to react. You know this, ja?"

Daniel glared as Schneider laughed and joked with the other prisoners ahead in the line. Try as he might, there was no suppressing the rage he felt toward Klaus Schneider. He would need to get control of it or there would be trouble.

Heimee cleared his throat. "Danny, I must ask you something, but you don't need to answer. Maybe it is none of my business?"

Daniel composed himself. "What is it?"

"Well, mein Freund, is it true? Did you really flirt with the pretty nurse? Because, Kumpel, if you did, I completely understand." He grinned, twisting the cigar between his teeth and tongue. "You talk much of her, ja?"

Daniel fought hard against his feelings. He would have given Heimee a hard shove and told him to shut his mouth, but what his friend said was true, and he knew it well. He'd been drawn to Nurse Robbins since the first day he saw her at the back fence. Her smile. The ever-changing color of her eyes. The way she looked at him when she passed the ball over the fence and into his hands. He'd had very little contact with her, but her image wouldn't leave his head. The last thing he needed was to get himself or the young nurse into trouble. Yet he'd done nothing wrong.

"I have only spoken to you, Heimee, mein Freund." There was sarcasm in Daniel's tone.

Heimee shook his head. He stepped in front of Daniel, placing both hands on his shoulders. "On my honor, I have said not a word, Danny." He looked Daniel square in the eyes. "Listen, Danny Boy. You don't need to say anything at all." He leaned in, flashing a brown-toothed grin. "It's written all over your face."

12 |

The summer trudged along, an endless string of monotonous days that blended one into another. As a child, Adina loved the summer months. She and Jeanie would spend lazy hours soaking in the river or lying beneath the tall trees on the cool grass in Jeanie's front yard.

Summer meant the celebration of harvest and the grape crush—the reward to a farmer's long, laborious year. Yet this summer harvest, like the last, and the one before that, lacked the celebratory joy that should normally accompany it. With so many fathers and sons gone, whether fighting or dead, it was nothing more than another harvest.

The days crept along, hot and dry, with no end to the daily tasks Papa filled Adina's schedule with. From home visits to medicine deliveries to hours on end at the clinic. No matter how full her day was, the hours seemed to move in reverse with no end in sight. She felt as though she were waiting for something to happen, yet nothing ever did.

Adina finished up the morning hours at the clinic. The air indoors felt warm and heavy, which only intensified her restlessness. She craved some time alone, if only to close her eyes and breathe some non-antiseptic fresh air.

Outside, she sat down under the maple tree in the front garden and leaned her head against its trunk. Some of the leaves at the top were already starting to change colors. The warm, dry air made her sleepy, and her mind wandered. She pictured the camp and the soldiers and wondered why she and her father hadn't visited much lately. She felt full of purpose at Camp Windsor. It wasn't that the needs of the townsfolk weren't important, for they very much were. But Camp Windsor was electric, like a magnet pulling her out of the ordinary. She was drawn to these men and wanted to know more about them. Especially Daniel.

"Adina," Papa called out. He stood at the clinic door holding the all-too-familiar brown paper sack with a white script stapled to the outside. "I have one more prescription for you to take to Carl Sanderson." He held the bag out at arm's length in front of him. "I told him you would drop it off to him at the market."

She stood, brushing leaves and creases from her skirt. "I'll leave as soon as I grab my kit, Papa."

Some days, there was no end to her father's demands. Was she a nurse or a delivery girl? "Maybe I should sell Beemans chewing gum and Lucky Strikes on the side," she mouthed under her breath.

The front basket on Adina's bicycle overflowed with brown paper sacks. Six deliveries to be made from one end of town to the other. She'd be lucky if she made it back home before dark. She pedaled steadily under the beating sun, making her way down Redwood Road. She was thirsty and thought about grabbing a cola at the Groceteria when she dropped off the prescription for Mr. Sanderson. She could almost taste the icy sweetness on her tongue and wished it was her first stop instead of her last.

The ride into town proved ordinary until she drew closer to the Quinn home. Parked along the curb in front of the house was a dark gray sedan. Adina's heart sank when she saw the words *Western Union* on the door. There were only two reasons a Western Union car would drive into her small town: either the driver was lost or had bad news to deliver. She rode over to the sedan and stopped. A man in a gray wool coat with the WU insignia on the lapel stood on the Quinns' front porch, a cream-colored telegram clutched in his hand. He removed his cap and knocked on the door. Adina stood, frozen. She knew all too well what this could mean. She hoped she was wrong.

DJ began to wail. Instinctively, Sally bent down to pick him up but stopped suddenly and moaned, supporting her lower belly with both arms as though attempting to hold the baby up and in. "Oh God...it's coming!" she yelled.

"Sally, stop. You can't lift DJ now. He'll be all right." Adina placed her hand on Sally's back, helping her to stand upright. "Let's get you inside." She scooped up the toddler, supporting him on her hip. "It's okay, DJ. Mama's gonna be just fine." Glancing down, she noticed the telegram on the porch. She grabbed it, stuffing the wet paper into her pocket, and followed Sally inside.

____

The tone rang over and over in Adina's ear. "Come on, Papa. Please pick up." There was no answer at the house or the clinic. She hung up the phone and wiped her sweaty palms on her skirt. Sally moaned from the bedroom. "I'll be right there, Sally."

Adina's mind raced. *Come on, pull yourself together.* She squeezed the back of her neck with her hand as her eyes scanned the room, looking for something—anything—that would jog her memory. She was trained for this, but she felt stymied, like a cold engine struggling to start. Her eyes caught sight of the kitchen. She ran to the sink and filled an empty pot with water, placing it on the stove to boil. She then opened drawer after drawer, finding one filled with clean dish towels. She grabbed every single one. Another drawer contained a ball of cooking twine. *That'll do.* She left the water on the stove to boil, took the towels and twine, and went into Sally's bedroom.

Sally lay on the bed with her eyes closed, taking deep, calculated breaths. DJ was curled on his side next to her. He was exhausted and almost asleep. Sally gently stroked her son's curls, oblivious to much else around her.

"Sally?" Adina said. "Let me take DJ to his bed."

Sally's breathing intensified. She moaned and rolled onto her side.

Adina carefully scooped the boy into her arms and quickly carried him into his room. If Sally were to yell out in pain during her labor, it could terrify the child, sending him into hysterics again. Then what would she do? She'd have to attend to a screaming toddler *and* deliver a baby. She laid DJ on his bed and quietly shut the door.

When she got back to the bedroom, Sally was standing, her body hunched over the side of the bed. Her blond hair stuck to her forehead in damp clumps. She breathed in through her nose, puffing air out through her mouth in rhythmic beats. She looked up at Adina, her eyes red and swollen.

"Sally, let's get you back on the bed so I can take a look at where the baby's at."

Through puffs and moans, Sally obeyed. She still wore her wet skirt, but her soiled undergarments lay in a heap on the floor. She squeezed her eyes shut as another contraction came.

"Breathe, Sally," Adina said. "Breathe through it."

The wave passed, and Sally looked at Adina. Tears streamed down her cheeks. "I can't," she said. "I can't do this... Not without Donald."

Still, Adina had no words. Nothing would bring Donald back. This baby would be born without him.

Another contraction came, more intense than the last.

Adina looked at her watch. "Sally, listen to me. That contraction was only two minutes from the last. I need to feel the position of the baby." She lifted Sally's skirt over her belly and felt for the baby. She could feel the head positioned low toward the pelvic bone. This was a good sign. But the baby was face up, the back of its head pressing on Sally's spine. *No wonder she's been moaning*, Adina thought. *The absolute pain of that.*

Another contraction came, and Sally yelled out.

Adina nudged Sally's leg. "I need you to sit yourself back against the pillows, Sally...and bend your knees."

As soon as Sally did, Adina saw the baby's head crowning. She grabbed the scissors from her kit and laid the towels and twine within reach. She cut a length of twine from the ball. There would be no time to get the water from the stove in the kitchen. She took a deep breath to steady her nerves.

"Okay, Sally. When I tell you, I want you to push and count to ten."

Sally moaned. "Oh God, my back. It hurts so bad."

"I know. The baby is face up, Sally. Sunny side up. I need you to give me a push. I'll try to turn the baby's head."

Sally nodded as another contraction mounted.

"Push, Sally!"

She bore down, eyes shut tight.

Adina counted. "One, two, three—that's it—breathe, seven, eight."

Sally screamed.

"Almost there...nine, ten. That's it."

The head was out and turned to the side. The baby's eyes were closed. No sound came from its blue-tinged lips. Adina cupped her hand to its soft, warm head.

Exhausted, Sally lay her head back against the pillow. The respite was short lived as she was hit with another fierce wave. She braced herself upright, grabbing hold of her knees.

"Okay, Sally," Adina said. "This is it. This may be the last push, so make it a home run, you hear?"

Sally nodded, then took deep breaths in and out to prepare.

"Push, Sally, push!"

Sally shut her eyes, clenched her teeth, and cried out.

"That's it, Sally. One, two, three, four." Adina supported the baby's head as its shoulders broke through. "Almost there, seven, eight." She gently grabbed the baby under its arm. "Just a little further. Push!"

Sally pushed with one last burst of exertion, allowing Adina to guide the baby all the way out. She gently laid the slippery, warm infant on Sally's belly. The baby started to cry.

"Here she is, Sally. It's a girl."

Sally reached for the baby. "Oh, Donald," she whispered. "It's a girl. We have a beautiful baby girl." She wept.

Adina carefully tied the twine around the cord, just above the baby's navel. She then cut the cord right above the twine. With a towel, she wiped the baby the best she could, wrapped her in another clean towel, and handed the sweet bundle to Sally.

The water on the stove had boiled dry, and the pot was ruined. Adina plugged the sink and filled it with water, then placed the soiled dishtowels in to soak. She was finally able to reach her father on the telephone. He was on his way to examine mother and baby.

The day definitely had not gone the way Adina had originally planned. The fact that she had been riding by Sally's house at just the right time was pure fate. The Western Union man wouldn't have had the slightest idea what to do. She was proud to have been able to step in and take charge. What would Papa say to her now? She'd delivered that baby from start to finish. He'd certainly see how capable she was, wouldn't he? As hard as she tried, she couldn't fight back the desire for her father's approval. He didn't want her to leave with Jeanie Mae, saying she was needed here, for the town. Was it for the town? Or was it for him? If for him, then why did he push her away?

There was a knock at the front door. Adina opened it, relieved to see Papa standing there, medical bag in hand.

"Papa, I'm so glad you're here now." Seeing him made her suddenly realize just how exhausted she was.

He stepped into the living room and glanced around. "Adina Luisa, where is Mrs. Quinn?"

She stared at him, bewildered. He didn't even ask her how *she* was doing. No acknowledgement whatsoever. But she was far too exhausted to question it or to even care. "In the bedroom, Papa."

"Take me to her, please," he said. He followed her into the hallway, then stopped. "The prescriptions. Were you able to deliver them all?"

She stood with her back to him. Was that all he cared about? The prescriptions? Was he truly that hardened? "No, Papa," she answered him. "But I comforted Sally, who just found out her husband was killed overseas, and then I delivered her baby. I did not deliver any of the prescriptions." Smothering the ache in her heart, she led him into the bedroom.

Sally sat propped up and dressed in a fresh nightgown. Her eyes were closed, and she cradled her infant daughter to her breast. DJ, now awake from his nap, sat next to his mama, staring in wonder at his new baby sister. Papa set his kit on the dresser and quietly walked to the bedside. Sally opened her eyes, still swollen from labor and tears.

"Mrs. Quinn, I'm so very sorry for your loss," Papa said, laying his hand on her arm. He stumbled for the right words to say. "Your husband, Donald—he would have been overjoyed at the sight of your beautiful baby girl." His voice was soft and genuine, full of love and compassion. "Tell me, did you give her a name yet?"

Sally tenderly stroked the baby's cheek with the tip of her finger. "I'm calling her Madelyn, after Donald's late mother. I think that would have made him happy."

"It's a beautiful name. I agree, your husband would have loved it, and her."

Adina watched him. She wondered how it was that just a few moments earlier, he entered the house cold, unfeeling, and oblivious to his own daughter's presence. Now here he stood, the soul of compassion. She remembered this side of her father. She missed it.

Sally took hold of Papa's hand. "Thank you, Dr. Robbins. I still can't believe Donald's gone. I don't want to believe it. I know I need to be strong now for Donald Junior and for this little one." She gazed lovingly into the newborn's eyes. "That's what Donald would want."

Papa stepped back and reached for his kit. "I would like to examine you and the baby now, Mrs. Quinn. If you don't mind, that is."

"Oh, that's quite all right, Dr. Robbins. I don't think there's a need for that. Adina took care of both me and the baby."

Papa's eyebrows raised. "Indeed?" He glanced at Adina.

"She even wanted to scrub out the sheets and my undergarments, but I told her there was no need to fuss over it now. I've called my parents. They're coming up from LA to be with me. I'm sure they're in the car, driving right now."

Papa glanced in Adina's direction yet seemed to have trouble looking her in the eyes.

"Truly, Dr. Robbins. Adina has done so much for me today. I'm not sure what I would've done had she not shown up when she did."

Papa struggled to find his words again.

"Unless you think it's necessary?" Sally said.

Papa regained his self-assured composure and smiled. "No, of course you are right. Adina is a perfectly capable nurse. If it is as you say, I am sure she oversaw all that was needed."

Adina wished she could shrink into the shadows behind the door but stepped forward instead. "Sally was incredible. So brave. Only three pushes, and she moved that baby right out. I could only hope to be as brave as she was, someday."

Papa stood silent for a moment, making Adina feel all the more uncomfortable. He then walked back to Sally, taking her hand in both of his. "If you would like, I will stay with you so that Adina can go home and get some rest."

Sally's eyes filled with tears. "Thank you, Dr. Robbins. I appreciate the offer. Truly, I'm all right. Sore, but all right." She gazed lovingly at her son and baby daughter. "I think I just need to be here, alone, with my babies. I'll need to talk with Donald Junior about his daddy." She closed her eyes, pulling the toddler close to her side.

"If you are certain you are all right," he said, concerned.

Sally nodded.

"Very well. We will let you rest." Papa grabbed his medical bag. "Adina, I will wait for you in the living room."

Adina packed up her supplies. Her thoughts raced despite her exhaustion. "Are you sure you're all right, Sally? I can stay until your mother and father arrive, if you'd like."

Sally's eyes remained closed. "Adina, I don't know what I would have done without you today. I'm grateful. Go home now. Get some rest."

Adina slung her kit across her shoulder. "I'll come by and check on you and the baby first thing tomorrow."

Papa stood waiting in the living room when Adina emerged from Sally's bedroom.

"You didn't have to wait for me, Papa. I have my bicycle. Besides, I still need to deliver the prescriptions—"

"I will make your deliveries, Adina Louisa. It is almost seven. I have the car. The deliveries will be made much faster if I do it."

He was a complex mystery. The harder she tried to figure him out, the more frustrated she became. She looked at him, and her heart swelled.

"Thank you, Papa. That's very kind of you."

He turned and walked out the door.

Just then, Adina remembered the telegram. The paper was crumpled and stained, the ink smeared. She smoothed it and carefully laid it on the coffee table. She then walked out, quietly closing the door behind her.

Henry's Tears

Adina lay on top of her floral bed comforter. The setting sun bathed the room in a dusky purple. She had been so physically exhausted after Sally's delivery that her emotions wouldn't allow her to stay awake. She didn't even bother to remove her shoes. Falling straight away into the softness of her bed, she slept deeply.

But now, something had pulled her out of sleep. Rubbing her eyes, she looked at the alarm clock. It was eight thirty, and her bedroom was dark. She pulled the cord on the bedside lamp, slipped off her shoes, and sat back against her pillows, basking in the memories of the day. She had delivered a strong, healthy baby girl. She did it alone. She relished her sense of purpose and longed for more opportunities like it. Not just delivering babies, though. What she really wanted was more reasons to go to Camp Windsor. It had been weeks since she and her father had visited.

The house was unusually quiet. The growling of her stomach broke the silence, reminding her she hadn't eaten since breakfast. Where was Papa? Had he looked in on her while she was sleeping? When she was little, he looked in on her every night at bedtime. Papa would come in and sit on the edge of her bed. She'd climb into his lap, curling up in his strong arms. He would rock her back and forth and sing to her soft and low. She could hear the old Lithuanian melody in her head. Safe and loved. That's how she felt in her father's arms.

Again, Adina's hunger interrupted her thoughts. She got up from the bed and opened the door. The hallway was dark but for the soft glow of yellow light coming from the living room. Wooden floorboards creaked under her bare feet, causing her to step tentatively. If Papa was in there, she didn't want to startle him. *He may have fallen asleep in the chair*, she thought. She stopped just before the archway entrance to the living room and peeked her head around the wall.

Papa sat hunched in his armchair. He held a framed photograph of Mama tightly against his chest, cradling it lovingly. Tears rolled down his cheeks.

Adina stood in surprised silence, watching as her father held tight to the photograph, rocking it back and forth, just as he used to hold and rock her as a child. Papa rarely showed emotion this way, at least not anymore. She wanted to run to him, to wrap her arms around him, to pour out words of comfort to him, to tell him how much she loved him. Tears burned behind her eyes.

"Mano meile," Papa whispered, the words choked at the back of his throat. "Please forgive me, my love."

Adina turned away, pressing her back against the wall. She clapped her hand over her mouth. She pushed back her tears and the ache in her heart. No matter how much she wanted to run to him, she couldn't. The divide between them, though just a few steps from hallway to chair, was far greater in her own heart. She couldn't see past it to the other side. He had shut her out when Mama died. At the very time she needed him the most, he turned away and stayed turned. She didn't have it within her to try. Her heart was growing colder to him, and it scared her more than anything.

She wiped her tears with the back of her hand, her appetite gone as quickly as it had come. As quietly as she could, she walked the long hallway back to her bedroom. As she passed the telephone stand, she glanced down, her eyes still clouded with tears. Four letters lay neatly stacked next to the telephone, where they would be easily noticed. She pressed her eyes with the palms of her hands and lifted the stack. Each was addressed to Miss Adina Robbins, stamped "US Army Mail," and postage dated weeks apart. They all must have arrived at the same time today. All of them were from Jeanie.

October 29, 1944

Adina tossed and turned, in and out of wake and sleep. Maybe it was the wind. Or perhaps it was the moonlight that beamed through the lace window curtains, causing flashes to graze over her eyelids. More than likely, it was the moving reel of dreams that cluttered her sleep. Cloudy visions of her father and mother, vibrant, youthful, surrounded in ethereal light and happiness. She was a child running to them. And then she was grown. Her feet felt like blocks of cement, her legs sluggish. Every step was fraught with effort. Indistinguishable shadows stood in her way. Uniforms, soldiers, faces. The silhouetted figures of her parents stood just beyond, close yet unreachable. A voice pushed forth through tears. "Papa, Mama," Adina cried out. She lay on her side, heart racing, eyes moist with tears.

The bedside alarm clock read one thirty a.m. Adina rolled onto her back and watched the spirited shadows dance on the ceiling. The sound of the wind through the trees outside calmed her. She thought about the dream and didn't like the confusion it caused.

The telephone rang, its clanging echoing through the silent house. Adina bolted upright.

Papa opened his bedroom door, his slippered footsteps shuffling down the hallway. Adina listened.

"Yes, this is Dr. Robbins." Papa's voice sounded muffled through Adina's closed bedroom door. She threw off the blanket and quietly stepped over to the door, opening it just a crack.

"Yes, yes. Fever, you say? It sounds serious. No, of course, it's not a problem at all. Keep him as comfortable as possible until I can get there. Yes, yes. Goodbye."

There was the click of the receiver, and then Papa's footsteps nearing her bedroom. Anticipating him, she opened the door.

"Ah, Adina. Good, you are awake. Quickly, get dressed. There is an emergency. I will need your help." He turned, walking back to his bedroom.

"Who is it, Papa? Where?"

"Camp Windsor. One of the prisoners is very ill." He entered his bedroom. "Hurry, Adina Luisa," he called back and shut his door.

The streets of Windsor were desolate. Papa drove with an urgency that differed from the normal leisure Adina was accustomed to. He was quiet and didn't run down a list of do's and don'ts. He didn't remind her of his expectations.

Adina stared out the front window, watching as the high beams caught the bends in the road and bounced off street signs and trees. She was thankful for the silence. It allowed her mind the freedom to explore the possibilities of what might await them at the camp. They had visited the camp together a total of eight times since the first day. They treated the prisoners for everything from the common cold to injuries sustained while working in the fields. She'd developed a rapport with some of the men, greeting them by their first names, as they did with her. She never imagined that she would have even the slightest care for these men— men she considered her enemy. Her heart was changing. She hated to think of any of them being desperately ill.

Papa finally spoke when he turned onto the camp road. "I will need you to stay alert, Adina."

She looked at him, perplexed. He made no other demands, only for her to stay alert. "Of course, Papa. I'm here for whatever's needed."

The private standing guard was already pulling the gate open as their car approached. Papa rolled down the window.

"We've been expecting you, Dr. Robbins," said the guard.

Light peeked through the blinds of the administration building as they drove up, and a moment later, Major Williams stepped out. Private Jenkins followed close behind.

"Thank you for coming out so quickly at this hour, Dr. Robbins," Williams said, reaching for Papa's hand. He appeared disheveled, his shirt untucked. Adina noticed he wore bedroom slippers on his feet. "Please, if you'll quickly come with me. I'm afraid he's worse off than when I first called you." He hurried toward the rows of tents. "It started yesterday. He made it through the day, working in the fields, never saying a word. Apparently, he was in a lot of pain, but he just kept working."

"Did he say where the pain was?" Papa asked, out of breath.

Major Williams stopped as he reached the last row of tents. "In his gut. Somewhere around this area." He motioned with his hand over his lower right side. "It got much worse after he worked in the fields. Vomiting and fever. Hurry now. This way." He turned left.

The major carried a flashlight, but it provided only a thin strip of light on the dirt pathway. Adina was grateful for the moonlight. Barbed wire lined the perimeter. They were at the back side of the camp. She heard hushed voices as they approached the last tent at the end of the row. A few prisoners stood whispering just outside, their faces obscured in shadows.

"Jenkins," Williams said, "you stay outside here. I don't want any of the other prisoners coming in. Understood?"

"Yes sir," the private replied. He eyed the prisoners standing nearby, then stood at attention, blocking the tent entrance.

Adina and Papa followed Major Williams into the dark tent. Men breathed and slept in the darkness, surprisingly so, considering all the commotion. One yellow light at the far end led them like a faint beacon.

Papa stopped at the bedside of the sick prisoner. Beads of perspiration reflected on the young man's pale face. His body shook and his eyelids fluttered open, revealing their blue irises, faded and distant.

Adina drew in breath when she saw who it was. Daniel Christensen.

Papa pulled his stethoscope from his medical bag. "Adina, remove the bedsheet from him and unbutton his shirt."

Without a second thought, Adina fell into step alongside her father. She stripped the bed sheet away and began unbuttoning Daniel's sweat-soaked shirt. Her fingers lightly brushed against his feverish skin. She gently rested her hand on his forehead. "Like fire," she said. She leaned in, close to his face. "Daniel, can you hear me?"

Daniel moaned. His fitful legs kicked and stretched. With watery eyes, he struggled to focus on Adina. "Fräulein, bitte, hilfe."

"He is saying, please help," Papa said, as he placed his stethoscope over Daniel's heart. He then moved it down to his abdomen and waited. Papa's eyes were calculating, yet his demeanor remained calm. Taking a penlight from his pocket, he lifted one of Daniel's eyelids, flicking the light back and forth.

"Doctor—bitte," Daniel moaned.

Papa pocketed the penlight, stood upright, and folded his arms. "Adina, what is your assessment?" His eyes remained on his patient.

Adina gaped at her father's question. To figure him out was like trying to decipher an impossible equation. He hammered and critiqued her in the day-to-day duties of nursing. He never seemed to have the time, let alone the wherewithal to be present for any of her emotional needs. He hid his reality from her, never admitting her into the depths of who he truly was. Yet somehow, it was in the urgent, the life-and-death scenarios, that he relied on her. It was in times like this that he trusted her and considered her his equal.

"Adina?" he repeated.

She stood straight, confident and professional. "We don't need a thermometer to know his fever is very high. His eyes are glassy. Pupils dilated. Pulse is rapid, and his abdomen is distended. I'm almost certain there's an infection. Possibly sepsis."

Papa nodded in agreement. Then, with one hand on top of the other, he pressed down on the center of Daniel's belly and quickly released.

Daniel cried out, his eyes wide. "Bitte, please!"

"Acute appendicitis, Papa," Adina said. "I'm sure of it. Ruptured, most likely. His symptoms prove sepsis."

"Yes, yes, Adina," Papa said, this time looking directly at her. "He needs to be taken to the hospital immediately."

"I'll call an ambulance," said Major Williams, turning to walk away.

"There's no time," Papa said. "My daughter and I will take him in my car. It will be much faster that way."

"That won't be possible, Dr. Robbins," Williams said. "He's a prisoner. I cannot allow him to leave the camp unsupervised."

Papa's eyes narrowed. "Major Williams, this prisoner is septic and will most certainly die if he is not taken to a hospital immediately." He stepped closer, standing eye to eye with the major. "As it stands right now, you should have called me hours ago, but instead you waited. It would be unfortunate for a prisoner to die on your watch, yes?"

Daniel moaned.

"Papa, we need to hurry," Adina pleaded.

Major Williams raised a finger, as though ready to refute Papa's veiled threat, but he stopped short of it. "Jenkins! Get in here, pronto."

Private Jenkins burst through the darkness of the tent opening. "Yes sir?"

"Quickly, take two men and grab a stretcher from the infirmary. Dr. Robbins and his daughter will be transporting the prisoner to the hospital." He turned to Papa. "I will call the hospital and let them know you are on your way."

Jenkins tipped his forehead with two fingers.

"Oh, and Jenkins," the major called. "You will escort them in the jeep."

***

Daniel lay curled on his side, wrapped in a blanket in the back seat of the Oldsmobile. His eyes were closed and his body shivered.

From the front seat, Adina craned her neck to watch him, fearing that if she looked away, he might die. She reached for his wrist to feel for a pulse. "Hang on, Daniel. We're almost there." She huffed in frustration, turning to Papa. "Why is this taking so long? Can't you drive any faster?"

Papa gestured with his hand toward the front windshield. "I cannot go any faster than the jeep in front of me, Adina Luisa."

She sat back, closing her eyes tight.

Papa's face softened and he took a deep breath. "We are almost there, Dukra."

Daughter.

It surprised her to hear him say it in his own language. How long had it been since he'd called her that? She stared out the window, remembering. She was seven years old. Papa ran alongside her, his hand holding onto the seat of the two-wheeled bicycle she was riding for the very first time. "*Pedal faster, Dukra...that's it.*" He gave a firm push, let go, and stood cheering her on as she rode ahead. She remembered him teaching her the meaning of the word. "*It means 'daughter,*'" he said. "*Say it, Adina. DU-KRA. You are my daughter, Adina Luisa. Papa loves his dukra.*" She pushed her thoughts aside as the blurred tree shadows and road signs passed by.

"Ah, you see?" Papa said. "We are here." He followed the jeep into the hospital parking area. Both vehicles stopped in front of the entrance. "Wait here, Adina," he said.

Private Jenkins was already walking toward the entrance. "I'll get the orderlies to help get him inside."

Within just a few minutes, two capable men dressed in white were wheeling a gurney toward the car. A nurse followed close behind. Papa got out of the car and met up with them, slamming his door shut behind him.

Adina watched helplessly from the car, unable to hear what her father was saying to the nurse. He gestured with his hands, then pulled his card out of his pocket and handed it to the nurse. The orderlies came over and carefully removed Daniel from the back seat and placed him on the gurney. His arm flopped like a rag doll's off the side. Private

Jenkins said a few words to Papa, then got into his jeep and drove away. Papa stood another moment, staring at the hospital entrance with his hands in his pockets.

Adina rolled down the car window. "Papa?"

Papa took his time coming back to the car. He situated himself back into the driver's seat and started the engine. Adina waited, giving him time to say something. But he remained silent as he drove out of the parking lot and back onto the highway.

"Will they perform the appendectomy?" she asked.

"Of course," he replied.

"Will he be okay?"

Papa looked at her, holding her eyes with his for just a moment. The silent exchange between them felt different to her. She studied him. Was it compassion? Concern? *Just say it. Say something...anything,* she thought.

He turned his eyes back to the windshield and the drive ahead. "That remains to be seen."

Jee

P.S. When you see my mom and dad, would you give them a hug from me? I'm not there, so you're the next best thing.

July 29, 1944

Adi,

It's Saturday afternoon. I have a few more minutes of free time and wanted to drop you a line to say hello and to let you know that I'm still alive. There's a saying around here: Join the WACs and die in training. Good one, right? It's like those girls said to me on the train, Basic is a bone breaker. Golly, that seems like ages ago. I think the Army is attempting to train who we once were out of us.

My bunkie, Cookie, found out that her cousin was killed. He was somewhere in Europe. She was close with him when they were kids. She did some crying, then bucked up. She said that it doesn't change why she joined up in the first place: to help put an end to this blasted war.

I miss you, Adi.

Jee

P.S. I started smoking cigarettes. Don't tell my parents. Besides, it's glamorous. It makes me look like Marlene Dietrich.

August 12, 1944

Dear Adi,

I did it! Basic training is over. I graduated. The ceremony was yesterday, and let me tell you, it was exciting. It was held here at the base. Many of the other WACs and GIs who were available attended, as well as some important people from the community. It was a real official event, to say the least. An Army band played as we marched in formation onto the field. The bleachers were filled with onlookers. I had no idea that graduating from Basic would be such a hoopla. But gosh, Adi, did it make me feel special. Both Cookie and I received commendations. I was recognized for special use of skill in administration and typing. I know it's not much, but it'll come in handy with assignments. Speaking of which, I already have an assignment lined up. Can't say anything about it though. Loose lips sink ships.

Last night, all of us were given special leave to go out and celebrate. A few of us girls paid for a taxi and went into Hollywood. Betty, another swell gal who graduated with me, knows a guy who's a cook at the Brown Derby. He was able to secure us a table, which isn't easy to do, since apparently the joint is always packed to the gills. Anyway, he got us in, and let me tell you, it was like a dream. We sat at the table sipping on Pink Ladies and eating shrimp cocktails. We got all the looks, too, since everyone is simply enamored with the WACs. Even had some folks want to take pictures with us. Can you imagine that? And then there were the GIs and sailors on leave who wouldn't give us space to breathe. You'd think these guys hadn't seen a woman in ages, let alone one in uniform. If I had a nickel for every time I was asked to dance, I'd be a high-falutin' millionaire. Every single one of them wanted me to promise to write. Some of them looked at me like they wanted to cry. It just breaks a girl's heart. I really did have the time of my life though. It truly was a last night for the books.

Speaking of last nights, tomorrow night really will be my last night at the base. Come Monday morning at four a.m., I'll be shipping out. I know it sounds crazy. I thought my first assignment might be somewhere in the US, but that doesn't seem to be the case. They're shipping me out of the country. I won't even know where until I get there. Even if I did know, I wouldn't be able to tell anyone, not even my parents. Everything is hush, hush. Every letter I write will be read over and blacked out by some "high upper" before it's sent. There's enemy eyes everywhere, or so we're told.

This will most likely be my last letter for a while. I have no idea how long I'll be traveling. And when I get there, I don't know what my living situation will be or when I'll be able to sit down with pen and paper again. Hopefully not too long. I'm not really sure how I feel about it all. I'm bursting with excitement, that's for sure. But at the same time, I miss home. I'm going to need you to be a faithful pen pal, Adi. You're my best friend. I want to hear all the news from home.

Now it's time for me to write a letter to Mom and Dad, as well as to about fifty sailors...wink, wink. So long for now, my sweet Adi Lou.

Yours,

Jeanie Mae

15

November 1944

Daniel's emergency appendectomy was a success. Two days after the surgery, the surgeon telephoned to inform Papa that if he hadn't taken the initiative to get Daniel to the hospital as quickly as he did, the young man probably would've died. Daniel ended up spending an extra two weeks in the hospital for the treatment of the infection and was then sent back to Camp Windsor to convalesce.

For Adina, the days and weeks that followed that fateful October night were not much more than business as usual. The same old routine of home visits, clinic duties, and medicine deliveries, with one exception —Daniel. He was the unusual change that came into her life. Daniel had taken up space in her mind and heart every day since she and Papa dropped him off at the hospital, though she hadn't seen him since.

Today's workday ended with one last delivery to Mrs. Hopper's home. Virginia Hopper, or Ginny to those who knew her best, lived west on Main Street, not far from Camp Windsor.

Adina's mind raced with an idea. Would she be able to stop by the camp to see Daniel? *Just to check in on him,* she thought. She pushed the craziness of it out of her head as she rode her bicycle up the long drive to the Hopper home. She climbed the porch steps to the front door. In the window next to the door hung a "Son's in Service" flag. The star in the center was gold. Next to it hung a black and white photograph of their son, Harland, with a handwritten inscription in the bottom right corner, "Killed June 6, 1942."

another." She handed Adina a piece of cake. "But enough about me. I want to hear all about you. How's your nursing coming along? I can remember when your mama worked alongside your father. She was a rare beauty. It was a sad day for this town when she passed away."

Adina wanted to leave but didn't want to be rude and hurt Ginny's feelings.

"I hear that you and your father have been visiting those Germans at that camp," Ginny said, her tone hardened. The word *Germans* spewed out like a foul curse. Her hand shook as she lifted the teapot to fill Adina's cup.

"As a matter of fact, we have," Adina responded, trying to sound more confident than she felt. "At least twice a month, sometimes more, depending on whether or not there's illness, or a broken bone, or—"

"They killed my boy," Ginny interrupted. She set her cup down on the coffee table and stared over at the photograph of her and her son. "Heartless bastards shot my boy." She shook as her eyes widened.

Adina touched her hand, causing the woman to pull away. "Mrs. Hopper, I—I'm so very sorry. Please try to understand. My father and I were asked by Major Williams to provide medical care for the prisoners as needed, nothing more." She realized there really wasn't much she could say that would bring a true comfort to the woman. Not that Mrs. Hopper's situation was unique. Far from it. If it didn't happen to you, it happened to someone you knew. Everyone suffered the loss of at least one family member—a friend, husband, co-worker. The war didn't have the common courtesy to discriminate. War has no conscience, it doesn't feel. It deceives and lures its victims to its bloody cause. The young and the willing eagerly run toward its siren call. War knows there will be no winners in its game. There will only be thousands of miles, snow, frostbite, darkness, and death.

Adina took Ginny's hand in both of hers, holding it securely, and searched the woman's eyes, hoping to impart to her just how much she really did care. "Mrs. Hopper, I'll try to come sit with you more often. Would you like that? There's really no reason I wouldn't be able to do that." She could feel herself rambling, trying to fill the empty spaces. "Again, I am sorry I—"

The mantel clock chimed.

Adina laid the lace napkin on the tray and stood. "I'm so sorry, Mrs. Hopper. I really do need to go. I had no idea how late it was. My father will be home very soon, and I still have one more stop to make."

Ginny dabbed her eyes with her napkin. "Well, I'm sad to see you go so soon."

Adina walked out of the parlor and toward the front door. Ginny followed close behind.

"Where's your last stop? Is it something that can wait until to-morrow? Maybe I can ring up your father and let him know you'll be a little late."

Adina stopped at the front door. Her heart beat anxiously. "Oh…um, that's not necessary. This shouldn't take long at all. Plus, I don't know the exact time my father will be home. He was seeing quite a lot of patients today," she lied. She snatched her medical kit and slung it over her shoulder. Quickly, she ran down the steps and over to her bicycle.

"Adina," Ginny called out. "You be careful, ya hear? Make sure you only go to that camp when your father's with you. Understood? You can't trust a German."

Adina swung her leg over the bike and rode down the drive. "I'll come back and visit you real soon, Mrs. Hopper," she yelled back, and rode toward the main road.

––––––––––––––––––––

Adina pedaled toward the end of the dirt drive, a cacophony of emotions overwhelming her heart and mind. She stopped suddenly at the end of the drive. Placing one foot on the ground, she steadied herself and waited. The wind carried the scent of burning leaves. She loved this time of year. Closing her eyes, she focused to slow her breathing and concentrate. Looking to the left, she could see the road to Camp Windsor. To the right was a two-mile ride back home. *I can't do it*, she thought. *Papa will kill me if I'm late again.*

It was true, she couldn't deny the irresistible desire she had to see Daniel again. It pulled her like a magnet. Yet the risk of something going wrong and having to explain to her father was way more than she was ready for. She pulled out, turning right on the main road to head back home. This time, her pace was less frantic, more controlled. Two blocks into her ride, as she approached the railroad tracks, the battle in her mind picked up once more. *There's nothing wrong with wanting to see him...*

Without another thought, she turned the bicycle around and headed west toward Camp Windsor.

An Unsanctioned Visit

Clouds of dust trailed Adina's bicycle, encircling her skirt and legs. Majestic oaks lined the road, their staggered arms sprinkling a sunset starry show of light and shadow on the dirt trail. Windswept leaves grazed Adina's face and lodged in her hair. She would be a mess when she got there, but she didn't care. Her heart sank when she glanced at her wristwatch and saw that it was already after five.

The barbed fencing soon came into view. Ginny Hopper's words repeated in her mind. *You can't trust a German.* But this German was different. This one wasn't a killer. He was gentle and kind. She knew it the very first time she looked in his eyes, clear and blue.

"Hold it right there!"

Adina kicked her right foot down, skidding the bike to a stop right in front of the guard at the camp gate.

"What's your business here, ma'am?" he asked and stepped closer.

Adina read the name on his uniform shirt. *M. Baxter.* She took note of the sidearm holstered on his hip. Her left leg started to twitch, knocking itself on the bicycle frame.

"I said, state your business," he said again.

Another gust of wind swept Adina's face, steadying her and bolstering her courage. She swung her leg over her bike and took a few steps closer to M. Baxter.

"Well, hello there. Private Baxter, is it?" She wet her lips.

He took a step back, gingerly laying his hand on his sidearm. "I need you to tell me why you're here, ma'am. I believe I've asked three times now."

She recognized him now. He was the guard who opened the gate the night of the emergency. It had been dark, and he wouldn't have seen her clearly.

"Actually, you only asked twice," she said, stepping a bit closer. "I mean, it would be three times if you count the very last time you asked just then. Forgive me, Private. I thought you would have recognized me. I'm Nurse Robbins. My father, Dr. Henry Robbins, and I were here last month for a prisoner emergency. You remember that, don't you?"

M. Baxter shined his flashlight in Adina's face. She squinted, shielding her eyes with her hand.

"Could you drop your hand, please ma'am, so I can see your face?"

She let her hand drop to her side and opened her eyes wide in the light, trusting that if anything might persuade Baxter, her eyes just might do the trick. She smiled, hoping it would help the golds and greens to dance.

"Oh yeah. I do remember you," he said. How are you this evening, Nurse Robbins?"

Adina let out a nervous laugh, pressing her palm to her chest. "I'm just fine, Private, and thank you for asking. Lovely fall evening, isn't it?"

He reached for the clipboard hanging next to him on the gate post. Shining his flashlight on it, he flipped through the pages. "Miss Robbins, I'm not seeing any medical visits on today's schedule. In fact, it says Dr. Robbins was just here two days ago." He hung the clipboard back on the post and again shined the light on Adina's face. "So, you need to tell me what business it is that you have here." He tilted his head, pointing his finger. "And come to think of it, why are you here without Dr. Robbins? It's not safe for a woman to be out here alone."

Adina's mind reeled. She knew she was taking a risk coming to the camp by herself. The weight of it sat heavy on her chest. She trembled and thought for sure Baxter could see it. "I'm sorry, M...is it Mark?" She turned up the corners of her lips and walked a little closer.

Baxter scratched his temple. "Um, it's Michael, or Mike, if you prefer."

She tucked a loose strand of hair behind her ear. "I'm so sorry, Mike. I thought for sure word was sent over that someone would be stopping by today to check on Prisoner Christensen." She laid her hand on her medical bag. "He's due for a bandage change."

Baxter's eyes darted from the medical bag and back to Adina. His fidgeting made her even more nervous. Was her plan failing? There had to be another way to get through to the blockheaded private. Then it came to her.

"Say, Mike, does all the staff here know about the Christmas dance that's being planned for the town this year? We're all very excited about it—what with this war and all, and everyone so down in the mouth about it. A town holiday party is just the right medicine, don't you agree?"

Baxter shuffled his boots, looking down at the ground. "I believe we've heard a little something about it. As a matter of fact, the powers that be may even allow some of the prisoners to attend. But I can't say I understand why." He straightened his back. "These prisoners are allowed more privileges than should ever be afforded to criminals."

She shifted her weight a bit closer to him, looking him right in his eyes. "But *you'll* be there...right, Mike?"

That did it. Baxter straightened his shoulders and flashed a toothy grin. "I believe so, ma'am. I hope so. Guys like us need a little fun now and then." He adjusted his cap, stepping closer to Adina. "You'll be there too, won't you— I'm sorry, ma'am. I didn't catch your first name."

She extended her hand to him. "Adina."

"Adina," he enunciated slowly. "Now that's a real nice name." He leaned in toward her. "Ya know, you've got two of the most beautiful eyes I've ever seen. I'm not really sure what to call that color," he said, clearly more comfortable now with her unannounced visit. He tipped his cap up out of his eyes and shimmied closer to her side. "Say, maybe you could save me a dance or two at the Christmas party."

She glanced at her watch. "Yeah, sure...sure, Mike. We'll dance." She looked past him, into the camp. "Anyway, I do have other stops I need to make after this one. Can I get in now to see Prisoner Christensen?"

Baxter pursed his lips, then re-adjusted his cap. "Well, most of the men haven't returned from field work yet. Should've been back by now, though. I guess it's a good thing that most of them are still out. Safer for you, that is." He reached for a walkie talkie hanging from the fence. "Let me just radio up to the office and see if someone can come down to escort you to the prisoner's tent."

Adina placed her hand on his arm. "Oh no, there's no need for that. I know where the tent is. Remember? I was here the night of the emergency. Besides, Mike," she gave his arm a squeeze, "you can just watch me as I walk there, right from where you're standing. Keep a little eye on me?"

A quirky smile curved on his lips. He glanced over at the administration building, shuffling his boots again. "I guess it'd be okay to let you through, just this once. You can't stay long though. Checking bandages shouldn't take much time, right?"

"I'll need to take his vitals as well. I need to be absolutely sure he hasn't developed an infection. You understand the necessity of all of that, don't you Mike?" She poured on her charms, touching his arm and smiling, then worried she might be pouring it on a little too thick.

"Sure, sure. I understand." He removed a set of keys from his pocket. "But you'll have to leave that bicycle here. I'll keep an eye on it for you." He unlocked the padlock on the gate.

"Thanks Mike," she said, winking at him as she walked past and through the gate.

She had done it. She was in. Her heart beat wildly as she walked toward the rows of tents.

"Hey, Nurse Adina!" Baxter called out.

She stopped dead in her tracks, afraid that he'd realized he made a mistake. "Yes?" she said, glancing back over her shoulder.

"Don't forget. You owe me a dance."

She exhaled. "Oh, right. Sure thing, Mike." She waved at him, heart pounding as though it would break right through her chest.

The sun had all but set, making the prisoner tents look like ghostly mountains against the deep purple sky. The whole place seemed empty, adding even more excitement to the adventure of coming to the camp uninvited to visit the prisoner alone.

The front gate, along with Private Baxter, grew distant behind her, and as the last row of tents grew closer, Adina questioned herself. Why was she doing this? Like the force of a magnet pulling her, she'd turned her bicycle in the opposite direction and come here, just to see one prisoner: Daniel. Why him? Every ounce of common sense screamed that this was the wrong thing to do. But something deep inside her kept telling her this German prisoner was different. He was nothing like that Klaus Schneider, that was for certain. Also, she couldn't ignore her erratically beating heart, its every pulse urging her closer and closer. Common sense didn't seem to matter anymore.

She slowed, turning left at the last row, and reached into her medical kit to confirm she had everything she'd need. Her hands recognized a bottle of antiseptic, scissors, bandages, and tape. At the very least, she'd be prepared to treat the patient. All else remained unknown behind the folds of the tent.

Adina paused just outside and took a deep breath. She pushed the canvas flap to the side and stepped inside. Warm yellow light spilled from the far corner, just as it did the night she and Papa had come, when they'd rushed through the half-darkened tent to save the prisoner's life. This time, she'd take things a bit slower.

The tent was empty, quiet. At least twelve cots were visible in the hazy light. Each prisoner's area was unique, telling its own story, like a home away from home. A ukulele sat atop a makeshift crate-turned-bedside-table; stained sheet music sat nearby. She saw a beautifully hand-carved wooden ship, about the size of a child's toy. Possibly a father's gift for one of the children in the photographs that were pinned to the canvas siding near the cot. There were so many photographs. Children, wives, girlfriends in the arms of their beaus. Mothers and fathers. These were the faces of those back home, waiting for their loved ones to return. Adina felt like an intruder, treading on sacred ground. Who were these men, so very far from home?

"Guten Abend," the voice said, catching her by surprise.

Daniel sat in his cot, propped up by pillows. His hair was pushed up against his head on one side, as though he had just woken up. His eyes looked tired, but he was smiling at her, as though he'd been expecting her to come. It was a smile that undid everything she thought she knew about herself, about why she came, about him.

"Guten, I mean, hello," she said. "I came to check you...your incision. To see if you were okay." Her voice shook. She was already babbling nonsense. Her feet felt as though they had sunk into cement. Was she paralyzed?

"Ah, yes. Good," he said, struggling to sit up a bit more. He grimaced.

"Be careful," she said, moving closer to his bedside.

"Oh, it's good. The pain is not so bad." He placed his hand on his right side and groaned. "It only hurts when I move." He laughed, lighting up his tired eyes.

Adina laughed with him, covering her mouth with her hand, utterly taken by the sound of his laugh.

"What would you like for me to do?" His eyes didn't leave hers.

"I'm sorry?"

"You said that you wanted to check me?"

Adina blushed. "Oh yes, of course."

She lifted her medical kit over her head and laid it on the small wooden table next to his cot. "If it's all right with you, I'd like to take a peek at your incision, just to be sure there's no infection." She paused, nervously tapping her fingertips together, waiting for him to make the first move. "Maybe it would be better if you lay back down."

As she moved the pillows from behind his back, a small, faded brown-leather journal fell to the ground. She reached down and picked it up. Burned into the front cover were the initials D.M.C. Gently, she ran her fingers over the letters. "This is you?" she asked, handing him the book.

"Yes, danke." He set the book on the bedside table.

She placed her hand on his back to gently support him as he lay back down.

"Dankeshön," he said again, intently watching her face as she worked.

Something about the way he looked at her put a knot in her stomach, as though he saw something that she couldn't see. She felt weakened by it. Normally, she didn't appreciate being made to feel weak, but right now she welcomed it.

"How have you been feeling?" she asked him. "Any pain or discomfort? Fever?"

He stared at her, not answering.

"Yes? No?" she asked again.

"No," he answered. "I mean yes." He laughed, the glow of the lamplight reflecting off his face. "How do you say it? I feel super?"

"Super? You almost died, Daniel."

His eyes widened. "You remembered?"

She raised an eyebrow. "I'm sorry? Remembered what?"

"My name. You remembered my name."

"Well, yes, I did. But I can't quite remember your last name," she lied, afraid he might think she was coming on too strong.

"Christensen. Daniel Christensen."

"Ah yes, that's right. Christensen. I'm Adina," she said, tapping her chest with her thumb.

"Yes, I know," he said, chuckling.

"Okay then, Daniel Christensen. Let's take a look at that incision." She reached down to lift his shirt, then snapped back. "Um, would you

mind pulling your shirt up a bit? And I'll need you to lower your pants, just enough for me to see the wound."

He did as she asked, revealing a four-inch bandage on his lower right abdomen.

Adina removed the antiseptic, scissors, and bandages from her kit and laid them out on the table. "Would you mind if I sat next to you on the bed?" she asked.

He nodded, inching over to make room for her.

She sat next to him and began to examine the area around the bandage, gently pressing the skin to feel for heat. "Does this hurt?" she asked, willing herself not to look in his eyes.

"Not too bad," he said, smiling as her fingers lingered on his skin.

"I'll need to remove the bandage now," she said. "Let me know if it causes you any discomfort." Starting at the corner, she carefully peeled the tape that surrounded the padding and gauze. "So, Daniel Christensen, how is it that you speak English so well?" she said, hoping a little benign conversation would distract him from what she was doing.

"I was taught English in grammar school, in the small village where I grew up." He stretched his neck to the side, trying to see what her hands were doing.

"Is that so?" she said. "Why would you need to learn English? You lived in Germany, didn't you? Or am I mistaken?" As soon as the words left her mouth, she regretted her sarcasm.

A smile turned up at the corner of his mouth. "Many people all over the world learn how to speak English, Adina Robbins. Not just Americans. Of course, you know this, ja? Or is it just you privileged Americans who are allowed to speak the English language?"

She blushed, too embarrassed to look up at him. "Touché," she said. She had finished removing the bandage and could see the incision. A four-inch, c-curved cut on the lower right side of his abdomen. She tenderly ran her fingers around the perimeter of the wound. "The surgeon did a wonderful job. The incision is healing nicely. You should be able to have the stitches removed in a couple days." She poured antiseptic on a tuft of cotton and cleaned the area on and around the incision site. Then she applied a fresh bandage.

Daniel asked, "How long have you been a nurse?"

She secured the last piece of medical tape. "I've had my certificate for about a year now. Why do you ask?"

"Because Fräulein," he grinned shyly, "you are very young."

She stopped what she was doing and looked him in the eye. "I'm nineteen years old. I graduated high school when I was sixteen, which is much earlier than most of my friends. And thanks to this damned war and the fact that God knows why so many nurses left here to go be heroes, I was able to earn my nursing certificate in just one year, thank you very much." She hated feeling like she always needed to prove herself to anyone. "So, you see, PW Christensen, I am old enough. Old enough to nurse the folks in this town, and certainly old enough to nurse you." Standing abruptly, she began putting the supplies back in her medical kit.

Daniel adjusted his pants and strained to sit back upright. "Adina," he said, his eyebrows raised. "I believe you misunderstand me. I only meant—" He raked his hand through his hair, long overdue for a trim.

Adina took a deep breath and reined in her runaway thoughts. "It's okay," she said. "I always seem to overreact. At least my father says I do. Don't pay any attention to me."

Daniel shifted his legs over the edge of the bed and faced Adina. "No," he said, his eyes much clearer now. "What I am trying to say is, you have been very kind to me. You came here to the camp alone. I understand how that might be a risk for you." His eyes took in every detail of her face. "It's just that... I've never seen someone as beautiful as you before, not ever, and I—" He looked down and smiled. "I think I am speaking too much."

Adina felt lightheaded, as though the ground under her feet swelled like the ocean. So much wonder filled her head as she looked at him sitting there, his tousled red hair falling into his eyes. "You don't know me," she said, her voice almost a whisper. "And I certainly don't know you." She held her hands together to steady them. He reached out, placing his hand on hers. His touch sent a current through her that made her catch her breath.

"I felt I knew you the first day I met you...at the fence," he said. "I know it sounds odd. I can't explain it myself. I only knew then that I must know you better, Adina Robbins."

Tentatively, she sat back down next to him. The corner of her eye caught sight of the journal. She took it in her hands, running her fingers over the soft, aged leather. "Tell me about this," she said and handed it to him.

"This—" he looked at the journal, holding it firmly in both hands. "I am a...how do you say it in English? I like to draw things."

Her eyes lit up. "You're an artist?

"Yes, an artist."

"May I have a look?"

"Of course." He untied the strap and handed the journal to her.

She laid it in her lap, opening to the first page. Written at the top in a delicate cursive was an inscription.

Für meinen Sohn. Wenn du die Welt siehst, ziehe dein Herz. Mein lieber zu dir, immer, Mutter.

Beneath the words was a beautiful full-color sketch of a lush green valley, with wooded hills against a sunset sky.

Adina touched the foreign words on the page. "What does this say?"

"Let me show you," he said. Taking her hand in his, he formed her finger to point to each word as he read out loud.

"*For my son. When you see the world, draw with your heart. Much love to you always, Mother.*"

"This journal was a birthday gift from my mutter many years ago. I've been sketching in it for a long time. It goes everywhere I go." He didn't let go of her hand.

"Your mother? Where is she? Does she know you're here?"

He shook his head, eyes distant. "Nein, I don't know where she is. I was forced to leave her against my will. There was no time for me to ensure her safety. I have no other family in Germany. At least none that I am aware of."

Adina tilted her head, searching his face. Who was this gentle young man with wavy red hair? How could it be that he had no family back home? What could have happened that he would need to leave his mother so quickly? The very thought of it. What kind of horror caused their separation? It troubled her, yet she couldn't deny the relief she felt in knowing it wasn't his choice. He wasn't a Nazi. And now here he was...a prisoner.

"You can turn the page," he said, interrupting her thoughts.

She gently turned the first page, then the next. Page after page filled with skillful, detailed sketches. Some were drawn with colored pencils, others in black and white. Pictures of buildings with pointed roofs. A village with cobblestone streets and a schoolhouse. Pages of people and faces. A hunched old man leaning on a walking stick, the lines and creases in his face and around his eyes intricately and painstakingly drawn. The smile on his face, warm and friendly. Another page revealed a sketch of a handsome young man who looked a little like Daniel. The young man's head was thrown back in laughter. Daniel had captured the joy on his face perfectly. Adina stared in awe, chuckling under her breath. On the opposite page was a snowflake, sketched in exquisite detail, crystalline and ice-like. She ran her fingers over it, half expecting it to feel wet and cold. "Fascinating," she whispered.

When she turned the next pages, the sights became more familiar. A vineyard scene. Row after row of grapevines surrounded by hills. A giant old oak tree, its branches curling and stretching like spindly arms, ancient and majestic. Next, she turned to an ocean scene. Cliffs with trees and detailed foliage, overlooking a sea of waves crashing against jagged, craggy rocks. This one was in black and white, but color wasn't necessary to convey the power and depth of that sea.

Adina closed the journal, tied the leather straps, and handed it back to him. Again, she searched his eyes—for what, she still wasn't quite sure. But she knew she wanted to know more. She found it difficult to ask him questions. Her words seemed to be stuck somewhere between her brain and her heart. When she finally did speak, "How?" was all she could say.

He raised his eyebrows. "How? I'm afraid I don't understand."

"Your sketches. They're incredible. You must have been taught by someone, in school perhaps?"

He smiled at her, clearly drawn in by the curiosity in her eyes. "No, not in school. I taught myself."

Adina's mouth fell open. "The picture of the coast—so exquisite. Where exactly is that?"

"I've seen pictures of the ocean in books. Of course, I saw the Atlantic Ocean from the ship that brought me to the United States." He tipped his head back, closing his eyes. "But truly, I dream of one day being able to see the Pacific Ocean." Opening his eyes, he looked at her. "Maybe I will someday, ja?"

She stared at him, entranced by his voice, his eyes.

Daniel chuckled.

"I'm sorry, what did you say?" she asked.

"I said, I'd love to see the Pacific Ocean someday."

Adina blushed. "Oh yes, visiting the coast. That would be a swell thing."

Outside, the sound of truck tires on gravel alerted her. "Oh no!" she said, leaping from the bed to grab her things.

"It's all right," he said. "It's only the other men returning from the fields. Looks as though they worked late tonight."

She swung her medical kit over her shoulder. "I need to get outta here. I've stayed much too long." Frantically, she looked around the tent as though plotting an escape.

He laughed, pointing to the tent entrance. "There is only one way in and out, Nurse Adina."

Her face flushed and she tried to suppress her nervous heartbeat. She looked back at him. "Thank you...for sharing your sketches with me. You have a gift, Daniel."

With that, she quickly walked to the tent opening and ran as fast as she could back to the gate and Private Baxter.

"It's about time," he said as he unlocked the gate. "I guess it took you a little longer than expected, right, Nurse?" His voice was laced with sarcasm.

"Um, yeah. Guess I'm not so quick with those bandage changes after all." She jumped on her bicycle, turned on the battery-operated front light, and pedaled hard down the dirt road.

"You ride safe, Nurse Robbins," Baxter called out after her. "And don't forget about that Christmas dance. You owe me!"

17

Riding Home

It was dark, way past the time Adina would normally end her day. There was nothing listed on her schedule that would cause her to be out this late. Papa would know this. He would never understand her reasons for going to the camp without him. She didn't understand it herself. To think about her father waiting at home to interrogate her made her stomach knot. How could she ever tell him that she went to the camp alone to see the one prisoner she was wildly drawn to? The one who looked at her as though she were the only person who mattered. The one who haunted her thoughts, her dreams.

She pedaled hard and fast, the cold night air stinging her cheeks as the main road stretched into endless darkness in front of her. She sped past the Hopper home and recalled Ginny's warning to not trust the Germans. Truth be told, her trip to the camp had nothing to do with whether she trusted the Germans. As a matter of fact, Adina applauded herself for her ability to finagle past Private Baxter and walk right into that camp, bold and fearless. It wasn't until she stood alone in front of Daniel that she felt weak and undone. It was her own heart she didn't trust.

The businesses downtown were closing for the night. Carl Sanderson was hanging a "Closed" sign on the glass front door of the Groceteria. Adina rode with her head down, hoping he wouldn't notice her.

"Hello there, Adina!" he called. Stepping out the door, he walked toward the street.

She put on the brakes, stopping in the middle of the road. Her stomach sank, and she wondered where her newfound courage had gone. Looking nonchalantly from side to side, she turned her head, pretending to not know who called her name.

"Oh hello, Mr. Sanderson. You closing up for the evening?"

He walked into the street to meet her. "I am indeed. Boy am I glad I caught sight of you riding by. Your father came by late this afternoon, asking if I'd seen you. He seemed a little worried—said you weren't in the clinic or at the house. So, I told him I'd seen you riding west past here earlier today, but not since." He scratched the back of his neck. "I tell ya, Adina, he sure seemed concerned."

Adina's leg started twitching again. She placed her hand on it to steady it and took a few deep breaths. "What time was my father here?"

Carl wiped his hands on his apron and reached up to stroke his chin. "Well, let me see now. Couldn't have been that long ago. Around six, I suppose." He looked at her quizzically. "You're working a bit late tonight, aren't you?"

"A little later than normal, Mr. Sanderson," she answered with a nervous chuckle. "Guess I better get myself home. Thanks for your concern." Without hesitation, she hopped back on her bicycle and rode off.

"Are you sure you're all right, Adina?" the grocer yelled.

Without a response, Adina pumped the pedals hard, riding into the darkness. As she rode, she tried to reason out what she would tell her father. She could feign confidence in other situations, but not with Papa. With him there was a wall. With him there was dishonesty. How would she ever be able to be honest with him when he had hidden so much from her?

Rocks And Flowers

Adina slowed as she neared the house. The "what ifs" raced in her mind. She would need to get her disheveled thoughts into some kind of order before she went inside.

A sweet smell of woodsmoke greeted her as she turned onto the drive, bringing some comfort amid her anxiousness. Lights were on inside the house, making it appear warm and welcoming. She knew better and prepared for the worst. Stopping at the end of the drive, she got off her bicycle and walked the rest of the way. Just ahead of her, at the base of the front porch, was the rock and flower garden her mother had so lovingly designed and cared for. It ran the length of the porch, stretching around the side walkway that led to the back of the house. Rocks of different shapes and sizes sat in all manner of arrangements, nestled in their dirt beds. Circles, pyramids, and towers. She thought about the flowers that once grew in and amongst the rocky formations. Cobalt blue lilac, pink wild roses, orange poppies. And sweet peas. Those were her favorite. The delicious, sweet fragrance would drift on the wind, enveloping her whenever she played outside as Mama worked in the garden.

Adina stood, silently staring at what was left of the once beautiful display. The rocks were still in their places, but most of the flowers were spent, but for a bulb or two that would sprout up in spring.

A gust of wind blew, scattering fallen leaves across the drive. Adina shivered. She hugged herself, rubbing the sides of her arms. Confusion, frustration, and grief infiltrated her heart and mind. Tilting her head back, she looked at the blackened sky, star-speckled with a crescent moon. *Why am I still here*? she thought. Her best friend was gone, somewhere far away, fighting for a cause that really mattered. *Did I miss my chance*?

Dropping to her knees, she reached down and ran her fingers over the damp soil. She closed her eyes, breathing in the cold night air, and saw her mother kneeling in the dirt beside her. She was planting gladiolus, her delicate, bare fingers covered in dirt. All the flowers were in full bloom in and around the rocks. Vibrant colors of yellow, purple, and gold. Adina heard Mama humming a melody, haunting and sweet.

She knew this one. It was the lullaby Papa would sing to her. *"Sleep, sleep, my little girl. Sleep, sleep, my little one..."* She could hear the melody, clear and true, yet struggled to remember the rest of the words. How she wanted to remember those words. She heard her mother's laugh, her voice. *"Adina Luisa, come help Mama move the rocks around."* How she loved to help her mother in the garden. *"That's it, Adina. Move the dirt with your hands...like this."* Tears streamed down Adina's cheeks. She desperately missed her mother, needed her, wanted to hear her voice. The ache of losing her was ever present, so deeply rooted inside. Adina opened her eyes, reaching her hand out as if to touch the memory. "Mama?" she whispered, blinking back tears.

"Adina,"

Her mother looked so young, so beautiful. Adina could see her eyes.

"Adina Luisa!" a voice came, deep and forced.

She jumped and looked up to see Papa standing on the front porch, pipe in one hand, newspaper in the other.

She wiped away her tears with dirty hands. "Sorry, Papa. I didn't see you standing there." She looked back at the garden, rocks and spent flowers just as they were when she first walked up. She stood, brushing the dirt from her hands. "I'll take my bicycle around back and be right in," she said, walking toward the side yard.

Papa said nothing and walked inside.

18

Confrontation

Adina walked up the back porch steps and stood quietly by the door. She thought of her mother, of her strength and her grace. "I wish you were here with me, Mama," she whispered.

Something was bubbling on the stove that smelled of steamed cabbage. Papa had been cooking. Adina always tried her best to make it home before Papa, in order to have dinner on the table for him. She had learned this from her mother. Luisa Robbins brought comfort and consistency to their home. She had a way of making everything she touched beautiful. Papa came alive whenever Mama entered a room. It could be the gloomiest of days, but if Luisa Robbins walked in, the sun would shine for Papa in all its splendor and glory. He adored her. And when she died, it was as if the sun stopped shining. A dark cloud had covered Papa ever since. Adina very much wanted to be a comfort to him. She stepped into Mama's roles, cooking, cleaning, and nursing alongside him. But for all of her trying in earnest to please him, she felt like a failure. Nothing she did seemed to ease his suffering. In fact, she felt she caused the opposite. No wonder she wanted to join the WACs and serve overseas. Any effort anywhere was better than here. Her heart was growing tired.

She walked into the living room. The cast iron stove warmed the room while Papa sat in his armchair next to it. His pipe sat in its dish on the round end table next to him. He didn't look up from his paper.

"Sorry I'm late, Papa," Adina said. She removed her medical kit and coat, hanging them on the coatrack in the entryway.

"You should always return your supplies to the cabinet in the clinic, Adina. I have told you this before," he said, eyes still not leaving his newspaper.

"Yes, I know, Papa. I'll put them back after dinner." She fidgeted, waiting for him to respond. When he didn't, she said, "What have you got cooking on the stove? It smells wonderful. I can finish up and have dinner on the table in just a few minutes." She turned back toward the kitchen.

"Please leave it, Adina. I want to hear about your visits today first." He looked up from his newspaper, directly at her.

She bolstered every bit of courage within herself, telling herself that she had done nothing wrong. If looking in on the recovering prisoner was wrong, then why was she a nurse in the first place? She removed her red wool beret, twisting it in her hands as she walked to the floral sofa and sat down across from her father.

Papa peered at her over the rim of his glasses as he folded the newspaper. "Were you able to see Mr. Murray today?"

"Yes, Papa."

"And how was he? His pain from the gout?"

"He's fine. I examined his feet and left him the medicine you prescribed." She eyed him timidly, ever twisting the beret in her hands.

"And Mrs. Quinn? You saw her and the baby today, yes? I hope that you measured and weighed the baby. Mrs. Quinn was concerned the child was not retaining enough from the breast." His eyes needled her.

Adina wondered at her father's questioning. Why didn't he just get to the point? "Sally and the baby are just fine, Papa. In fact, the baby has gained a few ounces since my last visit." She glanced at her medical kit hanging in the entryway. "I can check my log if you like." She realized she'd been wringing the beret in her hands and set it down next to her on the sofa.

"And how about Mrs. Hopper? You delivered her prescription?"

"Yes, Papa. Ginny invited me to stay for a cup of tea, so I did. But I didn't stay long." Adina wanted the interrogation to be over with.

It was obvious her father knew something. Why didn't he just come out with it?

"Not for long?" he asked, his posture unchanging, eyes fixing on her over his glasses. "Mrs. Hopper's would have been your last stop, yes? You are home late, Adina Luisa. You must have had another visit, one you added to your schedule, yes?"

Papa's accent seemed to thicken with each question. Adina was so accustomed to the sound of it that she barely noticed it. Except when Papa was angry. Then the accent distinguished itself, and his questions ended with a yes or a no.

Adina wasn't sure how to respond and found herself second-guessing his tactic. Did he know, or didn't he? Ginny Hopper did say she could ring up her father to let him know she'd be late. Maybe she had. Adina wished the old woman would just mind her own business. That was the problem with living in a small town. Everyone knew everything about everybody, sticking their noses in where they didn't belong.

She straightened her back. "You are the one who gives me my visiting schedule every day, Papa. Shouldn't you know if I had a late appointment?" Even she was shocked by the bite in her tone.

Papa removed his glasses. "Why are you speaking to me in that way, Adina?" he said, sitting forward in his chair. "I am only asking you a question. You came home late. I was worried."

His skirting around was wearing her down. Why the unnecessary questions? Was he purposely tormenting her to teach her a lesson? Her face reddened. "You worried?" she asked. "I suppose that's why you made a special trip to the market to ask Mr. Sanderson if he knew where I was."

"Adina, that is not why I asked Carl if he'd seen you," he said, stiffening his back. "I had a phone call from—"

"Ginny Hopper called you, didn't she?"

"I do not understand," Papa said.

Adina buried her face in her hands. "I knew I shouldn't have stayed for tea. There wasn't enough time. That woman just has to put her nose in where it doesn't belong."

Henry's eyes narrowed. "Yes, Mrs. Hopper did phone me." His impatience mounted. "Enough time for what, Adina Luisa?"

She removed her hands from her face and looked at him, her eyes red with tears. "What is it you're asking me, Papa? Ginny Hopper obviously told you that I went to the prisoner camp."

The look in Papa's eyes sent Adina's heart racing. She thought for certain that Ginny had put it together that she went to the camp alone. Did her father really not know? Had she just given herself up, all on her own? She straightened and wiped her eyes. "Papa, you knew, right? You've been asking me all these questions when all the while you knew what my schedule was. You had to have known that—"

Papa's chin raised and his eyes tightened. He held up his hand. "What possible explanation could you have for going to that prisoner camp alone...and at night? There is no good reason for it, Adina Luisa."

She turned her face away, not wanting to acknowledge the look in her father's eyes, as though she'd betrayed him, when she herself felt so utterly betrayed by him. She'd been trapped—strung up by his questioning until she gave herself up. Again, she felt as though she were shrinking before his eyes. Finally, she spoke.

"I'm tired, Papa," she said, her eyes searching the carpet on the floor. "Tired of you treating me like a child."

Papa sat back in his chair and folded his arms. "That was not an answer to my question, Adina Luisa. If you want to be treated like an adult, then stop behaving like a child. Raise your head and look at me when I'm speaking to you."

Look at him? If she truly did look at him, who was the man he'd allow her to see? Here Henry Robbins sat, demanding honesty from her, yet he himself hid so much.

Adina lifted her head. She studied his face and sharp features. His heavy, dark eyebrows and beard seemed grayer with each passing day.

She peered into his eyes, seeking the love she knew was in them somewhere. Even though time and trial had aged him, Adina still thought of him as the handsomest of men. As a child she imagined herself growing up to marry someone just like him. He was her prince, her knight in shining armor. But not anymore. His joy was gone. All that was left of him was work and formality. The ache of losing her father in this way sickened her more than anything else.

"Adina, answer me," he demanded.

She straightened, tilting her chin up so he would know she heard him. She could hear the crackling of the burning wood stove and the swaying tick of the grandfather clock in the entryway, yet the silence between her and her father was deafening.

"I went to the camp to look in on the prisoner, Papa," she said. "It had been two days since you last visited him. I didn't see any harm in just looking in on him." The chasm between them seemed to widen with every word she spoke.

Papa sighed. Removing his glasses, he rubbed his eyes, then looked at her. "You went to the prisoner camp alone, Adina. Was I not clear in the beginning that you were to not go there alone, ever? And yet you assumed that this would be the right thing to do. What were you thinking?"

The familiar feelings of inadequacy and frustration buffeted her. He had just told her to stop acting like a child, yet he had the unmitigated ability to make her feel like one. She couldn't think, she couldn't reason. She wanted to stomp her feet, throw herself in a heap on the floor and scream and cry. But she wouldn't do that. She already gave into it when he told her that Ginny Hopper called him. Papa had a power over her that she struggled to understand. It was as though on that day, when she had intruded upon that hidden, sacred part of his life, when she saw him embracing his faith where no one else could see, a line was drawn. Henry Robbins erected a fortress around himself that Adina couldn't penetrate. From that day forward, she would have to fight to pierce that barrier and prove to him that she was worthy of his respect and honesty.

She wanted to be brought into the truth of who he was—and of who *she* truly was. At the very least, she felt she deserved that. But it was always easier to surrender rather than fight for her right to be included in her father's trust.

As she looked at him, pondering these things, something changed in her heart. It was as though this unsanctioned visit to the prisoner camp to see Daniel had released her from her own prison—the prison she allowed herself to be locked in. She felt a freedom she'd never felt before. As though being with Daniel, this so-called enemy, opened her eyes. Daniel wasn't evil. He wasn't violent. He didn't speak expletives of hate and destruction as she had so often heard the grotesque Hitler spewing out over the radio waves. Daniel Christensen was gentle. He was kind. He was human. She was drawn to him. She drew strength from him. For the first time in years, Adina felt strong. Strong in who she wanted to be. There would be no more living in regrets and no more hiding. Not from her father, or from herself. And she decided right then and there that she would not hide from Daniel Christensen

"Adina Luisa!" The force of Papa's voice sobered her.

"Yes, Papa. I heard you." Head held high, she walked to the fireplace mantel and picked up a framed photograph of her mother and father, one that had been displayed for as long as she could remember. Papa and Mama sat on a snowy embankment surrounded by tall, leafless trees, snow and icicles clinging to their bare branches like crystals on a chandelier. Both wore full-length woolen coats, fur-lined boots and thick, knit mittens. What intrigued Adina the most wasn't the oddity of the couple sitting in the snow—she actually found that amusing. It wasn't even how young they looked. What most intrigued her was how tightly they held one another, cheek pressed to cheek. The smiles on their faces radiated love and laughter. The last time she remembered Papa that happy was before her mother died. Mama looked like an angel in the snow.

"Papa, where was this taken—the one of you and Mama in the snow?" She turned, showing him the photograph.

"It was in Lithuania, many years ago. You know this, Adina. You've seen the picture many times." He stiffened. "Why are you asking me a question you already know the answer to? Are you purposely trying to avoid me?"

Adina gripped the photograph tightly to her chest. Her temples throbbed as her anger rose. "Me?" she said, piercing him with her eyes. "Avoiding *you*? Papa, you are the one who has avoided me." She stepped closer. "I don't even know you anymore." She held the photograph in front of his face. "You speak as if I should know about the life you had in this picture. But how would I know?" Her hands shook. "You've closed that part of you and locked it up tight. You've lived in this town as the good Dr. Henry Robbins for years and years. You've healed the sick and delivered the babies. Day in and day out, you tirelessly make your rounds. Yet God forbid anyone ever know who Dr. Henry Robbins really is...especially his own daughter."

Papa looked away from her, shaking his head. With his handkerchief, he wiped his eyes, then placed his glasses back on his nose, carefully fitting the wires around his ears. "You have no idea what you are talking about, Adina," he said as he stood from the chair. He walked toward the kitchen, then stopped short to turn and look at her again. "You risked many things today. Your reputation, as well as mine and that of my practice in this town. Not to mention risking your own safety. From this day forward, you are not to visit the prisoner camp. I will personally speak with Major Williams in the morning to be sure this doesn't happen again."

Adina stood aghast. *Risking her safety*? She wasn't afraid. There was no danger. She felt much more at ease at the prisoner camp with Daniel than she did at home with her own father. "Daniel isn't a monster, Papa. He would never have hurt me. The very idea is absurd. Not to mention that he's still convalescing in bed from the surgery."

Papa clenched his fists, fingers extending and contracting. "Ah, I see that you and this prisoner are on a first-name basis now." His face reddened. "What else do I not know?"

"Papa, don't be ridiculous," she huffed. "How could you even think that he would—"

"He's a German!" Papa yelled, face contorted. "A Nazi! A Jew killer, Adina Luisa! He enlisted to serve his Führer for one purpose and one purpose only: to kill the innocent." He turned on his heels and strode away.

She watched him, clenching her fists like him, her eyes widening, failing to hold back her anger. "And you are a fearful Jew!" she yelled, the words flying out of her mouth before she could stop them. She said it—the name—out loud. Jew. It hung suspended in midair even as it echoed there in the small living room. How many years had she wanted to confront him with this? There would be no more hiding. No more regrets. "I can't pretend anymore, Papa. I want to know who you are— who I am. You don't need to be afraid of—"

"Silence!" He held up his hand. "You are a foolish girl, Adina."

"Please Papa, won't you just talk to me about this?"

His eyebrows knit. "You will speak no more of this. Is that understood?" He left her and walked into the kitchen.

Adina stood silent, just as her father commanded, just as he always did when an argument was over for him, and in his estimation, there was nothing left to be said. She felt helpless, broken, as though a precious heirloom was torn from her hands. To try to hold on would be futile. She would have to let go. She could hear him in the kitchen, stomping around, clanging silverware, opening and shutting cabinet doors. She felt like crying, and normally she would. But crying didn't make sense to her right now. She had said "Jew" out loud. How could anything remain normal after that?

Papa again stood in the kitchen entrance, stoic, a dish towel draped over his shoulder. He cleared his throat. "Oh yes," he said. "I had forgotten what it was I wanted to tell you in the first place. Mrs. Hopper did telephone me. It was to tell me that the medicine I had you deliver was for an older prescription, which she doesn't use any longer." He wiped his hands on the towel and walked back into the kitchen. Adina heard him place the pot from the stove onto the table. "Adina Luisa, please come to the table for dinner," he said.

"Yes Papa," she replied.

But nothing would be the same.

19

December 1944

The changing season didn't hold the same joy for Adina. At least not since the confrontation with her father. It was the first week of December, and not a word of the incident had been spoken since that dreadful night two weeks ago. She had played the entire event over and over in her head, wondering if there was something she could have said or done differently. She cringed at the thought and berated herself for her cold, harsh words, "*You are a fearful Jew.*" She remembered the look of hurt in her father's eyes. The vision of it wouldn't leave her alone. Who did she think she was? What in the world possessed her to act that way toward her father?

Daniel.

She closed her eyes, forcing her mind to recall every detail of him. His rusty red hair cut close on the sides over his ears—thick, unkempt waves tumbling loose over his forehead to the top edge of his eye on the right side. His skin slightly darkened by the sun. The soft pecking of freckles over his nose and cheeks, probably due to the same. She thought of that hot summer day when she saw him in the back of the truck, his arms and shoulders sure and strong, glistening in the summer sun. He wasn't an overpowering oaf, like so many of the GIs who passed through the town on leave. The ones who always hit on her during their visit for a check-up at the clinic, expecting her to fall for them at the wink of an eye, begging her for that one drink or that one dance. When she turned them down, they looked at her in disbelief, as though she'd denied a god. Those men were Jeanie Mae's type. She always gave in to those guys.

Adina giggled at the memory of her best friend, missing her terribly. If only she could pour out all her secrets on Jee's eager ears. What would she say about the prisoner Adina was so drawn to? The one who haunted her thoughts and captivated her with his eyes. She closed her own eyes tighter, trying to ignite the perfect picture of Daniel's eyes. They were blue like the ocean. There was something about his eyes she found difficult to put into words. How they were set, cradled in an arc of pillowy, darker skin underneath, as though he hadn't had enough sleep the night before, or possibly the result of a life filled with sorrow. She longed to know which it was.

Adina mourned the idea that her visits to Camp Windsor were now a thing of the past. Two days ago, Papa made a trip there alone to attend to a prisoner's sprained ankle. He didn't ask her to assist him. For the last two weeks, Papa filled her schedule with home visits, medicine deliveries, and hours upon hours working in the clinic, reordering and stocking medical supplies.

Sitting at a table in the clinic supply room, Adina stared at the pages of a supply ledger. She rubbed her tired eyes and looked at her watch. It was almost five. Papa would be home soon. She closed the supply ledger and stood from the table. It was then that her eye caught sight of the December calendar hanging on the wall, locking onto Saturday the sixteenth. She herself had circled it boldly in red, writing inside the box, *Christmas Dance.* The town of Windsor was in full-swing preparations for its yearly holiday event. The townsfolk seemed even more excited for it than in years past. News of the successful Allied invasion of Europe gave a reason to hope and even more reason to celebrate the season. The whole town was decked in holiday fare. Main Street light posts were hung with green wreaths and red ribbons. Shop windows were draped with garland and stringed colored lights. Many donned flyers on doors and windows advertising the much-anticipated event, aptly titled,

A Christmas Hope for Victory Dance,
December 16, 1944, 6:00 p.m. at the Windsor Grange

Adina stared at the red circle and remembered her conversation with Private Baxter at the Camp Windsor gate. Did she really promise to dance with him? Would he expect her to make good on that promise? Then she remembered something else he had said. *"The powers that be may let some of the prisoners go."* Some of the prisoners, meaning Daniel. Would he be going to the Christmas dance? She believed she would do just about anything if that were true. Even a dance or two with Private Baxter would be endurable if it meant she could see Daniel again.

As Adina walked to the front entrance to leave the clinic, she realized something very important: she had nothing new in the way of a party dress, let alone a Christmas party dress, to wear to the dance. She suddenly felt like Cinderella with nothing to wear to the ball. Adina wasn't anything like Jeanie Mae when it came to clothes. Where Jeanie had mountains of clothes, old and new, Adina would make do with the same wardrobe for years if she could get away with it. She had dresses, maybe even a nice one, at that, but none of them were special enough for this particular Christmas dance.

Mama had owned beautiful dresses. She and Papa always dressed in their finest for parties and dances. Adina had a faint memory of the last Christmas dance they attended, the one before her mother became ill. Mama wore a lovely green velvet dress with shoes to match. She remembered how her mother sparkled from the top of her shiny auburn hair down to her toes, illuminating everything around her. Papa beamed with pride when Mama walked into the living room that evening. She wore a beautiful string of pearls around her neck with a matching bracelet that Papa had given her for their anniversary. He loved to lavish Mama with gifts for every special occasion.

Standing in the open doorway, as the vision of her mother became clearer, Adina wondered if her father had gotten rid of everything. She remembered how, with a blank stare, Papa bagged and boxed up her mother's things within two days of Mama's death. It was as though he were attempting to eliminate any spark of memory of Mama. When Adina asked if she could help with her mother's things, Papa told her he didn't need her help and to go to her bedroom until he had finished. She snuck an embroidered handkerchief and a pair of white gloves from a box left in the hallway when he wasn't looking. The items were infused with the lingering scent of Mama's perfume. How bitter of Papa to discard everything else without asking her if she wanted to keep any of her mother's things—that is, if he *did* get rid of it all. She'd never thought to search until now.

She locked and closed the clinic door behind her. The evening winter air hit her face, cool and crisp. The sun, already beneath the hillside, left the slightest glow to light the way back to the house. Papa's car wasn't in the drive. Adina was excited at the thought that she just may have some time to do her own searching before her father came home. She'd start in Papa's bedroom, then she'd look in the attic.

The Attic

Adina combed through the closet in her father's bedroom. There was nothing other than shirts, slacks, and suit coats, each item hung in orderly fashion. Shirts were buttoned and lined up by color, the majority being white. Slacks were crisply pressed with straight, lined creases and hung over wooden bar hangers. He had five pairs of leather shoes, three black and two brown, each meticulously arranged along the closet floor. An extra blanket and pillow were tucked on the shelf above. Other than that, there were no items of her mother's to be found.

It was the same in the ornate bureau next to the window. One drawer contained her father's wool socks. Another, his white undershirts. Still another drawer held his monogrammed handkerchiefs, each one folded into a perfect square. Papa was very particular when it came to having a clean handkerchief in his pocket every day. Adina marveled at her father's meticulous attention to his clothing. He didn't have many things, but what he did have, he took great care of.

Adina helped with the laundry on a weekly basis. When the clothes finished drying on the line, she would bundle Papa's as neatly as possible in a basket, leaving it outside his bedroom door. He insisted on folding and putting his clothing away himself. She assumed it was on account of he didn't want her wandering through his bedroom. Though when Mama was alive, it wasn't just Papa's bedroom, it was *their* bedroom, and Adina was always welcome. As a child, when she had a nightmare, she'd run down the dark hallway, through Mama and Papa's bedroom door, jumping into the soft sheets of their bed and their comforting arms. How she missed those arms.

Quelling her feelings, Adina scanned the rest of the bedroom. Seeing that there was no place else to look, she made her way down the hallway to the small door directly across from her bedroom—the door that led to the attic. It had always been a wonder to her that the door was shorter and narrower than any other door in the house, though she never questioned it. Reaching for the handle, she had the stark realization that she hadn't been up in the attic since the last Christmas they celebrated together before Mama died. All the holiday decorations had been packed in their boxes to be stored away until the next year. Mama was too weak to make it up the stairs, so Papa had Adina help him haul the boxes back up to the attic. Adina had had no desire—and no reason—to go back up there, until now.

She opened the door wide, allowing the light from the hallway up into the stairwell. A waft of cold, musty air tunneled down over her, sending a shiver with it. The stairs were steep and narrow, more like a ladder than a staircase. Holding on to the walls for support, she climbed, grateful for the bit of light behind her. Above, the dark opening awaited. She glanced down at her feet and the bottom of her climb. *Seems higher than what I remember*, she thought. Or maybe she was just older. When she reached the opening, she stood, eyes straining through the darkness, and bent down so as not to hit her head on the top of the door frame. Floorboards creaked as she walked into the center of the dark, waving her hand above her to locate the ball chain of the one hanging lightbulb.

After a few waves, she grabbed hold of it, made a wish, and pulled the chain. The bulb lit, cascading a cone of hazy yellow light.

Low, sloped ceilings vaulted up to a single center beam. A four-paned window at the front end of the room revealed the dark of night outside. A lifetime of memories and keepsakes cluttered not just the floor space, but the rafters as well. Travel trunks and tattered boxes lined the floor perimeter. Stacked wicker-bottom chairs with velvet hat boxes on top sat in one corner, fishing rods with a tackle box next to an antique brass lampstand in another. Empty baskets, tennis rackets, and a rusty camping lantern hung from the exposed rafters above, and so much more than what she could see in the dim lighting.

Adina turned to look around and started at the sight of herself in a cracked, wood-framed mirror leaning against the sloped wall. She grasped her chest, sucking in air. Excited, she continued scanning the room. There was so much more than she expected to find. *Where do I begin?* she thought.

She knelt to the boxes at her feet. Some were sealed shut, others were open, their contents spilling over onto the dusty floor. One open box contained another tennis racket, its handle splintered. Soiled gardening gloves, a pair of cracked reading glasses, and several books written in Lithuanian filled the rest of this eclectic box. Next to it were sealed boxes labeled *Medical.* They were heavy, most likely containing textbooks and desk references. She shoved them aside.

Her eyes strained through the hazy yellow light. She wasn't exactly sure what she was looking for. A mountain of items piled almost as high as the vault in the ceiling sat just to her left—folded blankets on top of boxes, on top of who knew what. She lifted a dust-covered pile of blankets, revealing boxes labeled *Christmas Decorations*, the very ones she brought up with her father years ago. She lifted them, jingle bells tinkling inside, and set them aside. Then she spotted two storage trunks. One was black with brass hinges and a brass latch. The other, a wooden-hinged box about half the size of its neighbor. She placed both hands on the black chest, running her fingers over the contours of the brass latch. The tarnished name plate above the latch read *"Luisa."* Her heart ached as she touched each letter.

There was no lock. She wiggled the latch, loosening it upward. With both hands she lifted the lid of the chest until it fell back, resting on the mound of items behind it. The acrid scent of mothballs stung her nose, making her eyes water. She ignored it, too enthralled with what lay inside. Reaching in, she pulled out a white, lace-trimmed tablecloth with something wrapped inside. Carefully, she peeled open the delicate, aged fabric, revealing two sterling candlestick holders, as well as a sterling wine goblet. Carved pomegranates and grape clusters encircled its rim. She laid them aside and continued with the search, finding a white head covering, also trimmed in lace, like the one she remembered seeing Papa wearing the day Mama died. Then she spotted a small cardboard box and lifted it out. Inside was her mother's nursing certificate and nurse's pin. There were other official-looking documents, though written in Lithuanian. Adina found herself wishing she'd had an opportunity to learn the language, at least enough to read it.

She closed the small box and looked at her watch. She'd been up in the attic for twenty minutes, and still her father wasn't home. Wanting to see more, she found a pair of white leather baby shoes and some frilly pink-and-white infant dresses. She knew they were hers.

Her eyes then caught sight of a rather large photograph. The yellowing picture showed a youthful Luisa snuggling a tiny infant Adina to her face, pressing the baby to her cheek. The photo had been hand-touched with bits of color. Rosy lips and cheeks on Luisa, and the tiny flowers on her long, flowing dress with a pattern of pink and green dots. Baby Adina's lips and cheeks matched her mother's. The dress, which just about swallowed the baby's tiny body in frills and lace, was also a wash of light pink. Adina's eyes filled with tears. Why was this photograph packed away in this dark, dusty attic? She lifted the frame to have a closer look when something caught her eye. Emerald-green fabric. She stopped, resting her hand on the velvety softness. Heart pounding, she lifted it out. It was her mother's dress—the one she'd remembered. Her father hadn't gotten rid of everything.

Adina grinned, her heart skipping a beat as she lifted it from the trunk. The dress was more beautiful than she remembered. Folds and folds of buttery soft emerald velvet draped over layers of crinoline. The dress crinkled and swished as she held it up against her body to look at her reflection in the old, cracked mirror. The length fell to just above her ankles. *Perfect.* She would need to try it on to be sure it fit, but from what she saw in the mirror, she and her mother were very much alike. Also inside the chest were a pair of Peau de Soie pumps, dyed to perfectly match the dress. Their satiny silk fibers still glistened.

She brought down the lid of the trunk, carefully closing the brass latch, when her eyes locked onto the smaller wooden trunk. Curious to know what was inside, she knelt in front of it. The trunk, by no means ornate, had a plain wood-slat construction, black handles and hinges, and a single black latch. There was no name plate, nothing to distinguish it as important. She lifted the lid. Her enthusiasm was quickly dispelled when she realized the only things in this mysterious trunk were document folders and some books. Though tucked tightly in the corner next to the books was a small, drawstring pouch. She lifted it out. It was made of soft linen, and embroidered Hebrew lettering in blue and gold lined the border. She loosened the ties and pulled out two dark-blue yarmulkes and a small black book. It, too, had Hebrew wording. These items didn't surprise Adina. She figured they belonged to her father. He closeted his Judaism in fear, angrily stifling any questions she would ask him. Of course he would pack up any semblance of that faith and hide it away in the dark attic.

Adina grew nervous, remembering that Papa would be home any minute. She'd need to speed up her investigation. Lifting out one of the document folders, she unwound the string and opened it. Again, she recognized Lithuanian writing on another official document. A medical license. The right-hand corner name and signature read *"Henrikas R. Rabinovitz."* She stared at the name, mouthing it out loud. "Rabinovitz?

Papa?" Her heart beat faster as she flipped through page after page in the file, each containing the unfamiliar name.

She set the file aside and lifted out another. Inside she found a marriage license for *Henrikas and Luisa Rabinovitz, 1920, 4, 10,* as well as what appeared to be a certificate of birth for *Adina Luisa Rabinovitz, 1925, 10, 29.* All the documents were written in Lithuanian.

Adina sat, baffled and trembling. What *was* this she was looking at? She had never seen or heard the name "Rabinovitz" before. Did her father change their name upon coming to the United States? What possible reason would he have for doing such a thing? And why would he keep it from her? More betrayal. More lies. More bricks in the ever-growing wall of separation between them. How would she ever be able to look at her father the same again?

She closed the file, winding its string tight, and placed it back inside the dark trunk. Tears stung behind her eyes as she pined for the life she had been denied, the one that had been hidden from her. She wasn't sure who she was anymore. Adina Luisa Robbins? The name wasn't even real. Once again, she felt like the lost little girl, wishing for a life that would never be. It was a feeling that had become all too familiar. How much longer could she wander through the barren wasteland of her relationship with her father? She had given up the WACs. That ship had sailed. Camp Windsor had been a source of meaning and purpose for her. Now, even that was taken away.

But then she remembered Daniel. His face filled her mind. He was the reason she combed the attic in the first place, looking for her mother's dress to wear to the Christmas dance. It was because of him that she discovered the truth.

Adina closed the wooden trunk, along with its secrets. Quickly, she stood, gathering up the velvet dress and shoes. Reaching up, she pulled the chain on the light and heard the Oldsmobile coming up the gravel drive.

20

Christmas Hope for Victory Dance

The day of the Christmas dance finally arrived, a Saturday morning, cold and crisp, with the sky spread out endless, clear, and bright blue. A thick layer of frost lay on rooftops and porch railings.

Adina shivered at the thought of having to ride out in the cold. She hunkered down under the warmth of her bed covers, tucking them beneath her chin, knowing she couldn't stay in bed, no matter how much she wanted to. Papa had scheduled her for a half day of work today, on a Saturday, no less. It didn't make any difference to him, nor did he care that it was the night of the Christmas dance and she still had much to prepare. As Papa enjoyed announcing, "There is no rest for the wicked." And so, Adina would ride out in the cold today, making deliveries, or home visits... Whatever it was that her father deemed necessary. Truth be told, she didn't mind it at all. She was too excited for the night that lay ahead. She couldn't remember the last time she had something to look forward to, let alone be excited for.

Sitting up in bed, she ran through a mental list of what she would need to accomplish today. Only three medicine deliveries, which were close together. This was a good thing. It was unusual for her to have any scheduled home visits on a Saturday, and there was only one listed on the schedule for today. Maybe her father was a bit more on her side than she thought. Her last stop would be a visit to Ginny Hopper's. Adina had dropped off the green velvet dress two days ago. It was a bit big in the shoulders and needed a tuck or two. Ginny was a whiz with a needle and thread.

"What made you decide to go to the dance in the first place?" Ginny had asked the day Adina dropped off the dress. "Did someone ask you to go? Tell me, who is it?" The woman's eyes were full of curiosity. "Will you be hanging on the arm of a handsome GI? Is one of your old school chums home on leave? Oh, Adina, you'll look like an angel in your mother's dress. Your father will be so proud."

Proud? Adina wasn't so sure of that. Papa was unaware of her quest up in the attic. She hadn't shown him the dress, nor was she ready to address the documents she had found. When she could finally get a word in edgewise, she said, "I'm going to the dance alone, Mrs. Hopper."

"Going alone? Now that's just not right at all," Ginny protested. "What's wrong with all the men in this town? Don't they know a beautiful, available young woman when they see one?"

Apparently, what Ginny Hopper didn't realize was that all the eligible young men were on the other side of the world somewhere, fighting a war, leaving the town with the crippled and aged to hold down the fort. Still, it warmed Adina's heart that despite the Nazis' brutal murder of her only son, followed by the death of her husband, Ginny was able to find room in her heart to keep an eye out for her. The fact that she must have had a sense of Adina's secret trip to the camp that evening yet had kept it a secret despite any concerns she may have had, endeared Ginny to her all the more.

By midday, Adina was able to pick up the dress from Mrs. Hopper.

"What made you decide to wear your mother's dress?" Ginny asked as they sat in the parlor. A plate of fresh-baked cookies sat on the coffee table. "I remember the Christmas she wore it, gliding into the dancehall on your father's arm. She lit up the entire room." Her eyes wandered. "That was her last year with us, isn't that right, Adina?"

Adina hesitated, remembering it as though it were yesterday. "No, Mrs. Hopper. My mother passed away the following year, in the fall."

Ginny scratched her head and adjusted a hairpin at the base of her scraggly gray bun. "Ah, yes. I remember now. Your mother didn't come out of the house much after that. Poor thing became so sick. Your father wouldn't allow anyone else to tend to her, you know." Warmth filled Ginny's eyes. "He's such a good man, your father. He loved your mama so much. Like a treasure." She lifted the plate of cookies to Adina. "You were probably too young to remember much about those days. How old were you? Ten?"

Adina stared through Ginny and the plate of cookies as the memory of her mother wearing the beautiful green dress, and the day she died, looped over each other in her thoughts. Too young to remember? It would forever be etched in her mind. She would never forget.

"Adina? Would you like a cookie?"

"I was twelve, Mrs. Hopper," Adina said. "And no, thank you. I really must be going."

Ginny set the plate down. "But you haven't tried on the dress. Don't you want to be sure of the fit?"

Adina stood. "I'm sure it'll be just fine. I trust your skills, Mrs. Hopper. I still have so much to do before tonight."

"Well, if you insist. It's hanging in my sewing room. I have some brown wrapping paper in the kitchen. Let me get it wrapped up for you. It would be dreadful if you dropped it in a puddle on your way home."

Ginny returned with the dress, neatly wrapped and tied with twine.

"Thank you, Mrs. Hopper. This means so much to me, truly." Adina took the package and kissed Ginny's cheek.

The woman reached for Adina's hand. "You're going to look like an angel, Adina. Just like your mama."

Sparkles and Pearls

Adina finished the half day of work in record time, making it home by two in the afternoon. Papa was nowhere to be found, so she made sure to make good use of her time alone. In her bedroom, she unpackaged the dress and hung it up on the standing mirror so that any wrinkles could work themselves out. It was then that she was able to see the work Mrs. Hopper had done. Adina stared, awestruck. Sewn along the sweetheart neckline, as well as in various places on the bodice, were emerald crystals and creamy pearl beads. The sunlight peeking through the bedroom window reflected off the tiny gems, bouncing their light off the mirror. Sparkles danced around the room, igniting a sense of wonder within her. Now, Adina felt sorry that she'd been in such a hurry to leave Ginny's home without trying on the dress in front of her. Ginny would have been able to admire her own handiwork. Each bead—there had to be at least one hundred of them—had been painstakingly hand stitched onto the velvet dress. It was hard to fathom the hours it would have taken, not to mention the sore, cramped fingers and tired eyes. Ginny hadn't just made simple adjustments to the shoulders, she had turned the dress that once belonged to Luisa into something unique, with Adina in mind.

With the few hours that were left, Adina knew she needed to do things right, starting with a hot bath. She slipped into the tub and sank down, resting her head on the porcelain edge, the water just beneath her chin. The hot water soothed her. She closed her eyes, breathed in, and smiled. She felt a happy expectation of something that she couldn't explain. Even the war seemed to be changing for the good. The troops were making their way through France. Soon they may even be in Berlin. Maybe Jeanie would be coming home soon. Adina had been enjoying her work more as well. There was the excitement of getting to know the PWs.

And there was the excitement of Daniel. The thought of him made her shiver. She scooped warm water over her knees. Her heart raced as his face materialized behind her eyes, so real she wanted to touch him. Why was she so drawn to him? She thought of him in a way unlike any other man she'd ever known. Was it because he was taboo? Forbidden fruit? She was so angry at her father. Was Daniel her way of getting back at Papa for his coldhearted neglect? The rapid beat of her heart told her otherwise. The feelings that just the thought of him produced throughout her body proved to her that Daniel was so much more to her. Adina wanted more.

Once she had bathed, she dusted on some Dubarry talcum, pinned her hair into curls around her forehead, and made her way back to her bedroom. Apparently, she had soaked in the tub much longer than she'd intended. The bedside clock read four. She had two hours and wanted to be ready with some time to spare. Maybe she would eat some food to settle her excited stomach.

Papa's car rolled up the drive. Adina stood to the side of the window, peeking through the curtains. If anything could dampen her excitement, it would be her father. Yet she felt that not even he could take it away.

She pulled on her silk slip and her nicest pair of stockings. Standing in front of the mirror, she ran her fingers over the green velvet dress, pausing on the handsewn gems. She removed it from the hanger and, savoring every moment, placed the dress over her head, allowing it to fall into place. She buttoned the single pearl button at the back of her neck. Under it was a keyhole opening, revealing the bare skin at the top of her back. She stood, looking at her reflection in the mirror. The dress fit to perfection, from the shoulders and cap sleeves to the snug-fitting bodice on down. It was exquisite. Tilting her head, she looked at the figure and the face looking back at her. Visions of her mother filled her head. Memory after memory, ending with this same night, long ago. Her throat tightened, yet she stood tall, straightening her shoulders. Pulling the full, flowing skirt out at the sides, she smiled at her reflection and spun around, glancing over her shoulder as she did. She giggled, watching the sparkles dance at her side.

"Adina Luisa," Papa called from the kitchen.

She stopped spinning. "I'm in my bedroom, Papa," she said, listening at the door.

"I'm cooking dinner. You should eat before you leave," he called back.

She breathed a sigh of relief. It had been days since she mentioned wanting to go to the dance. It sounded as though he was still on board with it. She could only hope he would still be agreeable to her use of the Oldsmobile.

Too Made Up

The Peau de Soie pumps echoed down the hallway as she entered the living room. She laid her evening coat and white gloves over the chair.

"I've heated a can of soup for us. You can toast a slice of bread if you—" Papa stopped just short of the entrance to the kitchen. He was still wearing his tie and had a dish rag slung over his shoulder. His glasses slipped down a bit on his nose, revealing red, tired eyes. He stared, speechless.

Adina smiled. Delicate waves of shiny auburn hair fell to her shoulders. Her face, lightly powdered, and lips a Christmas red, accentuated the myriad colors in her eyes. The emerald dress sparkled in the lamplight. Mama's pearls hung at her neck, with the matching pearl bracelet on her wrist, Mama's wristwatch beside it. "Well, Papa. What do you think?"

Henry's eyes moved from the dress to the pearls and back up to her face. He squinted and blinked, fumbling with the dishrag on his shoulder.

She tilted her head and picked at the tip of her fingernail. Did he think she looked pretty? Did he recognize the dress—remember that it was her mother's? Was he capable of remembering at all?

"Papa?"

He straightened, clearing his throat. "Your face is much too made up, Adina. Is that necessary?"

Just like that, the spell was broken. Her smile melted. She looked down, smoothing the velvet folds of the dress. "It's a party, Papa. It's Christmas. The dance is called 'A Christmas Hope for Victory.' It's a celebration meant to lift the town's spirits."

"And where did you get that dress?" he asked, eyes narrowed.

She hesitated. "Up in the attic. In one of the trunks." She felt as though she were shrinking beneath his gaze. But for a moment, she thought she saw his bottom lip quiver, and, just maybe, Papa realized how beautiful she looked tonight—so much like her mother. Adina waited, anticipating it, with just the slightest bit of hope, when finally, he spoke.

"There's been no victory yet, Adina," he said, wiping his hands on the dish towel. He turned his back to her and walked into the kitchen. The sound of silverware and dishes being placed on the table was Papa's way of having nothing left to say.

Adina followed him into the kitchen, the callus over her heart thickening with each step she took. Why did he have to be so difficult? Why couldn't he understand that she loved and missed her mother just as much as he did? His heart wasn't the only heart to break the day Mama died. Adina not only lost her mother that day, she lost her father as well.

21

The Dance

The drive to Windsor Grange gave Adina a much-needed reprieve to clear her head. She was too excited for the night ahead to hold onto any regrets regarding her father. Her only disappointment was Papa's demand for her to have the car back no later than eleven thirty.

"The dance ends at eleven, yes? Thirty minutes is more than enough time for you to say goodnight and have the car back home by eleven thirty," he said.

I'm almost twenty years old, and he still insists I come home early, she thought. *No wonder I have no boyfriend.*

She pulled the car into the dirt lot of the Windsor Grange. The eaves of the simple building were draped in green garland and white lights. At the front entrance sat a hand-painted sandwich board sign that read, "Windsor Hope for Victory Christmas Dance, 1944." Surrounding the words were painted swipes of red and gold ribbons and Christmas ornaments, with an American flag eclipsed in the background. A lineup of townsfolk, all dressed in their best and bundled in coats and scarves, stretched out the front door and down the walkway.

Adina put on her coat and stepped out into the crisp evening air. She looked up. Her anticipation rose as high as the stars she saw in the crystal-clear sky. *No regrets,* she thought.

She was greeted by a few hellos as she waited in line. The rumble of drumbeats and horns amidst the celebratory voices inside intensified her excitement.

Crossing the threshold into the foyer, she saw that the holdup in the line was due to the coat check. She handed her coat to the teenage girl who stood at the table and took her claim ticket in return.

"Merry Christmas," the young girl said.

Adina stopped, caught off guard by the girl's sweet gesture. Did she forget how to respond? So many holidays had fallen by the wayside over the years. She glanced over at the closed double doors that led to the dance hall. Swags of holly and Christmas cheer adorned their entrance. Entrance to what? *Maybe something new, with no more regrets*, she thought.

Beaming a smile back at the young girl, Adina said, "It really is, isn't it?"

The girl cocked her head and snickered.

"I mean, Merry Christmas to you as well," Adina said, as she walked toward the double doors. On the other side, the sound of the drums, horns, feet stomping, and voices raised in laughter grew louder. Taking a deep breath, she pushed the doors open with both hands.

The hall pulsed to the sound of the band and the cadence of dancing feet. Swags of ribbon-adorned evergreens and twinkling lights hung overhead like a net of forested stars. A thick cloud of cigarette smoke hovered beneath. At the far corner stood a fir tree lit with colored bulbs and covered in ornaments and tinsel.

The room was filled with people standing in groups around the edge of the dance floor and tipping cups of red punch and glasses of champagne. The dance floor itself was a swarm of movement. Happy couples swung in rhythm to the music of an eight-piece band—not the usual jukebox fare. Feet stomped, arms swung, legs kicked, skirts twirled. Whistles, hoots, and hollers echoed above it all.

Adina tapped her foot, mesmerized by the scene, itching to get out on the dance floor. She scanned the thick crowd, hoping to see some of the prisoners from the camp. Any familiar face would do. Who *were* all these people? They couldn't all be from her small town. Word of the celebration must have gotten around.

"Well, if it isn't Nurse Adina."

She felt a tap on her shoulder and turned, surprised to see Private Baxter standing behind her in full dress uniform. He gaped, eyes examining her from head to toe and back around again. His nose and cheeks flushed red, possibly from the cold outside, or maybe from too much champagne. Adina bet on the latter. She had hoped to avoid this encounter, yet here he was.

"Oh, hello," she said curtly, turning her head as though searching for someone in the crowd.

"Come on, baby. Don't tell me you don't remember me." He swayed in closer, breath reeking of something much stronger than Christmas punch.

She squinted her eyes. "Uh, is it Mark, or maybe Matt?"

Baxter's mouth hung open. "Nah, baby," he said, shaking his head. "It's Mike. Mike Baxter. From the camp. Remember me? I'm the guy that let you through the gate that night for the sick Kraut." He wiped the sweat from his forehead. "You sure are prettier in the light, Nurse Adina. You sparkle about as much as that big ole Christmas tree over there."

His stare made her feel like a piece of strung-up meat. "It's Nurse Robbins, if you don't mind," she said, trying not to make eye contact as he swayed closer.

"Hmmm," he responded, playfully tapping the puff of her dress sleeve. "I'm remembering a very special promise you made me that night. And if memory serves me right, you, Nurse Robbins, promised me a Christmas dance," he said, attempting to wink.

"Did I?" She fidgeted with the tip of her glove, eyes searching the crowded room for someone—anyone—she could impose upon as an escape from Mike Baxter. All she saw was a sea of bodies on the dance floor in front of her.

"You sure did," he said enthusiastically. "You wouldn't wanna disappoint me now, would you? I mean, I allowed you through the gate that night. I could've gotten in a heap of trouble. But I did it for you,

Nurse Robbins, and I never told a soul." He eyed her, determined. "To be honest with you, Adina…I was thinking about coming clean. You know, filing a report on the whole thing that night."

She narrowed her eyes. Did he honestly think he could blackmail her —all for a silly dance? He really was a piece of work. He'd have his dance with her, and then she'd be done with it. Taking a deep breath, she forced a smile. "All right then, Private Baxter. One dance," she resigned, as the band played "In the Mood."

"Let's make it two," he said, pulling her by the hand onto the dance floor with such force, she almost fell over.

The crowd pushed in around them. Baxter swung Adina out, then pulled her back in, slamming her body against his. He held her tight, pressing his moist cheek against hers, all while stomping his feet to the beat of the band, and stomping her feet a few times in the process. His sour breath was nauseating. She felt herself crash into the backs of other dancers on the floor. It was odd how nobody seemed to mind. This was her first dance of the evening, and already she was overheated and felt faint. It was obvious this guy loved to dance. She loved to dance, too, but this was enough to make her want to give it up for good.

Just when she thought she couldn't stand another twirl, the song ended. The crowd applauded and thinned as some of the dancers made their way to the refreshment tables. Adina pulled back and was about to excuse herself, when the band began a sultry slow tune.

"Not so fast, baby." He pulled her back into himself, pressing his hand firm against her back and twisting her hand in against his chest. "Remember? I said two dances. Besides, they're playing "Embraceable You," my favorite song. It ain't Billie, but the band ain't too shabby. Not too shabby, right?"

She was trapped. "I'm a little thirsty, Mike. I'd really like to get some punch." She hoped he'd get the hint. Instead, he held her tighter, slowly moving her around the dance floor.

"Sorry, Nurse Adina. The song ain't over yet," he said, his half-closed eyes staring down on her. "By the way, I haven't seen you much at the camp these days. Only your old man comes by to check on the men now and then. What gives?" His mouth curved into a quirky smile. "Don't you like us anymore?"

Baxter had no idea just how much she wished she could go to the camp, but not to see him. How she wanted to learn more about the lives of the prisoners, especially Daniel. How her day-to-day nursing duties paled in comparison to nursing at Camp Windsor. But she would never tell Private Baxter any of that. She didn't want to make conversation with him. She wanted to push herself out of the man's sticky grip.

"Actually, my schedule has been very busy with other appointments." Her patience was wearing thin, and she threw up a silent prayer that the song would end soon.

Baxter peered into her eyes. "Well, maybe me and you could meet up for a bite to eat sometime."

She didn't respond.

"Ya know, you have the prettiest green eyes I've ever seen. Or are they brown? Maybe brown and green...or blue?"

The song ended. Adina pushed herself away. "Thanks again, Private Baxter." She made her escape, brushing past him and skirting around couples in a desperate attempt to get off the dance floor. As the band struck up another tune, she heard Baxter's voice call out.

"Okay, baby. Save me another dance for later. And don't worry about finding me. I'll come find you."

As Adina elbowed her way through the crowd toward the refreshment tables, she sensed heads turn and eyes following her.

"Merry Christmas, Adina. You look stunning tonight," someone said.

"That dress is divine. Where on earth did you get it?" said another.

She smiled her acknowledgements, determined to get to the other end of the hall for a glass of something to drink and some space where she could breathe.

Two long tables draped with red tablecloths sat along the back wall. Every square inch of one was laden with homemade Christmas cookies, breads, and pastries, as well as decadent pies and cakes, all happily donated by the townsfolk. In the middle of the other table sat a large, crystal punchbowl filled to the brim with a frosty, red punch. There were bottles and bottles of wine and champagne, generously donated by local vineyards, with plenty of overstock on the floor underneath.

Adina reached for a cup.

"Let me get that for you, Adina. And don't you look lovely tonight." Carl Sanderson stood behind the table. He ladled a healthy portion of punch into Adina's cup.

"Thank you, Mr. Sanderson," she said, taking a long drink, cool and sweet with a hint of rum. "This is delicious. Did you make it?" She downed the rest in one gulp and held the cup out for a refill.

"Not me. That's the wife's department. She's minding the cookie table right now." He watched as Adina gulped down half her refill. "Slow down there, little missy," he said with a nervous laugh and a glance to the side. "Is your father here with you tonight?"

She peered at him over the rim of the cup. His question made her uneasy, though she wasn't sure why. She had every right to be there, alone or otherwise. Yet even she couldn't understand why her father wasn't here with her to celebrate with the town. Now she needed to come up with some pathetic excuse to tell Mr. Sanderson why Papa didn't come.

"He stayed home tonight, Mr. Sanderson. I'm here alone," she said, sipping her punch a bit slower.

"Well, I'm sure sorry to hear that," he said.

Just then, Major Williams stepped up to the table, and thrust his hand out to Mr. Sanderson. "Merry Christmas, Carl. A glass of your finest champagne, please." He, too, was in full dress uniform.

Adina liked Major Williams. His mannerisms were kind, and he was always welcoming to her when she visited Camp Windsor.

She tapped his shoulder. "Hello, Major Williams. Merry Christmas."

"Nurse Robbins, Merry Christmas to you as well," he said, toasting with his glass of champagne. "And aren't you lovely in that green dress?"

"Thank you, Major. Please, call me Adina. After all, I'm not working right now." She smiled at him, the buzz of the rum helping her to relax.

He flashed a warm grin back at her. "All righty then, Adina it is. I have to say, your small town sure knows how to throw a party." He took a generous sip of the champagne. "My men sure have been looking forward to it. This sort of thing is always a good distraction. Great for morale."

She wondered which men he was referring to. "Oh, I completely agree. As a matter of fact, I just had a dance with Private Baxter." She hoped the mention of Baxter might lead to more talk of the prisoners.

"Ah yes, Baxter. Good man. Not very bright," he said, sipping again from his glass. "You know, Nurse Rob— I mean, Adina," he winked, "this war is far from over. Our troops are taking a beating in Belgium as we speak."

She watched his face as he reiterated the struggle of US troops in the snowy, forested mountains, living in frozen foxholes with severe frostbite and minimal food. All the while the Germans relentlessly shelling upon them, almost as much as the falling snow.

The major's eyes wandered around the room as he spoke. "It's hard, you know...not being there with them." He drained the last drop of champagne from his glass. "But as our troops progress, I'm sure we'll be receiving more prisoners at Camp Windsor. And so, my duty remains here."

With that, she saw her opportunity. "Major Williams, I had heard that some of the prisoners might be allowed to come to the dance tonight. Is that true?" She regretted her question as soon as it left her mouth. Did the major know of her secret visit to see Daniel? From what Baxter just told her, he never reported it. Did her father speak directly to Major Williams? Or did he only forbid her from going back to the camp? And why did the major have that strange look on his face?

"You know what, Adina?" he said. "I think I need another glass of champagne. Can I get you another?"

"Umm, no thank you," she responded, not wanting to push her question any further.

He smiled warmly. "Of course, and please save me a dance…Adina."

Prisoners Are Here

Adina did a roundabout intake of the room and decided a walk to see the Christmas tree was a good idea. She bumped her way through the crowd, all the while hoping she wouldn't run into Private Baxter again, though she did feel a tinge of guilt for leading him on to get what she wanted in the first place. Still, there wasn't any way she would put up with his pushy advances. Not tonight.

The Christmas tree stood in the far corner of the room. Its fir branches drooped with hand-painted tin and glass ornaments and paper stars and snowflakes. Each sloped branch was draped with strings of colored bulb lights and tipped with silvery tinsel.

Adina stood, taken with the warm glow of the lights and spicy scent of evergreen. She found herself entranced by a single yellow lightbulb, transported in her mind back to a happier time. A time when Christmas trees and celebrations were a part of her own life. When Mama was here, and Papa was happy, and the three of them were together, always. The memories were permanently stitched inside her head. She reached up, gently moving her fingers through the wispy tinsel, when she felt a tap on her shoulder.

"Frohe Weihnachten, Fräulein."

She turned to see Daniel standing behind her. He wore a white button-down shirt with a blue tie and a plaid suit jacket, a little too big in the shoulders. The entire ensemble had probably been put together from charity donations. Sewn onto both the jacket and one pant leg were patches with the letters PW, so that even in dress clothes he could be identified as a prisoner. His wavy hair had been trimmed since she last saw him. He smiled, his eyes taking in every bit of her.

Adina stood, frozen, her lips parting into a soft smile.

He tilted his head. "It means 'Merry Christmas' in German."

Heat flushed in her cheeks. She struggled to catch her breath. "Yes, I gathered that's what it meant." She giggled, reaching out her hand to him. "Merry Christmas to you as well, Daniel."

He took hold of her hand. "My English has improved, don't you think?"

She stared at him, as though finding it hard to believe he was real. "Your English?"

"Yes, my English, Nurse Robbins. I should think I speak it very well, having been here for almost six months now."

The lights from the tree reflected off the blue in his eyes, and she felt at a loss for words. Or maybe she had forgotten how to speak entirely.

"You are surprised to see me?" he said, still holding her hand in his.

"Yes, I am," she finally said. "I guess I didn't think you would be allowed to attend. I mean, I didn't see you or any of the other men when I first arrived."

"Ah, so you were looking for me?" he asked, looking at her as though he knew things about her—things she herself didn't know. How quickly he was able to get inside her head.

Adina glanced around the room. She spotted Heimee at the refreshment table stuffing a piece of cake into his mouth with his hand. He caught sight of her and waved with frosting-covered fingers.

"Were you?" Daniel asked.

"Was I what?"

"Looking for me?" His voice was soft, pleading. His eyes held hers. "You just said that you were."

She felt lightheaded, as though her heart beat too fast, and the room spun wildly. *Could it be the punch?* she thought. Maybe she needed another cup? She fought to get control of her heart and her breathing, of the racing thoughts in her head.

The band began playing "Stardust."

"Dance with me," he said.

She watched his face, and for a brief moment, she wondered what people would think of her if she danced with a German prisoner. As he held tightly to her hand, leading her onto the crowded dance floor, she didn't care, not about the turning heads or the whispers. When she looked into Daniel's eyes, she saw no enemy. She felt warm and safe. He felt like home.

Daniel turned toward her, taking both her hands in his. She watched his eyes, waiting for his lead. He stepped to her, gently placing his arm around her back to move her ever so slightly toward him. He held her other hand to his chest and slowly began to sway to the music.

Adina watched over his shoulder as the other couples moved around them in patterns of light and shadows of bodies. She gazed above at the strings of lights and misty clouds of cigarette smoke. With each sway and every turn, the ethereal dream progressed. Daniel held her closer. Her heart accelerated against him. He pressed his cheek to hers, his lips next to her ear. He breathed, and she closed her eyes. The band leader sang, yet the words of the song seemed to evaporate. All she could hear was Daniel humming the "Stardust" melody in her ear. She pulled back and looked at him, eyes questioning.

"What is it?" he asked.

Her lips parted, but no words came.

"Say something," he said.

"I don't know you," she responded, tightening her arm to his shoulder.

He drew her in close, again pressing his cheek to hers, moving her body to the music. "You do know me, Adina," he whispered. "I think you know me better than anyone else."

She listened to his voice as her awareness of the other dancers slipped away, and the floor felt as though it moved on its own beneath her feet. She longed for what she was feeling, had craved it for as long as she could remember. To have someone genuinely want her, love her. She always figured she'd need to run away to find it. She never thought she would find it here in her small town. She didn't have to chase it. Love came to her.

Daniel allowed his fingers to graze the exposed skin on her back, then rested his hand at the base of her spine, holding her close to himself.

She pressed into his neck, breathing in the scent of him. "This has to be a dream," she whispered.

He tilted his head back, the look in his eyes soft, yet earnest. Like the brush of a feather, he stroked her cheek. He had stopped swaying and held her still. "It might be," he said. "If it is, I don't want to wake up."

"Me either."

The song ended. Onlookers stared and scrutinized, yet Adina and Daniel stood in each other's arms on a dance floor that had all but emptied, then refilled with new couples as the next song began.

"Pardon me." Major Williams stood next to them. He laid his hand firmly on Adina's shoulder. "May I have this dance, Nurse Robbins?"

Adina peeled her eyes away from Daniel, smiling awkwardly. "Oh, um, yes, of course, Major. I'd love to dance with you."

Williams placed his hand under her elbow, then turned to Daniel, sternly looking him in the eye. "I believe you'll find some of your comrades standing over there, Mr. Christensen."

Heimee and Freddie, along with a few other prisoners, stood at the edge of the dance floor, pointing and laughing at him, mouthing taunts in German. Just behind them, Klaus Schneider stood, sipping from a glass of champagne. He smirked, narrowing his eyes at Daniel.

Daniel caught Adina's eye one last time before making his way off the dance floor and over to his friends.

Heimee gave him a playful shove. "Ah, Danny Boy. You danced with the nurse, ja?" he said, laughing and ruffling Daniel's hair.

Irritated, Daniel shoved him back. "Ja, we danced. You act as though you've never seen someone dance before."

Heimee growled behind his cigar. "Not like that, Danny. Not like that."

The others snickered.

Trying to escape their teasing, Daniel pushed past them, only to run right into Klaus Schneider.

"Well, Merry Christmas, Soldat Christensen." Schneider glared behind a feigned smile. "Are you enjoying yourself this evening?" he asked, tipping back his glass with its last drops of champagne.

Daniel glared at him.

"Come now, Christensen," Schneider said, blocking Daniel from stepping past. "We all saw how you enjoyed your dance with the nurse." He moved in closer, lowering his voice. "And why shouldn't you?" He placed a firm grip on Daniel's shoulder, looking at him with menacing eyes. "We should all have a chance to enjoy the nurse. After all, it's Christmas."

Daniel shook himself free. "Shut your mouth, Schneider." Gritting his teeth, his face reddened, and he pointed his finger right between Schneider's eyes. "Don't you even look at her. Do you hear me?"

Schneider took a step back. He held his empty glass in front of his eyes, turning it between his fingers, as though examining a rare diamond. "Are you threatening me, Soldat?"

Daniel lowered his hand and took a deep breath. The last thing he wanted tonight was an altercation with Schneider.

"That's right, Christensen," Schneider smirked. "Your self-control does you credit. Let's hope it does the same for your...*other* weaknesses, ja?" He held up his empty glass to Daniel. "I would have liked to toast you Frohe Weihnachten, but it appears I am out of champagne. I do love our American hosts. So kind and accommodating." He turned on his heels and walked through the crowd toward the refreshment tables.

Daniel stood seething, trying to compose himself. The possibility that Schneider would dare to approach Adina raked at him. He would need to find her. His eyes scanned the crowded dance floor, peering through the swirling mass, but he didn't see her.

"Danny, come drink with us," Heimee called from the refreshment table, holding up a topped-off glass of red wine.

Daniel waved him off, working his way through the crowd to the other side of the hall, all the while his eyes darting and searching. Finally, he caught sight of Adina's green dress. She was standing at the Christmas tree right where he first saw her this evening. She turned as he approached.

"I knew you would think to look for me here. I wanted to have another dance with you, but there was just so much going on around me, not to mention Major Williams kept asking me questions about—"

He held his finger to her lips, nervously glancing around the room. He leaned in and took hold of her hand. "I want you to meet with me later tonight," he whispered. He could see Schneider talking with Major Williams at the other side of the room by the refreshment tables.

"I'm sorry, what did you say?" She sensed his uneasiness.

He stepped closer, eyes wide. "I said, meet me later tonight. It's just that...it's much too difficult here. I want to be with you, without all these people. I have a label on me, Adina. I'm being watched." A gentle smile curved on his lips. "You understand?"

She mulled over what he was asking of her, knowing she wanted the same. Here she stood, holding the hand of a German prisoner of war, an enemy combatant, basically a criminal in the eyes of most, if not all, Americans. She knew people stared and criticized as she danced with him tonight, but she didn't care. She saw so much love in his eyes, not to mention a whole life behind him that she ached to know. Adina didn't know if she believed in fate or destiny, but something was at work here. It was no accident that Daniel Christensen was brought across the continent to a prisoner camp in Windsor, California. He was here for her, and she was for him. She knew in her heart that was true.

"Just tell me where," she said, grabbing his other hand.

"At the back fence of the camp, where I first met you that day. A ways down from there is a section of fence that's broken, bent down." He smiled, letting out a chuckle. "I could have gone through that day to get the ball myself, but it was much more fun to have you hand it to me."

She blushed. "What time?"

"How about one? I realize that it is the middle of the night, but most of the men should be asleep by that time."

Her heart raced at the very idea of it. It didn't even warrant a second thought. "Yes, I'll be there."

He stepped in closer, his lips next to her ear. "I will be there waiting for you," he whispered and brushed a soft kiss to her cheek.

"Hey, Danny."

Startled, Daniel turned to see Heimee standing behind him.

"We are leaving," Heimee said. "Major says we've had enough."

Daniel turned back toward Adina. "I'll see you soon," she mouthed.

She watched as he disappeared into the crowd, excitement and anticipation mounting within her. Standing there, she looked at the glistening lights and the festive party goers. There was no one left she'd want to dance with. The whole affair had suddenly lost its appeal. All she wanted now was to be with Daniel. She stood by the tree, giving just enough time so as not to appear to any onlookers as though she were running out after one of the prisoners.

Was that really what she was doing? Running after Daniel? The thought of it was both absurd and magnificent at the same time. The battle of wrong or right she had wrestled with must come to an end. She'd been given a choice tonight. More like a second chance to grab on to what she wanted. She'd fought for her father's love and approval since she was twelve years old, longer, if she included the months her mother was ill. It was a losing battle. The saddest part of it was that Papa wasn't willing to fight for her. Or maybe he just didn't know how to. None of that seemed to matter to her anymore. She'd make the choice to love and to be loved in return. She'd run after Daniel, and not look back.

22

The Wait

Adina lay on her bed, fully dressed, listening as the leaves brushed through the trees just outside her bedroom window. The green dress she'd worn to the Christmas dance hung neatly from the standing mirror once again. She watched as the moonlight caught hold of the crystals now and again, wondering if tonight had been her one and only opportunity to wear it. How she wished for Daniel to be able to see her in it again, someday.

She came home from the dance much earlier than planned. When Papa questioned why, she lied, saying she was suffering from a terrible headache and just wanted to go to bed. Normally she'd feel some guilt for telling the lie, but the fib rolled off her tongue with the greatest of ease. She was much too excited for feelings of guilt. He didn't question her any further but instead told her to take her temperature before going to sleep.

Now, she lay on her side, forever watching the alarm clock on her bedside table, willing it to move faster. Over and over, she ran through her plan in her head. If she timed it right, she should be able to make the ride to the camp in less than thirty minutes. Twenty minutes from home to the O'Brien property, then a five-minute run on the backwoods trail from Jeanie's home to the back fence of the camp. It would be very dark, but she didn't want to take a flashlight, worrying it may draw attention from one of the guard towers.

She took slow breaths, attempting to remain still, and pictured Daniel in her mind. The evening felt like a dream. The way he looked at her when he asked her to dance. No one had ever looked at her that way before. She thought about the warmth of his hand on her back as he pressed her close to him and the feel of his breath as he whispered in her ear. Her thoughts weren't helping to calm her breathing or her racing heart. Was she crazy? Truth be told, she didn't feel crazy. She felt solid. She felt as real as that first day she first walked into his tent alone. When she held the leather-bound journal in her hands and looked at its sketches, now turning over in her mind, she was drawn to him even more. His drawings spoke of who he was, of his heart, and what he felt. She wanted to be a part of it all. Like the little girl who wanted to jump into the pages of her favorite books, Adina wanted to be a part of Daniel's life.

At twelve thirty she got up, wrapped a scarf around her neck, and put on her coat. She placed her red wool beret on her head, pulling it down close to her ears. "Time to go," she whispered. Carefully, she lifted the window, sitting on the edge of the sill. The sharp night air pierced her face, flooding into the room. She swung her legs over the side and jumped, hitting the ground with a thud. The four-foot drop felt higher than she'd expected. She left the window open and ran around to the front of the house. Jumping on her bicycle, she sped down the moonlit drive.

Adina was pedaling harder than she realized and would have passed the narrow road to the O'Brien property had it not been for the bright full moon to light the entrance. Slowing, she made the turn and brought the bicycle to a quiet stop. Her chest heaved, the cold air making it difficult to catch her breath. She took a moment to spy out the trailhead just behind the O'Brien home. Moonlight silhouetted the spindly limbs of the oak trees, making them look like bony arms waving in the wind. There was a time when she would've been spooked by the sight of it, but not tonight. She wasn't the slightest bit afraid of what awaited her down that dark, wooded trail.

With a light foot, she walked the bicycle across the front lawn and past the back shed where Jeanie's brother stored his motorcycle. A lemon tree grew just to the side of the shed. Some of its branches still hung heavy with fruit. She selected two good-sized lemons, sliding them into her coat pocket. She then laid her bicycle down on the damp, leaf-covered dirt behind two thick-timbered oaks. As she began her walk down the trail, she looked up at the clear brilliance of the starry winter sky.

"Perfect," she whispered, as her walk became a brisk run.

23

Meeting through Wire

Adina slowed as she drew close to the clearing. She ducked down, keeping an eye on the one visible guard tower, which was lit but with no guard in sight. She scanned the fence line for the section that Daniel said was bent down. The mix of moonlight and shadow played tricks on her eyes, and she remembered the day she first saw him. He held her with his eyes, and she couldn't move. Never could she have imagined she would be meeting him here again, this time, in the middle of a cold December night.

Slowly, Adina moved forward, eyes searching the fence line. Then, she saw it, just as Daniel had described it. The section of fence was only about three feet wide, pulled and bent down to the ground. She stopped, straining to focus through the shadows.

"Adina," Daniel whispered, crouched in the shadows on the other side of the fence.

Her heart jumped at the sound of his voice. "Yes, it's me." She ran to the fence, lowering to her knees in front of him.

He knelt and took hold of her hands, the bent, barbed fence between them. "I didn't believe you would be able to come," he said. The moonlight was just enough to reveal the outline of his face and the spark of excitement in his eyes.

"Of course I came. I wanted to see you again." She dug into her coat pocket. "I have something for you," she said, handing him the two lemons.

"Zitronen? They are beautiful," he said, holding the fruit up to his nose. "But how?"

She chuckled, pleased with the success of her stolen gift. "They grow all around the area. I picked them from the tree on the O'Brien property."

"O'Brien? This is a friend of yours?"

"You haven't met my friend, Jeanie Mae," she said, "She's the one who ran away scared the day I first met you. Remember?"

"Ah, yes. I do remember."

"She volunteered for the Women's Army Corps. Now she's serving somewhere in Europe." Adina pulled her coat close around her neck.

"You are shivering," Daniel said.

"Northern California can get pretty cold in the winter."

His lips curved into a smile. "Cold? No, Liebe. This is not cold. Where I am from, my home, it is very cold in winter." His eyes trailed off. "Snow. So much snow. Too cold for zitronen, that is certain."

Adina reached for his hands, bringing his attention back to her. "Tell me."

"What is it you would like for me to tell you, Nurse Adina?"

She watched his eyes, as much as the dim light would allow her to see them. "I want to know you, Daniel Christensen. I want to hear about your home and your family. What are your mother and father like? Do you have brothers and sisters?" So much remained hidden in the way he looked at her. It was so easy to become lost in that look.

"Oh, meine Liebe," he said. "That would be a very long story."

"Meine Liebe?" she questioned.

"My love." He stroked her cheek with his fingertip.

She knew what it meant, having heard her father speak German on occasion, even saying those same words to Adina and her mother. Papa encouraged her to learn the language, but she didn't understand why. Why on earth would she need to speak German in the United States? Tonight, she wished she had listened to her father and learned. Hearing Daniel speak the language was like the sound of sweet music.

"We have all night," she said, glancing over to the guard tower. "Or as long as GI Joe doesn't wake up over there." She paused, a smile curving on her lips.

"What is it?" he asked. "What are you thinking about?"

Adina wondered what he thought of her. "This isn't like me at all—out here in the middle of the night, meeting with a man I barely know." She blushed. "I can't imagine what would happen if we were caught." She searched the eyes that so intently held her own, trying to slow her breathing, even if she couldn't slow her heart. "You're not a killer, Daniel Christensen. I'm certain you're not even a Nazi. No matter how hard I try to convince myself that being here with you is wrong in every way, it's not working. I can't stop thinking about you. Since the first day I met you, right here, you've haunted me." She reached across and touched his cheek. "Please tell me it isn't just me."

He took her hand, pressing his lips to her fingertips. "It's not just you, Adina. I can't stop thinking about you either. I've wondered how obvious It's been."

She giggled under her breath. "Actually, Heimee may have said I was all you talked about."

He cleared his throat, casting a shy glance to the side. "Ja, this is true. I'm happy he told you." He pulled his coat collar up around his neck and puffed his warm breath onto their hands, its mist reflected in the moonlight. He looked at her. "My story isn't all happy, Adina. Some of it is very difficult to tell."

She squeezed his hand. "I'm listening."

Taking a deep breath, he began. "I come from a very small village in the foothills of the Bavarian Alps, along the Austrian border. It's beautiful, Adina. So peaceful. My papa died when I was five years old. I have almost no memory of him at all. The only family I have is Mutter and my older brother, Max."

"Max?" Adina asked. "Is he the one I saw in your journal? The handsome one who looks like you?"

Daniel's eyes grew distant. "Yes, he looked like me."

"Looked?" As soon as the question left her lips Adina realized that Daniel's brother must be dead. She shook her head, sensing his struggle. "I'm so sorry. I didn't know. If it's too hard, you don't have to—"

"No, it's all right. I want to tell you. My brother, Max—" The memory brought on a smile. "He and I were very close. He watched over me after our papa died. Max was bold and strong. I greatly admired him. But with his strength came a very strong will." He paused, looking directly into her eyes. "Do you understand?"

"I think I do. My father, well... He can be very stubborn. As you said, strong willed."

"I am not like him—strong willed. Max was not afraid to speak his mind. It would get him into trouble. He was always getting into arguments with his school masters, always speaking out of turn. I, on the other hand, was obedient, too timid to speak out." He turned down his eyes. "Sometimes I wish I had not been."

Adina marveled at how similar she and Daniel were. No wonder she felt so irresistibly drawn to him. Still, something he said confused her. "What do you mean that you wish you had not been obedient?"

"Max never agreed with Reich philosophy," he continued. "As life began to change in my country, Max's hatred of the Führer grew. All of us hated what the Führer was doing. It's just, Max had no fear of making his hatred known. Every night we would gather around the radio. Hitler would scream his hateful plans over the air waves. Max would curse, *'Der Drecksack! Doesn't know his head from his ass'* and he would shake his fist at the radio." Daniel chuckled, balling his fist to mimic his brother. "It was as though he stood face to face with the beast himself."

Again, his eyes ran distant. "Mutter would silence him. She was so afraid someone would hear. Nobody ever spoke against the Führer." He gripped Adina's hands tighter, moving his face closer. "You must understand, the Reich only allowed us to hear approved news reports. Even the music we listened to on our household radios had to be approved. We heard reports that all radios were banned in Berlin. The people were required to turn them in to government officials or face consequences. But not in my village. We still had a radio, but we only heard what the Reich allowed us to hear." He glanced over his shoulder, as though still worried someone might hear.

"Daniel, no one can hear you. You're safe here," Adina said, trying to stay the uncomfortable fear she sensed in him.

"Adina, you need to understand something. Max had another radio. A different kind. He kept it hidden in the back of our bedroom closet. It had a cord that ran from the edge of the closet door to the single electrical outlet in the bedroom. He would power it up late at night, after Mutter was long asleep. From my bed, I would hear it whistling as he tuned in to hear what the rest of the world was saying."

Adina listened, hanging on to every word he spoke.

"Max listened to the BBC, to Churchill. He heard about the true horrors of what Hittler had done and continued to do. He also learned that Hitler's efforts were failing. Germany wasn't winning the war as we were led to believe. We were being lied to."

Adina's mind reeled at the thought of being lied to in that way. The very idea of removing people's ability to know the truth. "And Max...what did he do?" she asked.

"Being the outspoken young man that he was, he wanted to shout it to the world."

"Did he?" she blurted, covering her mouth with her hand. "Did he shout it to the world? I don't know how anyone would be able to keep information like that a secret."

Daniel dropped his chin. "Fear, Adina. Fear is what makes us hide. Fear is what enables us to live within a world of lies."

His words struck a chord deep within her. She, too, felt as though she lived in a world of fear and lies, though she could in no way relate to a life lived under the grip of a tyrannical leader such as Hitler. But Papa could be cold and even oppressive at times, even though Adina knew he loved her.

Daniel took a deep breath and continued. "Mutter discovered the radio. She scolded Max, forbidding him from ever using it in our home again. '*They will know*,' she said. '*They will come and take you away from me*.' Mutter cried, begging Max to get rid of it. She wanted no evidence of the radio to remain."

"Did he get rid of it?" Adina asked.

"He stopped using it. But they still came, just as Mutter feared."

"They? You mean the Reich?"

"Wehrmacht recruiters," he said.

Adina's heart sank. She could feel Daniel's hands tensing and heard the strain in his voice when he spoke again.

"The German armies had been dwindling for quite some time, and Führer Hitler was desperate. There would be no giving up for the Reich, so they began to take anyone. Young, old, weak, strong. Even young boys, fifteen, sixteen years old. They put a gun in their hands and sent them to the front lines." Daniel paused, searching deep into Adina's eyes as though looking for a place to rest.

"It's okay," she said. "I'm here."

"They came last January. It had been snowing for days and days. It was bitterly cold. We hadn't been able to go outside much. Our food rations were low, but we were warm and happy just to be together. I don't remember the exact day it was when we heard the low growl of the army truck as they made rounds throughout the village. A voice announced over a loudspeaker, '*All males sixteen years and older are to report to the village square immediately! Those who don't comply will face swift consequences.*'" His eyes trailed again. "I can still see the fear in Mutter's eyes. She knew this day would come. She prayed against it, '*Please God, don't let them take my boys.*' Max bolted the door, swearing he wouldn't go. He was red-faced, defiant, and absolutely determined not to comply. So much the fool, Max was."

"Your poor mother," was all Adina could think of saying. She wanted to say more—a word of understanding or comfort—but nothing else came.

"Mutter begged him, '*Please do as they say, mein Sohn. Obey them so that you can come back home someday soon.*'"

Adina felt tears burn behind her eyes. She was sure that the worst was still to come and held tightly to Daniel's hands.

"They were pounding on the door," he said. "Pounding so hard, I thought they would break the door down." Daniel raked his fingers through his hair, shaking his head.

Adina squeezed his hand. "What did you do?" she asked, timidly.

His eyes narrowed. "I unbolted and opened the door. There was no other choice. The soldiers had rifles. '*Schnell!*' one screamed, while the other pointed the end of the gun in my face. Max cursed at them, and the one pointing his gun at me slammed Max in the shoulder with the butt of the rifle. My brother crumpled against the wall. Mutter screamed, pleading with the soldier. I helped Max to stand and begged him not to fight, if only for Mutter's sake. He glared at me but did as I asked. The soldiers screamed, pushing us toward the door. I begged them to allow me to go to my bedroom first. I could not imagine going anywhere without my journal and pencils. One of them followed me with the rifle at my back. He shoved me forward as we walked back. Max and I put on our coats and tried to say goodbye to Mutter, but we weren't allowed."

"Where did they take you?" Adina asked.

"They marched us through the snow with their rifles at our backs to the village square. It was only a half a kilometer, not far, but it was bitterly cold, and the snow was deep. We only had our coats. There was no time for boots or gloves. By the time we arrived at the square, I couldn't feel my fingertips. Standing and guarding the other men and boys from the village were about twenty Wehrmacht soldiers. They, too, looked cold and tired, some with sunken, hungry eyes, their uniforms soiled and torn. Some looked old enough to be my Opa."

Adina frowned. "I don't understand. They were just standing around, waiting in the cold? Waiting for what? Who was in charge?"

She found herself becoming anxious with the scene that was unfolding. "I'm sorry, Daniel. I'm being pushy. I don't mean to be."

"It's all right, Leibe. I understand. You are the first person I've told, other than Heimee, that is." He brought her fingertips to his lips, placing a gentle, warm kiss on them. "Do you still wish me to continue?"

Adina nodded. "I want to hear the rest. I need to hear."

"All right then. There was a commander. A tall, brash man, obviously more fit and well cared for than his lowly subordinates. He shouted at the men and boys from the village, telling them to get in line from youngest to the oldest. Some of the oldest were so feeble they could barely walk through the snow to put themselves into the lineup. Some were sick. The youngest ones were terrified, eyes as big as saucers. They cried for their mutters. The commander taunted them, pointing his pistol at them and shouting '*Stille*!' They stopped crying after that."

"And Max? Where was he?"

Daniel's eyebrows knit. "When all the men and boys had found a place in the lineup, I saw that Max had not moved from his place under a tree. He stood there, defiant. I tried to wave at him, encouraging him to come, but he would not look at me. I turned to the men who stood beside me, looking at them, doing my best to hide my panic. The young man standing next to me had been a schoolmate. He was born with a deformity in both of his legs. He wore—" Daniel motioned to his legs— "on his legs...like your Roosevelt."

"Braces?" Adina said.

"Yes, and he used canes to help him walk. This young man was whispering my name and shaking with fear. His eyes were begging me for help. I looked down at his pathetic, crooked legs." Daniel shut his eyes. "The poor wretch had wet himself. Poor, stupid wretch."

"Oh, Daniel. I'm so sorry." She squeezed his hands. "This is difficult for you. I can see that. You don't need to tell me anymore, at least not tonight. Maybe some other time."

"But what if there isn't another time? What if tonight is all we have? I want you to know my story, Adina. Now is the time."

She cupped his cheek. "Ja, Leibe," she said.

He pressed his hand over hers and continued. "The commander yelled at my brother, '*Get in line! Schnell*!' Max didn't move. He would not acknowledge the man. He only stood there, like a statue in the snow. '*Don't be a fool, Max*!' I screamed. But he would not even look at me. So very stubborn, my brother. The commander told two of his soldiers to guard the lineup with their rifles. If any of us tried to run, they were to shoot. We did as we were told, as he walked to where my brother stood. He spoke something quietly to Max, but I could not hear. He was too far away. Max gave no response. And then, the commander calmly removed his pistol from its holster and held it up so that Max could see. '*Get in line, Schnell*!' he yelled again. Max did not move." Daniel paused again, listening to the sound of the wind in the trees. His eyes grew wide, a look of wonder filling them. "But then, something fascinating happened."

Adina waited, watching his face as his memory seemed to materialize. "What was it?" she asked.

He looked at her and smiled. "It began to snow. Large, lofty flakes of snow. They fell softly all around us, landing on my arms and my hands. It is always so peaceful and quiet when it first begins to snow. It is as though all the world stands still to watch. At that moment, I remember being taken over by the beauty of the falling snow. Each tiny snowflake is its own masterpiece...an exquisite creation. Then I heard the click of the pistol. '*Schnell*!' the commander yelled. This time, I screamed at Max, and this time, he locked his eyes with mine. He stood straight. So strong. And he smiled at me. I jumped as the pistol fired. There was a plume of black smoke, and then Max lay on the ground. I screamed, watching as my brother's blood pooled onto the fresh, white snow. I wanted to run to him, but the rifles were pointed at us. I didn't want to die. There was nothing I could do but watch. Max was gone."

Tears streamed down Adina's face. She, too, wanted to scream out. It was too much horror and pain, unlike anything she could ever imagine. "I'm so sorry, Daniel," she whispered. "So very sorry." What else could have happened to him, from that horrific day until he arrived as a prisoner at Camp Windsor? She didn't want to know. All that mattered was he was here with her now. Saying she understood his pain wouldn't make any sense. Yes, she'd lost her mother and had to grow up with a cold and distant father who, for all she knew, blamed her for the loss of his wife as well. A father who lived a life of lies and facade, unwilling to be true to who he really was. She wanted to tell Daniel that truth, but she feared what he would think of her. Would he still want her?

Suddenly, Daniel helped Adina to her feet, drawing her closer to him, yet still separated by the bent wire at their feet.

"Daniel, wait," she whispered. "I need to tell you something. It's about my father...about who I am—"

He placed his hands on her cheeks. The soft glow of moonlight revealed the deep longing in his eyes, a longing with questions attached. Could it be that the war, as well as the death of his brother and the loss of his mother—that every bit of it happened to bring him here to this very camp in her small, obscure town...just so he could be with her? She would fill the empty longing, the deep hole that humanity's hatred had left him with. Maybe, just maybe, he wouldn't be left alone.

He gently traced her lips with his fingertip until he met them with his own. His kiss began tentatively, exploring, until he raked his fingers through her hair, pressing himself into her, the kiss now full and deep.

Adina closed her eyes, her heart wildly beating. She wrapped her arms around his neck, holding him tight, his breath warm on her cheek. His arm moved to her lower back, cradling her, supporting her close to himself. She kissed him, touching the soft waves of his hair, caressing the curve of his neck, and wanting so much more.

He grabbed her face, pulling himself back. "Meine Liebe, meine Liebe," he repeated, his voice hoarse and faint.

Something moved in the guard tower. Adina and Daniel stood still, quiet in each other's arms, and waited.

"You must go now," he whispered. "Before they see us."

She didn't care who saw them. She never wanted to leave him. When would she be able to see him again? She needed to tell him the truth about who she was. Meeting at the back of the camp was much too difficult. If only there was some way to get Daniel away from the camp, even for just a few hours. And then the idea came to her.

"Daniel," she said, her eyes wide. "Do you remember the night I came to see you in your tent? You showed me your sketches, and you said something to me?"

He smiled. "I said many things to you that night, my love."

"You told me it was your dream to one day see the Pacific Ocean. Remember?"

His eyebrows raised. "Ja?"

Adina's smile beamed bright. "I'm gonna take you there."

He narrowed his eyes, "Now listen to me, Adina Robbins. There is no way you would be able to—"

She placed a finger to his lips. "You just leave it to me and be on the lookout. I'll get word to you soon."

He took a deep breath and smiled. There would be no talking her out of her plan, at least not here and now. She would need to leave now, before they were caught.

Daniel brushed a gentle kiss to her lips. "Gute Nacht, sweet Adina."

She fell into his arms, nestling her face into the warmth of his neck. "Wait for me," she whispered. Then quietly, she turned. Stepping softly, she walked back toward the trail. She stopped once to look back to where they were kneeling at the fence, barely able to see his silhouette in the shadows as he waited for her to disappear. He held his hand to his lips, then raised it and waved. She disappeared down the trail, into the darkness.

24

January 1945

It rained more often than not in January. Wet and muddy conditions made tent living at Camp Windsor much less than comfortable. The gray and the gloom caused each day to blend into the next.

Inside the shelter and protection of the camp, aside from daily KP duties and winter pruning in nearby fields, the prisoners did their best to pass the time. Books and newspapers were readily available, and there was always the radio to listen to. The men exercised and kicked the ball at the back of camp, rain or shine.

A few of the prisoners who could play instruments threw together a band with instruments generously donated to the camp. Heimee, who oddly enough played the clarinet, would tuck his cigar in his pocket on occasion to play along. If weather permitted, performances were set up outdoors. Even the camp staff would attend, especially if Heimee was going to perform. From the time that Günter Schmeltz-Heimer first arrived at Camp Windsor, he made it his mission to befriend as many camp staff as he could. It wasn't difficult for him, given his jovial and sometimes brash personality. On many occasions he could be found as the center of attention of a group of guards, telling them a joke or two, then doubling over at his own punchline. They found him a hysterical distraction from their duties. Some even likened him to a German Lou Costello. Heimee's likeability garnered him extra chocolate bars and a case or two of beer, which was always a welcome extravagance for him and his tent mates.

Five weeks had passed since Daniel and Adina met at the back fence after the Christmas dance. He hadn't heard a word from her, which wore down his patience with each passing day. He longed to hear her voice and to hold her in his arms. In the doldrums of cold, rainy days, he would imagine a life with her. What would that life look like for them? She was a young American woman in love with a German prisoner of war. Would her father accept him? Would they need to leave—go somewhere far away in order to be together? That was fine with him. He had no idea if his mother was still alive. Once he was released, whenever that would be, there was nothing tying him to Northern California or the town of Windsor...except for Adina. Daniel was willing to do whatever needed to be done, if it meant he could be with her. Not being with her now was almost unbearable. Why hadn't she tried to contact him? Maybe someone saw them that night and she was now bearing the brunt of their carelessness. Of course, if that were true, something would have already been said to him, as well as action taken against them. So why, then? What could be keeping her from messaging him as she said she would?

Today, Daniel stayed behind at the camp. His day consisted of early morning kitchen duty, followed by latrine KP, after which he confined himself to his tent and the comfort of his cot. Taking his journal and a pencil, he turned to a blank page and began to sketch. He started with Adina's eyes. Having used up the remaining bits of colored pencils and chalk, he'd have to try to capture the uniqueness of those eyes through shading, shadows, and light. He closed his own eyes, drawing deep from the memory of the colors in hers: brown, green, gold. All of them combined to produce something brilliant, yet undefinable.

Once he had sketched her eyes and the shape of her eyebrows, he worked out her nose, remembering how it had a bump just beneath the bridge. He then drew her lips, taking care not to overemphasize the fullness of them but to bring forth the tender softness he felt as his lips touched hers. There would be no way to accurately capture it, but he had to try. When he felt he'd done the best he could on those features, he rough-sketched the contours of her face, adding a line here and a shadow there. Then her hair, loosely flowing in waves over bare shoulders. He sketched, erased, and smudged, working the page, then stopped. He stared at his work, as though looking into a dream. It was Adina, and yet it wasn't. He shut his eyes tight, again attempting to conjure her into the forefront of his memory. It wasn't working. What he needed was for her to be sitting right there in front of him, where he could reach out and touch the shape of her cheeks and run his finger down the bump on her nose, place his lips on hers. Not until then would he be able to do the drawing justice.

Outside the tent, the sound of marching feet on dirt grew louder. A company of prisoners was making their way back from a visit to town. Daniel went with the group the day before, as well as two days before that. With each trip into town, he had hoped to at least catch a glimpse of Adina. Maybe she'd be stopping by the Groceteria at the end of her workday or be riding past on her bicycle. But he never saw her.

The light outside grew dusky. Daniel had been sitting on his cot sketching long enough for his backside to go numb. The bell would be ringing soon for dinner.

Just then, the tent flap flew back. Two prisoners walked in with their sacks of penny purchases. Heimee barreled in behind them.

"Ah, Danny Boy. Here you are. I should have known you'd be sulking in your bed. Der Esel." He lumbered over to Daniel's cot, sitting himself down on the edge. Water dripped from his cap, off the tip of his cigar, and onto the blanket.

"Dummkopf, Heimee. You are making a mess. And you smell like a cow." Daniel shoved him with his foot.

Heimee let loose a guttural laugh. "Ja, Freund. It's raining, and I am wet." He removed his cap, shook it off, and threw it on the ground. He then reached into his pocket, and pulled out a small, brown paper sack. "I want to show you what I purchased in town." Reaching in the sack, he pulled out two newly wrapped cigars. Closing his eyes, he swiped one beneath his nose and inhaled. "Ah, Cubano," he said, eyes still closed, savoring the lingering aroma.

Daniel rolled his eyes. "That's delightful. Same as the one you've been chewing for weeks."

Again, Heimee laughed. Reaching his plump hand back into the crumpled sack, he pulled out a small, tightly folded piece of paper. Something was written on it in smeared black ink. "I have this for you as well, Freund. Thought you would like to have it." He handed it to Daniel.

Daniel held the folded paper in his hand. His name was written on the outside. With a wide grin, he looked up at Heimee.

"Sorry, Danny. It got a little wet in the rain."

Daniel's heart raced as he fingered the letters on the damp paper. It had to be from Adina. "But how? Who gave this to you?"

Heimee sat back down. "The nurse handed it to me herself. Who did you think, my Mutti?" He glanced over his shoulder and leaned in. "She asked about you, Danny."

Daniel sighed in relief. Just to know she was well and that she spoke of him was exhilarating. "Where was she? What did she say?"

"Slow yourself, Danny Boy. She didn't say much. Some of us had gone into the market, or the Grocer— What is it they call it? No matter. That is where I saw her. She quietly walked up to me in one of the rows of the food and shook my hand. That's when she handed that letter to me." He paused to unwrap one of his new cigars.

Daniel's impatience grew. "Then what did she say?"

"She asked if you came to town, and when I said no, she asked how you were. I told her you were the same lazy oaf you have always been." He held the cigar to his nose again, breathing it in as though it were a delicious meal. The smile then left his face. "Schneider was in the market as well, Freund. I believe he made the nurse nervous. She didn't talk with me for very long."

Daniel pushed further. "Come now, Heimee. She must have said something else to you. She knows you and I are good friends. She couldn't have only asked you if I was there or how I was feeling. Tell me all that she said."

Heimee ran his hand through his damp, matted hair. "Ja, now that I think about it, she did say something more." His eyes cut to the side, and his voice became a gruff whisper. "She asked if I knew anything about the guard schedule for the tower at the back of the camp."

Daniel's eyebrows raised, and he grabbed Heimee's arm. "She did? And do you?"

"Ja, ja, I do. There is one private who sometimes leaves his post at the back side every Thursday in the afternoon hours. He has eine Frau in Santa Rosa. He visits her."

"How do you know this? We are usually working in the fields at that time."

Heimee chuckled. "There is much I know that you do not, Danny Boy. But I think the better question would be, why would the nurse want to know when the guard would not be at his post?" He winked.

The dinner bell sounded, and Heimee grabbed his cap. "Come, Danny. Das Diner."

"I'll be right there," Daniel said. He looked at the letter in his hand. It was the closest he'd been to Adina since that night. He wanted to open it and read her words right then and there.

"Schnell!" Schneider barked, making his rounds up and down the tent rows. "Das Diner, schnell!"

Daniel stuffed the letter into his pants pocket. He would need to wait until after dinner to read it. He grabbed his cap and walked toward the tent entrance just as Klaus Schneider stepped in.

"Ah, you are the only one remaining, ja, Christensen?" He looked down his nose at Daniel.

Daniel looked around the tent and pulled his cap down onto his head. "Ja, Herr Schneider," he said with a smirk. "I am the only one remaining." His face melted into a stern glare.

Schneider placed his hand on Daniel's shoulder. "Soldat Christensen, we are friends here, ja?" His tone erred on the side of sugariness.

Not the usual for Klaus Schneider. "Christensen...or, um, Daniel. We come from the same fatherland, ja? The same blood. This conflict will soon be over, and we will be going home. It is only a matter of time. It would be beneficial for us to mend our differences. Better for you, better for us all."

Daniel kept his eyes forward, staring out into the rain. He listened to Schneider's words, almost shuddering from the feelings of rage building within him. The same fatherland? The same blood? Was Klaus Schneider truly that deranged? If there was one person who could destroy what was happening between him and Adina Robbins, it was the man standing next to him. He wasn't about to allow anything or anyone to interfere with it. Not Major Williams or Adina's father, and most of all, not Klaus Schneider. He reached into his pants pocket, feeling for Adina's letter. It was there, safe, and his confidence bolstered. He turned his head to Schneider, tilting his chin so he could look right into his eyes. For a moment, he said nothing, allowing the suspense to build—just the right amount of time to be sure he only said what needed to be said.

Finally, Daniel spoke. "Nein," he said, and walked out into the rain.

Schneider's eyes narrowed as he watched Daniel walk away, waiting until he reached the mess tent.

"Ja, Soldat," Schneider said under his breath. "We are not friends."

The Letter

Dinner ended without any further verbal communication between Klaus Schneider and Daniel. Schneider wasn't happy with Daniel's response to his question of friendship. This was made evident by his attempts to catch Daniel's eye to stare him down throughout the meal. Daniel wasn't the least bit unnerved by it. He knew Schneider didn't really want a friendship. What he wanted was complete and total obedience to the will of the Reich, and not just from Daniel, but from every

German citizen. Klaus Schneider wanted the new world order, and he believed it was still yet to come.

A movie starring Lauren Bacall was being shown in the recreation tent, complete with a bag of popcorn and a Coca-Cola for each PW. Bacall would be a big draw for the men, which meant Daniel would be able to read Adina's letter alone in his tent.

With KP duties finished, the men filed out of the mess tent, making their way in groups to the recreation tent. It had stopped raining, though dark thunderheads rolled above, gliding over a misty moon. Daniel slipped away from the group and walked in the opposite direction.

"Danny, where are you going? Frau Lauren, she's this way," Heimee yelled. Some of the others whistled and catcalled in response.

Daniel ignored them, quickly making his way to the tent and the comfort of his cot. He pulled the cord on the bedside lamp and retrieved the letter from the safety of his pocket. Unfolding the paper, he read the first line.

My dearest Daniel,

As I write your name on the paper, I can see your eyes and the way you looked at me the night we last were together. I write your name, and I feel your lips on mine and your arms encircling me with their warmth. You're in my head, vivid and clear. It's as though the writing of your name is my very own doorway, my magical escape to being with you. Does that sound childish? If it does, it's because I feel like a child in the most wonderful way. You've awakened something in me, Daniel. Something I was certain was dead, yet when I'm with you, it comes alive. It's absurd to think I would be falling in love with you. Wouldn't you agree? I barely know you. Yet I can't deny it. I'm falling in love with you, Daniel Christensen.

Now, as to the promise I made to you. I have a plan. It will take some coordination, but I believe I can pull it off. You remember I told you about my friend, Jeanie Mae? Her brother, Jimmy, keeps a motorcycle stored in a shed on their property. That bike is our ticket to ride to the coast. Now, I'd be taking it without permission, which is more like stealing. But then again, Jeanie is my best friend, and her brother is away fighting the war in Europe, so I'll just call it borrowing for now.

I promise you, Daniel, we will see the Pacific Ocean together. I don't know when, or if I have the patience to wait, but it's worth it if waiting means I'll be in your arms again.

Wait for me,

Adina

Daniel's heart quickened, and he wanted to read the letter again and again. Did he read it correctly? Yes, his English had improved, but speaking it and reading it were two different things. He read through the entire letter again. He didn't misunderstand. She loved him. She wanted him, just as he did her.

Outside, the rain began falling again, tapping out an erratic rhythm on the tent canvas. The wind blew, and the electric lamp flickered. He carefully folded the letter, looking around for a safe place to hide it. He picked up his leather journal. No one had ever attempted to look in it without his permission. It would be safe there. He tucked the letter between two pages where he had practiced sketching one of the many squirrels he'd seen in the oak trees around the camp. He then tied the leather straps and placed the journal under his pillow.

The tapping rain became a thunderous pelting, drowning out the sound of the cinema playing in the distance. Daniel lay down on his cot, placed his hands behind his head, and listened. How long would he have to wait? It didn't matter. He'd wait as long as it took. She loved him.

25

March 1945

Henry Robbins pored over the chart of seventy-eight-year-old Frank Murray. The old man sat on the examination table, hunched over, wearing only his undershorts and a stained undershirt, which was too small to contain his paunchy belly.

"How long have you been feeling poorly, Frank?" Henry asked, gently palpitating the glands in the man's neck. "You have said three days now, yes?"

"Well, let me think," Frank said, rubbing his temple. "It may be four days now. Yesterday was the worst. My ear is killing me."

Henry peered over the rim of his glasses. "You are most definitely running a fever. Stick out your tongue, please," he said, placing a wooden depressor to Frank's tongue. "Why on earth did you wait so long to come in? You should not be taking such risks at your age."

Frank mumbled something incoherent over the stick in his mouth until Henry removed it. "Well, I'm here now, ain't I? I would've stopped that beautiful daughter of yours if I could've caught up with her. She's been riding that bicycle back and forth past my house almost every day."

Henry's eyebrows raised as he examined the man's ears. He knew Adina's daily schedule very well. There would be no reason for her to be riding past the Murrays' house on a daily basis. "Has she now?" Henry responded.

"Yep, but she's riding too fast. I'd have to be standing at the end of my drive if I wanted to get her attention. I just figured she had something important going on."

Henry jotted notes in the chart. "You can put your shirt back on, Frank," he said. "It appears you have a virus and a nasty ear infection. I have a vial of penicillin. I'll give you an injection before you leave, but I won't be able to give you another until my order arrives. The war has made penicillin scarce." He patted Frank's shoulder. "One dose should start you on the road to recovery."

Frank buttoned his shirt. "Thanks, Doc, I surely appreciate it. Say, speaking of the war, I'm sure you've been hearing about those places they've been finding over there in Europe—about the camps them Nazis have been running." Frank shook his head. "It's a damn disgrace if you ask me. Those poor people. Apparently, they've been doing it for years—starving them, and God knows what else."

Henry worked in silence, filling the syringe full of penicillin. He knew all too well about the atrocities the Germans could inflict on human life. He fled his country before it could take hold of his own life, and the lives of his wife and child. News of the systematic mass murders in Lithuania came as early as 1941. Churchill called it "a crime without a name," but Henry knew its name was "hate."

"You came from that part of Europe, didn't you, Henry?"

Henry didn't respond.

"Doc?"

"Forgive me," Henry said. "Yes, I came from Lithuania."

Frank pressed further. "I guess that's why you brought your family here to the great United States of America. Ain't that right, Doc?"

Henry held the syringe and cotton alcohol swab in his hand. He took his time, avoiding eye contact with the man. He would need to weigh his words carefully. He'd lived a long time in the small town of Windsor. He was the respected Dr. Henry Robbins, and he was thankful that no one had ever pressed him for the details of his past. He had been able to keep his private life private. "To be quite honest with you, Frank, I had a good life in Lithuania. But my opportunities were limited. I knew that I would be able to further myself and make a better living as a doctor here in the great United States of America, as you say." He winked.

Frank smiled. "Indeed, I said it, Doc."

Henry gave the injection and sent Frank Murray on his way, all the while his stomach soured. How easy it was for him to live the lie. He hadn't left Lithuania to further himself. He ran away in fear. He left the few remaining members of Luisa's family alone to helplessly fend for themselves. Were they even alive anymore? There would be no way for him to know. When he left them, he denied the core of who he was. Henry knew that for them, he had been dead for a very long time.

———

Adina had been lying to her father for days, giving him excuse after excuse for why she'd missed or rescheduled an appointment or returned home too late to start his supper. Her tall tales encompassed everything from Sally Quinn needing help with her new baby's colic to someone falling off the curb and into the street downtown. Of course it was a visitor from out of town who did the falling, and of course Adina was called upon to help the poor fellow. She'd also used the excuse that she got tied up in conversation with Carl Sanderson at the Groceteria. This one actually made sense since it wasn't unusual for her to stop by the market at the end of a work day. Getting caught up in conversation with Carl was a common occurrence, and therefore, she thought it qualified as only a half truth. But she already used that excuse yesterday, so it was off limits for today.

It was a Tuesday afternoon. Spring was just around the corner, yet a chill lingered in the air. The sun had only just begun to venture down over the western hills. Adina sat hunched in the shade and shadows of the oak trees and shrubs at the backside of Camp Windsor. The same place she first saw Daniel and where she met up with him the night of the Christmas dance. She had come here most days at the end of her work day, sometimes even in the middle of her day, to sit in the shadows and watch. Maybe some of the prisoners would start up a game of football. Maybe Daniel would be with them. If only someone would walk by the fence line, possibly one of the prisoners she knew on a first-name basis. Then she would at least be able to give them a note to take to Daniel.

How many more chances would she have to pull off her plan? It was a plan she was fairly sure would work...if all the pieces lined up. Jeanie's mother and father both worked outside the home during the day. This would allow for easier access to the shed where Jimmy's motorcycle was stored. At least nobody would be around to see her take it. Then she and Daniel would have a full day to make the ride to the coast, spend a little time together, then ride back. If all went as planned, Daniel would be back at the camp and she would be home before anyone even noticed they were gone. If only she could get a note to someone.

She looked at her watch. It was five o'clock. She had been sitting behind a tree for over an hour. Her legs were cramping, and her stomach growled. Was she hungry or just nervous over what reason she would give to her father for her lateness tonight?

Just then, a few prisoners began mulling around the back row of tents. She heard their voices and saw the smoke trails from their cigarettes. They had no ball, so they weren't there for a game. It appeared they were out for a stroll and a smoke before dinner. Adina recognized one of them. It was Freddie. Her heart beat wildly, and she scrambled to reach into her coat pocket for paper and pencil. She hastily scribbled a note on the paper.

"Tomorrow, 12:30 p.m. Organize a football game at the back of camp. Bring Daniel. Be sure to kick the ball over the broken fence into the trees. Please send Daniel to get the ball.

Adina Robbins"

Fingers shaking, she folded the note and stood. Some in the group had already left for dinner. Only Freddie and another prisoner remained to finish their smokes. Freddie turned his head, and Adina took a few steps out into the open. Frantically, she waved her arms, then stepped back into the shadow of the trees. She was successful. He had seen her. With a nod to acknowledge her, and a cool demeanor, he turned back to the other and spoke a few words in German. The other prisoner laughed and went on his way to dinner.

Freddie lingered just long enough to be sure the other fellow was out of sight. He finished the last drags of his cigarette, stomping it under his foot, then made his way to the broken fence. Adina's eyes darted from side to side as she ran to the fence line to meet him.

"Hello, Nurse Robbins." Freddie smiled behind the surprised confusion in his eyes. "You should not be here. You know this, ja?"

"Yes, I know," she whispered. She looked toward the guard tower, then behind her. She then handed him the note. "Here, quickly, take this."

"What is this?" He turned the note over in his hand and raised an eyebrow. "Is it for who I think it is for?"

The look on Freddie's face caused Adina to second guess the efficiency of her plan. She now wasn't sure who she wanted the note to go to first. If Freddie gave it to Daniel and somebody saw, it might not go well for Daniel. Suspicions were high enough as it is. And she didn't want Freddie to read it. He was a sweet kid and all, but just naive enough to say something to the wrong person. There was only one other person she felt she could trust to see the plan through with discretion.

"Give it to Heimee," she said.

Freddie laughed out loud, then cleared his throat. "Günter? You want me to give it to Günter Schmeltz-Heimer? Are you certain of this, Nurse?"

Nervously, she stepped back, eyes pleading with him. "Yes, Freddie. Please, just do this for me. I have to go now." She turned, running back into the shadow of the trees.

Freddie watched her go, turning the folded note over in his hand. He shrugged his shoulders, stuffed the folded note into his pants pocket, and walked back toward the mess tent.

26

Escape, April 1945

The O'Brien home sat peacefully, with no cars parked in the dusty, dirt drive. All good signs that no one was home.

Adina stood next to her bicycle, looking out over the yard and toward the trail, the shed with Jimmy's motorcycle nearby. Standing at this distance from the main road, it was hard to hear much of anything except for the sweetness of birdsong, and the wind moving through the leaves of the giant Pistache tree.

The day was perfection itself, as the sun shone warm on Adina's face. Puffed white clouds passed over a crystal blue sky. Finally, a day with no rain. She looked down at the new growth of spring wildflowers in the lush, green grass. Reaching down, she plucked one and twisted it between her fingers. She remembered that day almost a year ago when she and Jeanie ran down the trail. She felt like a child, wild and free. How on earth could she have known what she was running to? When she saw Daniel for the first time, her stomach sank and her heart raced. When he looked at her, she felt exposed, defenseless. His smile made her weak.

Today, Adina stood ready and willing to steal a motorcycle from her best friend's brother so she could kidnap a German PW being held in a US military camp, just so she could take him on a day trip to the coast.

"Who do you think you are, Adina Robbins?" she whispered. She didn't recognize herself. This wasn't the dutiful, obedient doctor's daughter. The one who completed her daily schedule and organized the clinic supply room on a weekly basis, assisting her father whenever there was need. And she definitely wasn't the one who obeyed when he said,

"No, you cannot go, Adina Luisa. I need you here. The town needs you." Not anymore. One thing she knew for certain: she was falling madly in love with Daniel Christensen, just as he was with her. Today, she would make his dream of seeing the Pacific Ocean come true.

———————————————

Camp Windsor's grounds buzzed with activity as time neared the twelve thirty lunch bell. A company of men jogged around the perimeter, sounding off a German marching tune. Others waited by the pullup bar at the far right of camp, watching the one at the bar flexing under his reps. Everyone seemed pleased with a sunny day and no rain.

Heimee, Freddie, and Daniel walked briskly toward the back of the camp, red kickball in hand. There was nothing suspicious in their manner—nothing that would alert anyone of any ensuing mischief. Both Heimee and Freddie appeared genuinely enthusiastic to get to the back field to play a game of football. Freddie led the pack, with Heimee a few feet to his back. Daniel lagged behind.

"Schnell, Danny Boy!" Heimee yelled. "We don't have much time before the bell."

Daniel rolled his eyes. "There are only three of us," he yelled back. "How will we play a decent game?"

Ignoring him, Heimee lumbered a half jog to catch up to Freddie. "Freddie, position yourself to kick the ball out over the fence," he said between pants.

"Why me?" Freddie gawked.

"Because, Dummkopf, you kick harder than me. I am much too fat."

Daniel caught up to them and snatched the ball out of Freddie's hands. "Fine then," he said. "Let's kick for points. Freddie, you stand over there." He pointed toward the fence. "Heimee, you stand across, and I'll stand over to the left."

Freddie, eyes wide and mouth hanging open, looked to Heimee for direction.

"Umm, no, not that way, Danny," Heimee said, clearing his throat while spitting a few tobacco leaves to the ground. "Why don't you stand where Freddie is? That way he can get some much needed…umm, strength practice. You know, good strong kicking." He spit again.

"Fine, fine," Daniel huffed. He threw the ball to Freddie as they switched places.

"Wunderbar!" Heimee shouted, clapping his hands.

Freddie dropped the ball to the ground, effortlessly kicking it to Heimee, who danced a few fancy steps around it and kicked it over to Daniel.

"Are you going to mess around, or are we going to play?" Daniel yelled, pounding the ball with his foot so that it skidded right past Freddie toward the tents. "Ah ha," he gloated. "That's one point for me." He waited, hands on hips for Freddie to return with the ball.

Freddie returned out of breath. He held the ball out in front of him, calculating the fence line with his eyes.

"What are you waiting for?" Daniel shouted.

Freddie turned, as though ready to kick the ball to Heimee. Then in an instant, he pivoted toward Daniel. Taking a step back, he then swung his right foot forward with all his might as he simultaneously dropped the ball. The connection of foot to ball was made with a thud. The red ball soared high into the air, over Daniel's head, into the sunlight, and out of sight.

Shielding his eyes, Daniel watched as the ball catapulted over the barbed-wire fence and beyond the trees. He turned back toward Freddie, throwing his hands in the air. "Der idiot! I guess the game is already over."

"Nah, Freund," Heimee yelled back. "We still have some time. You run quickly and get the ball." He waited for Daniel's frustration to subside. "Come on, Danny." He pointed at the guard tower. "The guard isn't here today, ja?"

Daniel shot a glance toward the guard tower. "Scheisse," he muttered and walked in no particular hurry to the bent-down part of the fence.

"Schnell, Danny! It's almost lunch," Heimee yelled, winking at Freddie.

Daniel picked up his pace as he approached the fence. He slipped one leg over the wire to the other side, snagging and tearing his pants. He breathed another curse and walked toward what he thought was the direction of the ball. He couldn't see it and took a few more steps toward the tree line.

"Daniel," he heard a voice whisper.

He stood still, squinting his eyes toward the sound of the voice. "Who is there?" he whispered back.

"It's me, Adina."

Daniel's heart leaped as he walked toward the trees. There, crouched in the shadows, was Adina. She smiled, eyes brightening at the sight of him. She reached out her hand, beckoning him to her.

With one step, Daniel was next to her, lifting her to her feet and into his arms. "Leibe," he whispered, peppering her neck and cheeks with kisses. "What are you doing here? Are you crazy?" He held her face in his hands, covering her mouth with his lips.

Adina felt lightheaded in his arms. Knowing they couldn't stay there, she pushed back, placing her fingertips over his lips. "We have to go," she said, haste filling her eyes.

"Go? What are you talking about?"

"Didn't the boys tell you? I'm stealing you away to the coast today." She kissed his cheek.

He shook his head. "They told me nothing, only forced me out here to kick the ball around."

"It was all a part of the plan, my love," she said, planting a kiss on his lips. "Come on now, we need to get out of her." She pulled on his arm.

"Adina, I can't leave," he protested.

"Why not, silly?" she laughed, grabbing both his hands. "I already have the motorcycle hidden at the end of the trail." She tugged his arms, inching them both closer to the trail.

Daniel looked back toward the camp. Heimee and Freddie were gone, probably already in the mess tent for lunch. Both his friends were in on the plan with Adina this whole time. But would they cover for him if somebody noticed he was missing? His chief concern was Schneider. Heimee could hold his own with the tyrant, but Daniel wasn't so sure about Freddie. "But if we get caught—" He cupped Adina's cheek with his hand.

"Shhh. There are two hundred men at this camp, at the very least." The love she felt for him gave her all the confidence she needed. "You'll never be missed." She took hold of his hand and started walking. "Besides, you'll need to drive the motorcycle. I've never driven one before." She giggled as they ran down the trail hand in hand.

"And what makes you so sure I know how to drive a motorcycle, Fräulein?" he said, panting.

27

The Ride

The two-lane road stretched to the west, twisting and turning past rolling green hills and towering redwood trees. Brushes of color whooshed by with each turn. Every now and again with the curve of the road, a glimpse of the river could be seen, sunlight bouncing off its rippling green water.

Adina sat behind Daniel on the back of the motorcycle, clinging tightly to his waist. She laid her head against his back, taking refuge from the biting wind, listening for his heartbeat as she watched the scenery pass by. On occasion, a car or truck passed them in the opposite direction. She found it interesting that nobody seemed to pay them any attention. One would have thought that the sight of a young man on a motorcycle, his clothing branded with the letters "PW," and a young girl clinging to him might draw all kinds of scrutiny. But no one seemed to care. Whether a delivery truck carrying fresh fish into town or a family in a sedan driving back from vacation, all seemed to be blissfully in their own worlds.

Daniel's driving was smooth and calculated, eyes forward, so as not to draw any unnecessary attention to themselves. Adina understood his apprehension toward this crazy excursion. He was much more concerned about what would happen to her than he was for himself, should they get caught. Yet she wasn't concerned at all, and that was the beauty of it. She had been set free. Free from the bonds of obligation to her father and his expectations. How long had she lived feeling as though she owed her father; owed him her day in and day out support as his one and only nurse? Owed him the same love and care she watched her mother give? And the thing that goaded her the most, she felt she owed him her companionship. Papa had no one after Mama died. He was alone, and Adina was afraid to leave him that way. Yet time and time again, Papa brushed her aside. All her attempts to work her way into his heart were met with another brick in the wall. And then there were his lies. Her findings up in the attic were the last nail in the coffin. She wouldn't be playing the game of pretend anymore. She was free.

Adina hugged Daniel tighter, feeling his body relax into her. Her heart raced with the speed of the motorcycle. Closing her eyes, she made a secret wish. If it were possible, they would reach the coast, catch the next boat sailing anywhere, and never look back.

Suspicions

Henry sat at the front desk in the clinic waiting room. He fingered through a patient chart, jotting down final observations and notes from the day's visit. A stack of seven more charts sat off to the side. It was a regular part of Adina's duties to complete chart entries at the end of each day. He would meticulously write out the home visits, medicine deliveries, and clinic hours in his personal ledger. It would then be Adina's responsibility to copy it into her own ledger. He glanced over the rim of his glasses at the clock on the wall. It was almost three o'clock, and his daughter was nowhere in sight.

He sighed, removed his glasses, and rubbed his eyes. He was tired, and his day wasn't over yet. He had been invited to attend a special meeting at Santa Rosa Hospital. Several head physicians and hospital board members were gathering to develop a postwar care plan for returning servicemen and women. The outlook was positive. With Russia's Red Army zeroing in on Berlin, the war in Europe would be coming to an end, and the need for efficient medical care for returning soldiers would be upon them before they knew it. Henry understood the need all too well. And so, as a respected physician and war veteran, he was invited to represent the town of Windsor at the first meeting.

Henry knit his eyebrows, deepening the V between them. An uneasiness settled over him. Where was his daughter? He opened and rechecked his personal ledger to make sure he was remembering Adina's schedule correctly. No afternoon home visits were listed and only two medicine deliveries. He fidgeted with his fountain pen. Should he go look for her? Yet why would he? Adina was a grown woman. She would be turning twenty this year, the age Luisa was when he married her. Although Adina looked very much like her mother, she wasn't Luisa, and she was pulling away from him. He'd always been hard on her, but if anyone had asked him why, he wouldn't have been able to give an answer. He loved his daughter deeply. He cared for and provided for her, as any good father should. He truly believed that his rigid rules and high expectations were for her own good and protection. Surely she knew that. She must realize all he had done for them, from bringing his family safely to the United States and giving them a roof over their heads, to developing a thriving medical clinic in the town where he, as a physician, was trusted and respected. None of it came without cost. He sacrificed a great deal, and yes, he required great sacrifice in return. All of it he did for Luisa and Adina.

Closing the small, four-ringed black book, he tucked it in his medical bag, sat back in the chair, and folded his arms. If he wanted to make the meeting on time, he'd need to get on the road. Pushing his all-too-familiar fears aside, he took a sheet of paper from the desk drawer, and with his fountain pen, he quickly jotted a note.

Adina, please be sure to complete these patient charts with my exact notes. I will not be home until later this evening. Papa

He stacked the remaining charts in the center of the desk and laid the note on top where it would be easily seen. Grabbing his medical bag and coat, he placed his hat on his head and walked to the door. He stood there for a moment, tapping the outside of his pockets to feel for his keys and especially for his pipe. Satisfied, he opened the clinic

there had to have been so much life before that. What were his dreams? Did he want to attend a university to study art? Would he settle down someday and start a family of his own? How desperately she wanted to be a part of that life. She closed her eyes, listening to the repetitive crash of the waves and the screech of the gulls overhead.

Letting go of her hand, Daniel walked a few feet closer to the foamy water that pushed inward, smoothing the rocky sand beneath. He folded his arms across his chest, hugging himself. Suddenly, his hands dropped to his sides, and he fell to his knees in the wet sand. His body shook as tears tumbled down his cheeks. Digging his hands into the muddy sand, he wept.

Bewildered, Adina hesitated, then stepped slowly toward him. The waves continued to sweep in, surrounding Daniel, soaking his pants and shoes, entangling ropes of leafy seaweed around his fingers. Unmoved by the chill of the water, he cried, whispering words in German.

Adina knelt next to him. Reaching down, she lifted his hand, his wet fingernails caked with sand. She brushed and caressed his fingers, bringing them to her lips. She didn't know what else to do. If there was a way for her to take his sorrow, carry it for him, she would do it. She knew how to do the job well. She had carried her father's, as well as her own. She would do just about anything for Daniel. She held on to his hand, watching his eyes.

Daniel lifted his head, staring at the waves through fallen, damp strands of hair, like the bars of a jail cell. "Mutti, Max...Es tut mir leid. Es tut mir leid." He breathed the words like a mantra, over and over. "I'm so sorry," he whispered.

Adina lifted the damp hair from his eyes, sweeping it back over the top of his head. With her finger, she gently brushed tears and tiny grains of sand from his face.

The force of another wave swept in and around their legs. He looked at her, blue eyes pleading, seeking. "I could not help him. I didn't save him. I did nothing. Nothing."

"I'm so sorry, Daniel," she said, caressing his cheek. "It wasn't your fault." Her words rang hollow, even to her own ears.

"Why, Adina? Why? I did nothing. I am a coward...nothing more."

She held his eyes as she pondered the question. The burden of that three-letter word was too much to bear. He was begging her, by name, for answers. Why the loss of his brother? Why war? Why death? Why any of it?

Why, indeed. How could she be so all-consumed with herself? Always, it had been her past, her mother's death, her father and what he did or didn't do. Why did Jeanie go away, yet she stayed behind? Why was she the one who stayed to care for her father and take care of his patients, his clinic? Childish, that's what she was. Here Daniel knelt, in the waves and wet sand, in anguish over the memory of his brother. Max, shot to death in cold blood right before his eyes, while he could do nothing to save him. All the while, back here, in the comfort and safety of her small town, she was behaving like a selfish child.

And then, Daniel came. Her German prisoner. She'd done more, given more, and taken more risks for Daniel Christensen than for anyone else in her life, even her own father. It was Daniel. He was the answer to why.

She turned to him, cupping his face with both her hands. "Look at me, Daniel," she said, her eyes deepening with the ache of love in her heart. "I know you regret not being able to save them. How could you? Those beasts had their guns pointed at you. Had you moved you would have been shot. Don't you understand, Daniel? You couldn't save them. But you came here...and you saved me."

He shook his head. "Saved you? I don't understand."

She smiled, hesitantly. "I know it sounds silly, maybe even a little selfish. But just think about it with me. What are the chances? You were brutally forced to leave your home, forced to fight in a war at the demand of an evil dictator. You were then captured, a prisoner of the United States military, transported across the globe to not just any camp in the US but here, to my small, insignificant town in Northern

California." She looked out over the water and the misty clouds above it, searching for the words to help him understand. "The day you first saw me, at the back fence." She paused.

He turned toward her, pulling her to him. "Tell me, Leibe. Tell me about that day."

Swallowing hard, she looked in his eyes. "I was dying inside, Daniel. Every day seemed like a never-ending uphill climb. Ever since my mother's death I've worked for my father's approval, for his affection. But at the end of the day, I always seemed to come up short. So, when Jeanie begged me to join the WACs and serve in this stupid war, I thought, why not? I wouldn't even tell my father. I'd just go away." Again, she stopped to take in his face, his eyes, his mouth that tugged a bit to the left when he talked. Everything about him gave her courage and hope. "But then, you walked up to the fence line. You were smiling at me." She looked down at the water and the sand.

He tipped her chin up, searching her eyes. "And?"

"My heart started beating," she whispered, moving closer to him. "Maybe for the very first time."

The sea rushed in around them in waves of foamy gray and blue. Daniel pulled Adina into his arms, pressing his lips to hers. She gave herself completely to the force and honesty of his kiss, holding on to him with every ounce of her strength, feeling as though she couldn't get close enough. Daniel had awakened a desire within her she never knew existed. With every caress of his hand to her back, every rake of his fingers through her hair, the hunger inside her grew. She pressed her body to him, returning his kisses, willing him to know she belonged to him.

Prisoner Missing

Back at Camp Windsor, dinner was in full swing. Once again, the mess tent teemed with tired, hungry men, eagerly anticipating a delicious meal. The lineup at the food service tables was a boisterous clamor of men discussing their work day and bantering over encounters they had in town. Everything seemed to be in order, nothing amiss, except for the fact that one prisoner was not to be seen.

Heimee scanned the tables for an open seat. He carried two plates of food, one in each hand. The larger of the two was piled high with meatloaf and mashed potatoes, gravy dribbling off the side of the plate and onto his grubby fingers. The other plate had two slices of buttered white bread and a generous portion of Brown Betty for dessert. Freddie followed close behind. The two found seats at the far left of the tent alongside a small, chatty group of men.

"What's new, Damen?" Heimee plopped down in a chair, bumping into the table and sloshing gravy off his plate. It puddled onto the table. Heimee was well liked around camp, and the men laughed, finding amusement in his clumsy arrival.

Klaus Schneider, who happened to be sitting at the opposite end of the table, was not the least bit impressed. He glared over the top of his coffee cup at both Heimee and Freddie.

The prisoner sitting next to Heimee gave him a hard punch in his upper arm. "Who are you calling Damen?" he said.

"That would be you, Freund," Heimee replied with a wink. Laughing, he shoved a healthy scoop of potatoes and gravy into his mouth. He then caught sight of Schneider, which made him choke. Potatoes and gravy sputtered out of his mouth and onto his shirt, as well as onto the man sitting next to him.

"Dummkopf, Schmelz-Heimer! Watch yourself." The young man abruptly stood, brushing flecks of potato from his pants.

"Sorry, Freund," Heimee said, shooting a side-eye glance at Schneider. He then looked nervously at Freddie. "Schneider," he whispered, pointing his eyes toward the end of the table.

Freddie nodded.

Heimee remained calm and resumed his meal, taking care not to overstuff his mouth again. He made light conversation with the men, telling crude jokes between bites and stealing an occasional glance at Schneider.

Coolheaded, Schneider sat casually taking bites of food, dabbing the corner of his mouth with his napkin, and sipping his coffee. He said an occasional word or two to the man sitting next to him, but other than that, his manner gave Heimee no need for concern. Over the remainder of his meal, Heimee seemed to forget that Schneider was ever sitting at the end of the same table as him.

As the evening meal wound down and cleanup began, Heimee scraped the last smear of Brown Betty from his plate. "Mmm, das war lecker," he said, wiping his mouth with the back of his hand. Shoving his chair back, he stood. "Let's go, Freddie." He turned to the shock of seeing Klaus Schneider standing behind him.

"Hallo, Schmeltz-Heimer. A moment of your time, if you will?" His lip curled to one side.

Though surprised, Heimee managed to suppress his nerves. "Why of course, Herr Schneider." He smiled and rubbed his fingers over the sticky hairs of his mustache. "What can I do for you?"

Petrified, Freddie stood statuesque, eyes wide and darting between the two men.

Schneider stepped face to face with Heimee, chin high and nose to the air. Looking down at the stout, pudgy man, he stalled his question, a common technique he used to assert his assumed power.

"I am wondering," he finally began, "do you know what has happened to Soldat Christensen?"

Heimee, allowing the question to mellow, retrieved his half-smoked cigar from his pocket, sniffed it, then inserted it between his brown teeth. "And what makes you think I would know where Soldat Christensen would be?" he responded, fumbling through his pockets for a match.

Schneider tilted his head, narrowing his eyes. Answering a direct question with a question was not an acceptable response from a Soldat to his Oberscharführer. Schneider would not take it lightly. Still, he smirked as he examined the underside of his fingernails on his left hand. "We did not see him at the midday meal. And here again, he is not at the evening meal. You must think that is very odd, ja? After all, you are a friend of his. You bunk in the same tent, this is true?" Schneider's Aryan physique towered inches above Heimee, making his downward stare effective, yet the view up into his nostrils quite distasteful.

"There are many men at this camp, Herr Schneider," Heimee responded. "It is easy to become lost in a crowd, ja?" Wanting the questioning to end, he did his best to skirt past the man, though with little success.

"I see, so you are saying he is lost? That would be tragic indeed." Schneider turned to Freddie. "Wouldn't you agree, Soldat Becker?"

Freddie froze. "Well, um, I...yes, that would be. I mean, if he were lost it would—"

"Come to think of it," Heimee interjected, "Soldat Christensen did not look well earlier today." He nervously tumbled the unlit cigar over his teeth and tongue. "He's probably been sleeping in the tent this whole time." He grinned at Schneider, patting him on the arm. "I'll go there now and check on him. Maybe I should bring him a nice cup of tea, ja?"

Schneider looked down at his arm with disdain, brushing it off with his hand. "You do that," he said. "And when you find him, you will report his condition directly to me. Is that quite understood? After all, if Christensen is not well, as you say, he may need immediate medical attention."

Relief swept over Heimee's face. "Ja, ja, Herr Schneider," he said with a half salute. He then motioned to Freddie. "Come, Freddie. Let's go."

"Not so fast. Soldat Becker will remain here with me," Schneider said with a look of satisfaction.

Freddie looked at Heimee, eyes wide.

"Very well. I will go now," Heimee conceded, walking around Schneider and toward the tent exit.

"Soldat Schmeltz-Heimer," Schnieder called out.

Heimee stopped. "Ja, Herr Schnieder?"

Schnieder's eyes pierced across the room. "Don't ever touch me again."

29

Plans for the Future

Adina and Daniel sat snuggled together against a large drift log. He wrapped her in his warm wool coat, pulling her close to his chest. She listened quietly to his heart as the waves of the ocean ebbed and flowed out of sync with the beat.

Daniel gazed in wonder at the two monolith rock outcroppings protruding from the ocean. The closer of the two, a giant, gray, craggy box, was accessible from the beach by way of a rock jetty, leading all the way to the formation's base. He watched as an old man wearing knee-high, black rubber boots and a white bucket hat skillfully traversed the rocks. Occasionally, he would reach down to retrieve a shell or sea creature, carefully examining it to determine its value. If he deemed worth keeping, he placed his find in a netted sack hanging from his waist. All else was thrown back into the sea.

Yet it was the more distant of the two formations, the one to the left, that truly intrigued Daniel. It consisted of two mesa-like structures jutting out of the water, each connected by a rock bridge. Beneath the bridge was a circular opening, a sort of window to the vast sea beyond. Wave upon wave forced under the bridge and through the opening, catching the light of the setting sun, like pink and gold diamonds scattering onto the craggy rock.

"I don't see a goat," Daniel said, breaking the silence.

Adina giggled. "What is this you're talking about? A goat?" She looked out at the two rocks.

"You called it Goat Rock. Is that correct?" He pulled his coat tighter, holding her firmly against himself. "Neither of the rocks looks like a goat."

She gently touched the stubble on his chin. "Oh, that," she said. "I think the name has something to do with where the goats would feed on the grassy cliffs behind us, not the rocks in the water."

He looked down at her, a smile curving his lips. "Well now, that's very deceptive," he said and gently kissed her temple, then her lips.

She had never been kissed by a man the way that Daniel kissed her. It was as though his lips caressed every part of her being, tender, his breath warm and inviting. She loved the scent and the taste of him. When she kept her eyes closed, she became immersed in the magnificent sound of the pounding ocean waves and the intense longing to take him in deeper. And when she cracked open her eyes, she marveled at the length of his lashes and the shape of his freckle-pecked nose, and she would ache with love for him. She never wanted it to end.

Daniel's kisses stopped as he looked out at the ocean. The sun was close to the horizon, turning the entire lower skyline a deep orange with pink, sapphire-lined clouds above. "I wish I had my journal," he said. "I would sketch this memory. I would capture everything about it, especially the color. But I have no colored pencils or paint." He helped her to sit up next to him. "We should be getting back, Adina. It will be dark soon."

"Wait," she protested. "I have something I need to tell you. I've put it off long enough." She looked into his eyes, positive he could see her secrets. A wave of fear washed through her, stopping at her heart, intensifying its beat. Was she already doubting? Did she stop believing he loved her? Would he look at her the same way, desire her with the same passion if he knew the truth?

"What is it?" he said, his brows furrowing. He cupped her cheek. "There is nothing you cannot tell me."

She took hold of his hand and drew in a deep breath of crisp sea air. "My family has lived a lie. Ever since my father and mother fled

Lithuania, we've carried this lie with us." She watched his face, his eyes, for signs of worry or shock. She saw none, only the same love that had been there all along. "Before my father left Lithuania, he was a Jew."

"Ah, Juden," he responded, patiently waiting for her to continue.

"Yes, you see, he denied it and changed our family name. My mother's family rejected her for this. I have often wondered if I still have family in Lithuania. We've never had contact."

"And your father, he made you lie about this as well?" Daniel asked.

"No, I had no idea. My childhood was wonderful. We lived like everyone else, even celebrated Christmas for gosh sake. Nobody ever questioned us. There was never a reason to give any answers, until—"

"Until what, Liebe?"

"The day my mother died, on my twelfth birthday. I walked into my father's study when the door was closed—something I was told never to do. I saw him. He was praying in Hebrew. He spoke the prayers with such love and devotion." Tears filled her eyes. "I had never seen my papa do anything like this before."

"And what did your papa do? He must have seen you standing there, ja?"

The tears streamed down her cheeks. "He was so angry. He screamed for me to get out. I can still see the look on his face. I ran out as fast as I could and straight to my mama." She paused as the pain and sadness of that day flooded back in.

"And did she confirm what you saw?" he asked, waiting for her response.

Adina couldn't answer. She shut her eyes tight, the grief of the memory overwhelming her.

With one swift motion, Daniel took her into his arms and held her tight. "Oh, Liebe, meine Liebe. I'm so sorry."

Adina wept, holding him tightly. She wept out her fear and her doubt. She wept away the years of trying to achieve and attain acceptance. She cried until the tears were spent and all she could do was look in his eyes.

He swept the hair from her forehead and tears from her eyes.

"Daniel...I'm a Jew," she said.

"Ja, Liebe, you are," he said, not a trace of shock in his expression. Only the same spark in his eyes and soft smile on his lips.

"Maybe I'm not being clear in what I'm saying," she persisted. "My father denied his Jewish heritage. I didn't know this. How could I now deny something I knew nothing about? It was his decision, not mine. Ever since that day, I've wanted to learn more about who I am. I just haven't known how to go about it, especially without my father finding out."

"I do understand, Adina," he said. "Of course you would want to know and pursue the truth. This is who you are. I love you for this." He caressed her cheek.

Her eyebrows knit as she fought back the doubt. "But if we stay together? You are a German. I'm a Jew. How would that work? You would want a family, wouldn't you? Children?"

"Lots of them," he said. "With you." He kissed her lips with such sweet tenderness. "My sweet Adina," he whispered.

The sun was sinking beneath the blue horizon of the Pacific Ocean, leaving the sky glowing a deep purple.

"Come now," Daniel said. "We will have plenty of time to make plans." He helped her to her feet as she brushed away the caked sand from her still-wet slacks, her shoes, a swampy mess. He held tightly to her hand, and she watched his face as they walked.

"Daniel," she said.

"Shhh. All will be well, Liebe. The war is ending. We'll be together." He smiled, walking her briskly up the hill.

Schneider's Discovery

Klaus Schneider had no intention of waiting for Heimee to report back to him on Daniel's whereabouts. He was a man who prided himself on his sly techniques on the battlefield. His tactics fiercely motivated his subordinates to march for days without rest, then fight on the front lines, though weakened and ill equipped. For him, his capture and subsequent transfer to Camp Windsor was nothing more than an inconvenience to be patiently endured while waiting to return to his homeland. He would be certain his men were obediently ready to follow him when that time came.

With the evening meal finished, the men gathered in the recreation tent for cards and dominos, while others bantered and smoked outside.

Schneider strutted with determination with Freddie following sheepishly behind, struggling to keep up. He ripped back the flap of Daniel's tent and walked inside. The air was rife with the scent of damp canvas and sweat, and the lack of light made it difficult to see. He stomped to the back of the tent, stopping at Daniel's cot.

"Ah," he said, triumphant. "There is no sick prisoner to be found, ja, Soldat Becker?"

"Herr Schneider," Frederick pleaded, "is this necessary? It isn't right."

Schneider's icy eyes narrowed. His arms stiffened at his sides and zeroed in on Freddie.

"Not right, Soldat?" he said, his face just inches away. Even in the dimness, Schneider's face flashed angry and red. "A prisoner has gone missing, Soldat Becker." He reigned in his temper, attempting to appear calm and in control. "I believe you know something about this, ja? And if you are not willing to cooperate and tell me what you know, then I will be forced to find the answer on my own."

Schneider then moved to the small bedside table and pulled the cord on the lamp. Golden light flooded the table. Items lay scattered on its surface. A comb and small mirror, a few sheets of blank stationery, and two well-worn pencils. Also a book. More specifically, a donated novel, dogeared and tattered. He slid out the stationery, turning it over in his hands. He then swept the comb and mirror to the floor. Picking up the novel, he haphazardly leafed through its pages. Frustrated and unsatisfied, he flipped it over and shook it by the cover like a rag doll, dashing it to the floor. His eyes feverishly darted over and around the table, and back and forth over the cot. Taking a step back, he dropped to the floor on his hands and knees to peer under the cot. Seeing that it was much too dark underneath, he grabbed the bedside lamp and thrust it under, sweeping it from side to side. Two more books, some folded shirts and rolled socks, as well as the coat Daniel wore to the Christmas dance were the only items beneath.

Schneider stood, casually turning toward Freddie, eyeing him like valued prey. He moved slowly, as though he owned time itself. After all, he and the young man weren't going anywhere anytime soon. Once he had achieved the full effect of heightened anxiety, for this was the effect he was aiming for, he cocked his head, closed his eyes with eyebrows raised, and took an exaggerated breath in through his nose. "Becker, Becker, Becker," he said, just past his exhale. "Why must you make this so difficult? If you have information, tell me now."

Freddie stood silent, his eyes narrowing with disdain for the man in front of him.

"Becker," Schneider continued. "You are well aware that our American hosts have trusted me to oversee the men...or, um, forgive me, that is, to oversee the men from our own regiment. I have done a fine job of that, have I not?"

Freddie looked down at the ground and tapped the brutalized book with his foot. "If you are referring to morning wakeup calls and assigning latrine KP, then yes, they trust that you are doing a fine job." He tilted his eyes up at Schneider, anticipating the response he knew was coming.

With one swift step, Klaus Schneider stood face to face with Freddie. "Do not test me, Soldat." The words spit from his mouth. He pointed a finger between Freddie's eyes. "I can make life very difficult for you, as I am sure you remember well." Abruptly, he turned back around to face Daniel's cot.

"Herr Schneider, there is no need for this response," Freddie pleaded. "Why can you not understand? We are not at war here."

"We will see," Schneider responded. He ripped the blanket, sheet, and pillow from the cot with one motion, sending them to the ground in a heap. There, peeking from the folds of the blanket lay Daniel's journal. Schneider picked it up. "What do we have here?" he gloated, running his fingers over the soft brown leather.

Freddie stood helpless and defeated. He shook his head as he watched the merciless man.

Schneider untied the leather straps and took his time reading the inscription on the first page. "Quaint," he smirked. He began turning the pages. "Some of these are quite good." With the next page turn, he paused, raising his eyebrows. "Hmmm, Fräulein," he said. He continued thumbing through page after page, sketch after sketch, until he stopped. "Aha. I believe I may have found something." He held up the folded note pinched between his fingers like a scorpion and tilted his eyes toward Freddie, who looked at the floor in defeat. Schneider unfolded and quickly read the note. "Right," he said, refolding the paper and carefully placing it in his shirt pocket. He then tossed the journal on the cot and strutted past Freddie. "Clean up Christensen's things, would you please, Soldat Becker? It appears I have something very important for Major Williams." Smirking, he strode out of the tent.

Freddie stood alone. The light from the lamp lying on the floor cast eerie shadows onto the canvas above. Reaching down, he picked up the leather journal from the cot. Tenderly, he closed it, not wanting to look at the contents inside out of respect for its owner. He tied the leather straps, sat down on the bare cot, and buried his head in his hands.

30

The Dark Ride Home

Daniel drove, slow and steady, taking care on the twists and turns. The dim front light barely illuminated the road ahead, making the ride back feel all the more sluggish.

Frigid air beat against Adina's body. The ominous blackness of the road ahead and the moonless sky above added to her anxious anticipation. She felt sandwiched between both. Where was the moon? When she came up with her "perfect plan" to steal Daniel away to the Pacific Ocean, she was much more concerned with how she would get him out of the camp, not so much about how she would get him back in. She didn't consider things like time constraints or darkness. At the very least she should have found a way to check the battery on the motorcycle's headlight. Even she knew a bicycle light battery needed to be strong to see in the dark. She hadn't thought about food either. A picnic on the beach would've been nice. She berated herself for not being more prepared, though there wasn't much she could do about it now. No matter how much she wished for the motorcycle to go faster or its light to shine brighter, it wasn't going to happen.

She distracted herself with her memories of the day, still vivid and fresh in her mind. So much seemed like a dream, though she knew it was real. Daniel was real. She wrapped her arms tightly around him, snuggling into the warmth of him. She felt privileged that he allowed her to see him today, vulnerable and broken, and then to be his refuge, his comfort. And then, when she revealed her secret, he showed no shock, no disgust, only his unconditional love and acceptance. He wanted her. He wanted to spend the rest of his life with her. He said they would make plans for a future where they could be together, get married, and start a family. If it weren't for this horrid war, that future could begin now. But she reminded herself once again that if it weren't for this horrid war, she never would've met him.

Peeking her head around Daniel, Adina looked for any sort of familiar landmark that would indicate they were getting closer to home. Every turn looked the same in the darkness. Feeling her anxiety rising again, she pressed her hands to Daniel's chest, squeezing him close. "Are you all right?" she shouted over the sound of the motorcycle and wind that rushed past her ears. She could see a few points of light in the distance. They were getting closer.

"Cold, but I'm fine," he shouted back.

The bends and curves lessened, becoming the straightaway that would lead them back to civilization. The soft illumination of Santa Rosa lay just at the horizon. Adina poked her head around again. Two lights shone ahead on the highway.

"Look at that," she shouted. "Those are the first car lights we've seen since we've been riding back."

Daniel didn't respond.

The lights grew brighter in the distance. Adina watched as they transformed and became clearer. She felt her heart sink to the pit of her stomach. The lights were not from an oncoming automobile on the other side of the road as she thought.

Where Is My Daughter?

Henry stood on the front porch, anxiously looking down the driveway toward Redwood Road. It was dark and getting later. Adina still was not home.

The hospital committee meeting went much longer than he had anticipated. It was almost five p.m. by the time he walked out and said goodbye to his colleagues. He made a quick stop at a small market in Santa Rosa to pick up a loaf of fresh bread and some cans of tomato soup. He thought it would be a nice gesture, a sort of peace offering, if he were to cook up some grilled cheese sandwiches to have with a hot bowl of tomato soup for supper. The comforting meal had always been a favorite of Adina's, especially when she was a child. Would she still enjoy a meal like that? How would he know? He hadn't made it his business to know his daughter's likes and dislikes for a long time. Years, to be exact. Whether or not she still liked grilled cheese sandwiches and tomato soup didn't matter. He needed to make some sort of effort. It was much easier when she was little and Luisa was alive. Luisa would have known what to do. Beautiful, sweet Luisa. She was a healer, a mender of wounds who knew how to bring the sunshine with her on a dark and cloudy day. She would have the right words for Adina. Henry didn't even know where to begin. Maybe it was too late to try.

He frowned, nervously chewing the pipe between his teeth, its tobacco long burned out. For years, his pipes had been a comfort to him, like a pacifier to a baby. During the Great War, he smoked cigarettes like a fiend. Everyone did. But after the war, he switched to the pipe. For Henry, smoking the pipe was much more sophisticated, not to mention how he enjoyed the taste of a fine whiskey or cherry soaked tobacco. Even Luisa loved the rich, candied aroma whenever Henry lit up. Especially cherry. She loved it so much that for their last anniversary, she gifted him a beautiful new hand-carved pipe and two tins of cherry tobacco. He adored her for it. When she died, he threw out what remained of the tobacco that hadn't been smoked, as well as the hand-carved pipe. He hadn't smoked cherry tobacco since.

Henry turned the pipe over, tapping it on the edge of the porch rail. Bits of ash and unused tobacco fluttered to the rock garden below. He pulled out his pocket watch to again check the time and peered into the darkness toward the end of the drive, expecting to see Adina's bicycle turning onto it, just as he'd seen her do day after day for years. She may not have known he always watched for her, but he did. Where was his daughter?

Inside the house, the telephone rang, piercing through Henry's thoughts. "Adina Luisa, finally," he said as he burst through the door, running to the telephone in the hallway. He cleared his throat. "Hello, Adina, is that you?"

"Dr. Robbins?" said the voice on the other end. "This is Major Williams from Camp Windsor."

Henry gathered his thoughts. "Oh, yes. How are you, Major Williams? Is everything all right?"

There was a brief silence on the line, then some muffled words spoken to someone who must have been standing next to the major.

"Major Williams?" Henry said.

"Dr. Robbins, would you be able to come to the camp right away? We have a situation. I think it would be a good idea for you to be here." The major's voice was guarded.

"What is the problem, Major Williams? Has someone been hurt?"

"No, not that we know of yet. If you could just come here as soon as possible, I'll give you what details we have when you arrive."

Henry paused, waiting for more information from the major. Only silence. "Yes, of course. I will be there as soon as I can," he finally responded. "Thank you, Major." He put down the receiver and removed the handkerchief from his pocket to wipe the sweat from his palm, when he realized he still held his pipe, vice gripped, in his hand. Tucking it safely in his pocket, he wiped the soot stain it left on his palm, grabbed his coat and hat, and quickly made his way to the car.

31

Road Block

Daniel slowed the motorcycle as they approached the lights. The closer they got, the more certain it became. Two Army jeeps sat parked side by side, facing them in the middle of the highway, their high-beam lights obscuring Daniel's vision. He shielded his eyes with his hand. Two MPs stood next to the vehicles. Each carried a holstered sidearm.

Adina's heart beat voraciously, as though it would devour her from the inside out. Fear swept over her so that she couldn't catch her breath. What had she done? How could she have been so stupid, so selfish to think that this was a good idea? Silly, stupid, childish. These were the words that mocked her now. Her newfound freedom, the liberation she'd embraced and waved over her head like a victory flag... Would it now be her defeat? She held tightly to Daniel with trembling arms, whispering his name laced with regret.

One of the MPs walked forward with his hands raised, motioning for them to stop.

Daniel stopped the motorcycle, placing his foot on the ground. Adina held him, burying her face in the back of his neck. "I'm so sorry," she said.

"Adina, it will be all right."

She held him tighter, feeling like the little girl holding on to the lifeless body of her mother as her father tried to take her away. Letting go meant never seeing her mother again. It meant being alone. She laced her fingers together in front of Daniel. Hot tears stung behind her eyes.

"Step away from the motorcycle and raise your hands," one MP shouted, placing a hand on his sidearm.

Daniel grabbed Adina's hands. "Meine Leibe. It's all right." His voice was gentle and reassuring, though his eyes told a different story. "Please, Adina. You must let me go."

"I can't," she whispered in his ear. "They'll take you from me. I'll never see you again." The tears streamed down her face.

"You don't know this. It's different now, Liebe. The war is ending," he said, turning toward her and gently kissing her lips.

Reluctantly, Adina unlaced her fingers, allowing her arms to drop to her sides. She placed her feet on the ground to steady herself.

Daniel stepped off the motorcycle. He helped Adina off and laid the motorcycle on the ground. Facing her, he gently stroked her cheek, brushing a tear from her eye. "Ich liebe dich," he said, touching her lips with his finger.

"I said, hands in the air!" The MP removed his sidearm.

Daniel turned, raising his hands as commanded. "It's okay, Private. I'm coming. There is no need for the gun." Slowly, he walked forward.

Adina followed a few steps behind. "He didn't do anything wrong!" she yelled. "It was all my fault. We were only gone for the day, on our way back to the camp now. Please, don't do this," she begged as the tears caught in her throat.

The MP took Daniel's hands and handcuffed them behind his back. "What in the world got into your head, PW? Where did you think you would go? And with a civilian too."

Daniel walked in full cooperation with the MP to the jeep. "Yes, yes," he said. "It was a mistake. I know this. But I will not give you any trouble. Please, none of the blame should be on Nurse Robbins."

"Hey, you're the nurse that used to come to the camp," the other MP said to Adina. "Holy cow, what are you doing with this guy? That ain't safe, Nurse Robbins." He placed a hand under her elbow. "Come with me to the other jeep. We'll get you back to town safe and in one piece."

Adina ripped her arm away. "Let go of me, Private," she hissed. "I was never in any danger to begin with." She walked to the jeep without help, her eyes never leaving Daniel.

The MP muscled the motorcycle into the back of the jeep, its front wheel and handlebars hanging off the side. Adina sat in the front passenger seat, eyes staring straight ahead. She watched as the jeep carrying Daniel pulled out into the darkness of the highway and toward the city lights. She and the MP followed behind.

Private Baxter stood ready and waiting to open the gate at the first sight of the MPs' return to camp. He flashed a triumphant smirk at Adina as they passed through. She kept her eyes straight ahead, not giving him the satisfaction of acknowledging him.

As both jeeps pulled up in front of the administration office, Adina saw the Oldsmobile parked and waiting. Tipping her head back, she took a deep breath, bracing herself for the inevitable that awaited her inside.

Heimee and Freddie stood outside at the far end of the administration building, looking wretched and miserable. Two camp staff officers stood talking with them.

Daniel was quickly escorted away. Heimee shouted an apology in German to his friend, though Freddie couldn't bear to make eye contact. Daniel turned his head, catching eyes with Heimee, and smiled.

Adina watched, unable to say another word, as Daniel was led down the dark path toward the prisoner tents. Where were they taking him? Possibly to a holding tent? Or maybe back to his own tent? The unknown felt suffocating.

"Nurse Robbins?" Major Williams stood at the entrance of the administration office. "Would you come in, please?"

Adina stood shivering next to the jeep. Flickering light came from the opening of the recreation tent, accompanied by an occasional burst of laughter. Movie night for the men. Two prisoners stood outside for a smoke and to take in the other show across the way at the administration office. She thought she heard them snicker at her. She took one last look down the pathway where Daniel was led. He was gone. Only the darkness remained.

"Adina Luisa."

Papa stood at the office entrance, and Adina wondered at the look on his face. Was it worry or sorrow? His eyes were red and tired, the creases surrounding them appearing deeper than she'd remembered. She walked to the entrance and stopped, standing beside him. She thought, by the twinge in his eye, that maybe he would say something. His lip behind his beard and mustache quivered a bit, but he had no words for her.

"Hello, Papa," she said, walking past him with a casual air.

"Come in, Nurse Robbins. Please take a seat." Major Williams motioned to the two chairs across from his desk.

"I'd much rather stand, if you don't mind," she said, realizing as she spoke just how much her jaw was aching from clenching her teeth.

"Adina, please sit," Papa said.

Her eyes burned into him, the urge to cry just beneath the surface. But she was determined to not let her father see her cry, no matter how much she ached inside. Reluctantly, she sat in the chair. Papa took his seat next to her.

Major Williams clasped his hands on the desk in front of him. A folded piece of paper sat at his fingertips. He seemed hesitant to speak, his friendly demeanor now overshadowed by his duty. "Nurse Robbins," he began, "how long have you had a relationship with prisoner Christensen?"

She tensed in her chair. Looking down, she was oddly taken aback by her father's shoes. He wore the same black Oxfords he'd had since before the war. Her eye was drawn to a scuff on the left toe. He'd obviously tried to buff it out and cover it up with polish but without success. He refused to buy himself new shoes. *There is a war,* he would say. *"Nobody is buying new shoes."*

"Adina?" Papa said.

Aroused from her thoughts, she looked at him. "Hmm?"

"The major asked you a question."

"I'm sorry. What was the question, Major Williams?" she responded.

"Your relationship with Daniel Christensen. How long has it been going on?" he asked again.

She picked at her fingernails. "Relationship? We're friends—good friends, as a matter of fact. He has been very kind to me whenever I've come to the camp."

"Mr. Christensen never forced himself on you? Has he hurt you in any way?"

"What? No! Never." She fought the urge to stand in protest, gripping the edge of the chair. "Why would you ask such a question?"

"Nurse Robbins... Adina," Major Williams altered the tone of his voice, his eyes softening. "It's very important that I ask these questions in order to discover a reason, something that would make sense of what's happened today." He rubbed the back and sides of his neck hard enough to leave a pink streak on one side. "You see, I wouldn't put it past any of the prisoners to do just about anything to get out of here. They all know they'll have to face the music when they're sent back to Europe. I don't imagine that's a happy thought for any of them."

Raising her eyebrows, she shook her head. "I don't understand. What do you mean, 'do anything'?" She eyed the major's fingertips as he tapped at the folded piece of paper in front of him. She could see the handwriting on it. It was hers, the letter she'd written Daniel after meeting him at the back fence the night of the Christmas dance. She felt sick to her stomach, and the hot tears that were dammed up behind her eyes now freely tumbled down her cheeks. "Where did you get that letter? Did you search his things?" She whipped her head toward her father. "This is absurd," she said, her face reddening.

Major Williams held up his hands. "Please, calm down, Adina," he said, as he unfolded the letter, laying it open on the desk. "I won't read it out loud. It's just, the contents of this letter indicate much more than a friendship." He leaned forward. "Please, just tell me. Were you coerced in any way into writing this letter?"

Adina sat in her chair, feeling as though she were shrinking, like Alice after drinking the potion. She was falling down a hole and wasn't sure she would be able to climb back out. She shook her head in disbelief. What kind of a question was this? Coerced into writing the letter? Quite the contrary. Her feelings had never poured out of her so freely in her life as they did when she wrote that letter to Daniel. Seeing her handwriting, even now on the creased paper on the desk, only served to reinforce those feelings. She looked at her father. He, too, picked and fidgeted with his fingernails. He had a curious expression on his face. It wasn't necessarily anger. There was something in his eyes. Something from the past. Something familiar. "I love him," she said, looking at her father.

"Excuse me?" questioned Major Williams.

"I said, I love him. Daniel Christensen and I are in love with each other. He didn't force me to do anything; not write the letter or take him to the coast." With shaking fingers, she pointed to the letter. "But you already knew that, didn't you? And that's all it was—a day trip to the beach because he wished with all his heart to see the Pacific Ocean." She locked eyes with her father. "It was my idea to go, not his. Daniel had nothing to do with it."

Major Williams rubbed his eyes. "Nurse Robbins, do you understand the risk you took today? We are at war. Daniel Christensen is a prisoner of war. He is the responsibility of the United States government. What if there had been an accident, for instance, on that stolen motorcycle? The responsibility for that would be on me, not you. Not to mention that he's a German soldier and a product of the Nazi regime."

"He's different," she blurted, her anger working its way up her spine." He was forced. A conscript. He hates the regime. He hates Hitler." Her eyes narrowed at Williams. "And I'll tell you something else, Major Williams. If I could have found a boat and a captain who was willing, we would have taken it together and sailed away for good."

At that, Major Williams took a deep breath, and, with tired eyes, looked at Papa. "Dr. Robbins, do you have anything you'd like to say on this matter?"

Papa sat quiet, his stooped shoulders causing his coat to puff out at the top, making him look feeble and small. He turned his head toward Adina but would not look her in the eyes.

"Papa?" she said.

The sound of her voice forced him to look at her. The wordless communication between them was brief, fleeting, yet carried a lifetime of emotion. He, too, was tired, the fatigue settling deep within the core of who he'd become.

He then raised his head and straightened his coat. "I trust you will make the best decision for what is to be done, Major Williams," he said.

Adina sighed—her silent submission. "And what is to be done, Major Williams? What will happen to Daniel?"

The major removed his glasses, examining a greasy fingerprint on the thick lenses. "Not much, exactly." He pulled a handkerchief from his pocket and worked the lens. "He'll be kept in isolation for tonight. Of course his free time and passes to town will be revoked." He placed his glasses back on his nose. "And I'll need to file a full report with the war department."

Adina tried to relax her tense shoulders. "Thank you, Major Williams," she said.

"Besides," he continued, "these men will be shipping out soon."

Adina straightened. "Soon? What do you mean?"

"When the war is over. And mark my words, it'll be over very soon. When it is, all these men will be shipped out. There won't be a need for a prisoner camp here anymore."

She stood. "But where, Major? Back to Germany?" She knew the day would come when something would need to happen to the prisoners, she just never saw it through to completion in her mind, especially concerning her and Daniel.

"I've only heard talk, Adina. Some could be sent to England to help in the rebuilding effort. The Germans bombed the hell out of the Brits. But all of the logistics haven't been figured out yet. I'm sure the Russians will want to have their say as well." He stood up from his desk. "Dr. Robbins, Adina, I'm sure you'd like to be getting yourselves home. It's quite late, and I have a busy day tomorrow."

Papa stood, holding out his hand to the major. "Thank you, Major Williams. You've been more than understanding in the matter. I'm grateful."

Williams heartily took Papa's hand in a firm shake. "Of course. We're grateful for your services as well, Dr. Robbins." He then pointed a finger at Adina. "Nurse Robbins, I would appreciate it if you stayed away from Camp Windsor from here on out. I'll have direct orders out to all camp guards to comply with this request. Is that understood?"

She glared at him, waiting and watching to see if he would add anything else. Possibly an *"except for when there's an emergency,"* or something to that effect.

"Well, goodnight then," he said.

Papa walked to the door, holding it open for Adina. She walked past him, eyes to the ground. He followed behind her. "Adina Luisa, the car is this way," he said.

She stopped, turning to him. "My bicycle is back at the O'Briens'."

"Get in the car," he said, walking toward the Oldsmobile. "You can get the bicycle tomorrow."

She stepped forward, raising her chin. "I don't need a ride, Papa. I will get my bicycle, and then I will ride it home." She turned, walking away from him and toward the front gate.

"Adina!" he called out. "Don't be a child!"

"Stop treating me like one," she yelled back.

32

The New Normal

Franklin Delano Roosevelt was dead. The world was in shock. Few Americans really knew just how sick the president was and had been for a very long time. Of course, rumors concerning his health ran wild. Some who had seen him in public said he often looked fatigued and exhibited lapses in memory. Officials quickly squelched the hearsay, covering it up to keep appearances neat and tidy. Then, on April 12, as the president sat in a chair, posed for a portrait, he suffered a brain hemorrhage and died. The strong leader, whose leg braces and chair with wheels were often overlooked by those who leaned on him to guide the free world, was now gone. Vice President Harry S. Truman was sworn in the very same day.

Folks around Windsor appeared to move in a covey of mixed emotions. They deeply mourned the loss of the president, as well as the losses of those the war had stolen from them. At the same time, the Allies were making victorious strides in Europe, with both Russian and American troops encircling Berlin. There was reason to hope, and life moved forward.

Adina poured herself into her daily work, even adding to the schedule Papa set for her. Whether it was an extra home visit or checking and rechecking supply lists and reorganizing shelves in the clinic, she did whatever she could to keep her mind and body occupied from sunup to sundown. Avoiding Papa was her chief goal, though an impossible one, seeing as she worked alongside him almost every day.

The incident of the failed return from the coast was never spoken of again. Adina brought her bicycle home on her own that night, just as she had insisted upon. Papa stopped trying to intervene and drove home alone. He sat in his chair in the living room, still wearing his coat and hat. He sat in the quiet of the house as the clock pendulum swayed, counting out the minutes. Gripping the arms of the chair, he stared at the photograph of his sweet Luisa and waited for his daughter to come home. When she did, she silently went inside, walked down the hallway, into her bedroom, and shut the door. Henry sat in the chair, finally succumbing to fatigue in the wee hours of the night and went to bed.

In the days and weeks that followed, Adina found it was easier to interact with Papa as though he were a colleague or a landlord, rather than her father. That way, she could get through her workday without the plague of failure and disappointment that had sickened her relationship with him for so many years. It took a good deal of effort on her part to make this work. She began setting her alarm clock to go off an hour earlier in the morning, just so she could be dressed for the day and out of the kitchen before Papa came in for his breakfast. This way, she would be in the clinic, medical kit packed and slung across her shoulder, with not as much as a "Good morning" to Papa. She was out the door and riding down the drive before he could say a word. It was worth the extra effort if it meant less heartache for her. For the most part, it worked.

Henry, on the other hand, had begun to try to reach out to his daughter. Whether it was having a meal ready and on the table for her when she finally ended her day or giving her the option to have an afternoon off. "Why not take the Olds into Santa Rosa and go to the cinema?" he said one afternoon. She laughed, saying she had way too much work to finish and couldn't afford to waste her time taking in a movie. He even offered to take her for a cup of coffee at the diner. Her curt reply was, "Not today." For Adina, his efforts were a feeble attempt to rekindle something that had died out long ago. Too little, too late. But to Henry, it was the offering of an olive branch, and the cracking of his heart.

Adina increased her efforts to fill the passing days, to only have to think about and do the things that were necessary to get from one day to the next. But it was a losing battle. Daniel occupied every part of her. Every nook and cranny of her mind and heart belonged to him. She thought about him always and looked for him constantly whenever she rode into town. But she knew he wouldn't be there. He was in lockdown. There would be no free passes for him. Still, she rode past the camp daily. Some days, she'd stand on the streetside across from Camp Windsor, straining to see past the flagpole, waiting. She never saw him but held onto the hope that just maybe, someday she would.

At night, when she was alone in her bedroom, she lay on the bed, staring at the shadows on the ceiling. This is where, with Daniel on her mind, she would make plans—plans for their future and the beautiful life they would live together. When her eyes would close, she would see his eyes, blue and soulful. She would touch his face, feel his breath, his lips on hers, bringing back his scent and warmth. It was here that Adina would fall asleep, only to repeat the process the next day, and each day thereafter.

By the end of April, the fanatical dictator, Adolph Hitler, committed suicide. The war in Europe was ending.

33

May 1945

Stacks of newspapers sat on the sidewalk in front of the Groceteria. The headline read, "It's V.E. Day...The War Is Over!" There wasn't a resident or shop owner in town who wasn't reading the news or blaring it over the radio for all to hear. Laughter and singing, hugging and dancing, all occurring at once in an exhilarating symphony. There were tears of joy for the loved ones who would finally be coming home, as well as sorrow for those who wouldn't.

Hearts remained heavy for those still fighting in the Pacific, as a slow and steady flow of GIs from the European front began to make their way home, some bearing the visible scars of battle. Carl Sanderson's oldest son lost his right foot at the Battle of Cisterna. After spending months being rehabilitated in a hospital in England, he was fitted with a prosthesis and sent home.

Adina received a letter from Jeanie Mae. She would be finishing her service in England and coming home sometime toward the end of summer. The exact date was yet to be set. In typical Jee Mae fashion, she had a big surprise to share but wouldn't say a word to anyone until she was home, not even to her parents. Adina chuckled at the thought. With all that had consumed her heart and mind, she had forgotten just how much she missed her best friend. Adina and Jeanie shared everything with each other, yet there had been so little communication between them since Jeanie left. Adina wondered what Jeanie would think about her falling in love with a German prisoner and held on to the hope that someday soon, she would be able to introduce her best friend to Daniel Christensen.

Adina and Papa fell back into the cadence of their mechanical existence. Up at dawn, breakfast, appointments, clinic, and deliveries. Then home by five with dinner on the table by six, but only if Adina felt like it. She'd be in her room with the door closed by eight. She often questioned whether she was trying to teach her father some kind of lesson by not paying much attention to him. If so, what would that lesson be? That you can't keep denying a person love and attention, especially when that person is your own daughter, and then expect her to continue giving love and attention in return? She had fought that battle for years and lost. Her love and attention was now upon Daniel. There were plans to be made. She needed to come up with a way to stay in contact with him, especially now that the war was over.

End-of-May sunshine beat hot on Adina's head, flushing her cheeks and making her sweat. As she rode her bicycle, a gentle breeze blew softly through the short sleeves of her white cotton blouse, cooling her from the inside out. She savored the scent of the first blooms of star jasmine, a sign that summer was just around the corner. It was hard to believe that almost a year had passed since Papa said the words, "We will treat the Germans." Words that changed her life. How odd that it was her father's connections that enabled them to enter Camp Windsor to tend to the medical needs of the prisoners. The thought of this muddled everything she was feeling concerning him. If it weren't for her father, she never would have had the unique opportunity to meet these men and learn about their lives. Men like Heimee and Freddie. The pair, not much different from the folks around town she'd grown up with, proved themselves good friends when they were there for her in a pinch. Jeanie Mae was the only other friend she had who might have done the same.

And then there was Daniel. Especially Daniel. To think that if it weren't for her father, she never would have met him, never would have experienced the love of this unusual and beautiful prisoner. When

Daniel sat across from her on that first day, she looked into his eyes and knew he was different. His love would change her life forever.

Sally Quinn called the clinic early one morning, requesting a visit. Baby Madelyn had a drippy nose and was running a fever.

Adina knocked on the front door and waited. The sound of baby cries and child's play reverberated from inside. She glanced around. Piles of dried leaves and cobwebs gathered in the corners of the porch. Dust covered the porch glider. The front yard grass and shrubs were dry and overgrown. All sure signs of the struggles of a war widow with two children under the age of three.

The baby's cries grew louder, and Sally opened the door. A screaming, red-faced Madelyn sat on her hip. "DJ, I thought I asked you to clean up those wood blocks," she yelled back toward the living room. "Mama almost fell over them." She swiped strands of damp hair out of her eyes as she turned to Adina. "Goodness," she said. "It never stops. From morning till night. I can't keep up." Taking a dishrag from her apron pocket, she wiped the baby's wet face and runny nose. "I'm so sorry, Adina. Do you mind if we sit out here on the front porch? The house is an absolute disaster."

"Of course," Adina said, feeling sorry for Sally. They were so close in age, yet here was Sally, her husband gone, leaving her with two children to raise on her own. It was a common war story that Adina grew weary of hearing.

"Come on outside, DJ," Sally said. She held Madelyn tight to her hip while she wiped the glider down with the grimy dish towel. "Sorry it's such a mess around here. There's only so many hours in a day. I can't seem to keep up." She sat down on the glider, attempting to soothe the baby in her lap. DJ joyously bounced a red rubber ball up and down the porch steps, oblivious to his crying baby sister and clearly happy to be outside.

Adina reached for the baby. "Looks like you could use some help around here. Let me take a look at her." She lifted Madelyn under her pudgy arms, allowing her to bounce with her feet. She soon stopped crying and began to coo, curiously enthralled with Adina's smile. "That's a sweet girl. No more crying." Two rivers of thick, clear mucus flowed from each of the baby's nostrils. Adina placed her hand across her little forehead. "She doesn't seem to have a fever right now. Sally, would you get my stethoscope out of my kit?"

Sally handed over the instrument, and while Madelyn jabbered away, Adina quietly listened to her heart and lungs. "Everything sounds just fine. No chest congestion, only a strong, thumping heart," she said. Adina's attention was drawn to four beads of pearly white in Madelyn's pink, gummy mouth. The baby's chubby neck and front of her little dress were wet with drool. Adina took a handkerchief from her pocket and wiped off her index finger. She then gently massaged the back and lower half of the baby's gums. Madelyn's eyes scrunched up tight as she yelled in protest. "I think I just discovered the problem," she said. "She's teething. And not just one tooth. I felt at least three sharp little points on her lower gums. No wonder she's so uncomfortable." She wiped Madelyn's runny nose with her handkerchief. "The discharge from her nose is clear, a good sign that there's no infection. Everything else looks just fine."

Sally didn't seem too surprised by Adina's diagnosis. "Teething? I guess that makes sense. I'm remembering Donald Jr. getting all his teeth at once as well." She stared, expressionless, at her little boy. "Wonder why I didn't think of that in the first place?"

Adina's heart ached. How hard this must be for Sally. "You've got a lot on your plate right now, Sally. None of this can be easy for you."

Sally stood and reached for the baby, settling her back on her hip. "I guess now's as good a time as any to tell you," she said.

Adina had already begun packing up her kit. "Tell me what?"

"I'm leaving Windsor. Me and the kids, that is. Soon, actually." Sally looked out across her front yard, sorrow and fatigue now clearly visible in the new creases and dark circles around her eyes. Sadness had aged her, inside and out.

Adina stopped what she was doing. "Where are you going?" she asked. She didn't like what she was hearing. Ever since delivering Sally's beautiful baby girl, Adina felt a strong connection to her.

"We're moving down south to Santa Monica to be with my parents. I can't make it here alone anymore, Adina. Not without Donald. We have no family in Windsor. As a matter of fact, my closest relative, an aunt on my mother's side, lives in Modesto," she said, wincing. "I definitely don't want to go there."

Adina chuckled. "No, of course you wouldn't." She stood, slipping her medical kit over her shoulder. "I completely understand. It will be so good for you to be with your parents. DJ and Madelyn will get to be near their grandparents as well."

Tears filled Sally's eyes. She rocked the baby hypnotically from side to side. Finally, she looked at Adina. "I want to thank you. For everything. I don't know what I would have done if you hadn't come when you did...the day I found out about Donald...the day Maddie was born." She held out her hand to Adina. "I wish we could have become closer friends."

Adina wasn't quite sure how to respond. She would have loved a closer friendship with Sally, but life's course put them on different paths. Now, Sally would take her children and leave Windsor for good. Adina wondered if she were doomed to a mundane, duty-filled existence in her secluded small town, while the rest of the world moved away without her. That couldn't be true. Not when she had Daniel. He was her salvation. She wanted him forever. Even if wanting him meant leaving her father and all that she knew to start a new life on the other side of the world. She welcomed it wholeheartedly.

Adina smiled. "We can write to each other. As soon as you get settled down south, you can write to me with your new address. Then you can keep me up on how you and the kids are loving sunny Santa Monica, and I'll keep you up on all the Windsor news." She laughed. "Which probably won't be much."

Sally nodded and sighed. "Thank you again, Adina, for everything."

Adina squeezed Sally's hand and walked down the porch steps. Mounting her bicycle, she rode down the dirt drive. DJ kicked the red rubber ball in the overgrown grass. "See ya later, DJ," she called back. Turning left, she headed into town.

34

Gift for Daniel

The Groceteria was out of her way, but Adina made a stop anyway, using it to extend her day before having to go home. It was much preferable to secluding herself in the clinic, unnecessarily organizing supply shelves for hours.

Inside, the Philco was blaring a little louder than usual. Carl Sanderson stood behind the checkout counter, laughing with another gentleman, as though they both just heard the punchline of the funniest joke ever told. The air felt lighter, and everyone seemed happier since the war ended.

"Hello there, Adina," Carl called out over the gentleman's shoulder.

"Hi, Mr. Sanderson," she said with a half wave. She'd hoped to go in unnoticed. "Just picking up a few things before I head home." She grabbed a handbasket and made her way in. The market was a buzz of activity. Mothers with children in tow, filling their baskets with who knew what. Kids stopping in after school for penny candy or popsicles on a warm May afternoon. Servicemen, home now but still in uniform, congregated around the magazines and cigarettes, their eyes all turning to her as she walked by.

"Miss," one of them said, tipping his cap.

"Afternoon, fellas," she returned with a smile, hearing one of them whistle through his teeth. So much for going unnoticed. Instead, her confidence bolstered, and she held her head a little higher as she passed. She sensed a much brighter future just around the corner. She gave herself over to it and casually strolled down the canned food aisle. Having no reason to rush, she would take her time, absorbing the joy and levity that surrounded her. Her eyes scanned the shelf with the canned soups. They were stocked with soup at home, but she grabbed a can of chicken noodle and a can of tomato, placing them in her basket. At the end of the aisle, she saw the salted crackers and added those to the basket as well.

Next aisle, home goods and toiletries. Passing up the laundry detergent, bath soaps, and toilet tissue, she stopped at a small display at the end of the aisle. A narrow, five-tiered shelving unit stood with all things appealing to the female sex. The middle two shelves contained face powders and cheek rouge, as well as bottles of cologne and toilet water. The shelf beneath was dedicated to items for the hair—hair nets, bobby pins, and beautiful handmade barrettes and hair pins crafted by a local resident. The bottom shelf was strictly for nylon and silk stockings, which were tucked into a white wicker basket. It looked pitifully empty, with only one or two pairs inside, sadly crumpled and snagged. A handwritten sign tacked to the outside of the basket read, "New Stock Coming Soon!"

But it was the top shelf that sparked Adina's eyes. Tubes and tubes of lipstick glistened atop the glass-bottomed shelf. The Sandersons obviously had received a new shipment containing popular brands, and even ones with French names Adina had never heard of before. An advertisement with a gorgeous photograph of Lana Turner sat in front. The actress wore a juicy red color or her lips, glancing out the side of her eyes, as though she was saying, "You could have these lips too." Adina picked up the elegant gold tube that sat next to the picture. The name on the bottom read "Brick Red." Removing the top, she carefully turned the base, bringing the bullet to the top. It looked just as luscious as it did on its famous model, yet she couldn't understand why they picked a drab name like "Brick Red" to describe it. She doubted it would look as lovely on her but tossed it into her basket nonetheless and didn't bother to check the price.

She rounded the corner to the last aisle, which normally contained odds and ends of every kind, from pots and pans to brooms and mops. There were fishing rods and tackle, hammers, and boxes of nails and screws sitting right next to stationery items, writing paper, fountain pens, and the like. The plethora of items and their arrangement never made much sense, but Adina enjoyed exploring the shelves anyway. As she neared the stationery, something caught her attention—a solitary box of Faber-Castell colored pencils. It was the only one of its kind on the shelf. She had never noticed anything like it in this aisle before— possibly because her eyes had never been open to the beauty of art before Daniel. She remembered how when they were at the coast he marveled at the colors of the sky and sea, wishing he had colored pencils or paints to capture it. And now, here sat one lone box of colored pencils. Adina picked up the tin box and removed its lid, revealing twelve vibrant colors. Daniel would have no trouble mixing them to achieve more colors. She placed the tin in her basket, along with two new black-tipped pencils and a new notepad for herself, and walked directly to the front counter.

Carl was finishing up with another customer as the cash register rang out. "Have a nice day," he said. He looked up at Adina. "Howdy-do, Adina. How are you this lovely May afternoon?" he asked and began removing the items from her basket.

"I'm doing just fine, Mr. Sanderson. Thanks for asking."

He punched in the price for the soup and pressed the oversized Enter button with the palm of his hand. He then lifted out the lipstick. "Bet you're happy to see the new supply of these beauties," he said, waving the tube.

"I sure am. They're just lovely, Mr. Sanderson."

"You were smart to buy today. I just stocked those shelves late last night. They'll be empty again before you know it." He entered the price. The punch of his palm sent the numbers to the register's little window. One dollar and seventy-five cents. "That's a nice treat for you, Adina."

She raised her brow. It was a bit more than she would've wanted to spend. Brushing the guilt aside, she told herself she hadn't splurged in a long time.

Carl continued, ringing up the box of salted crackers and the two pencils and pad of paper, finally picking up the tin of colored pencils. "Are you taking up drawing?"

She straightened. "You could say that."

He peered over the top of the register, and she curved her lips into a soft smile, hoping the twinkle in her eye might suffice. When he didn't press her any further, she breathed a sigh of relief.

Finishing up, he hit the total. "That'll be five dollars and twenty cents."

Adina reached into her kit and pulled out her coin purse. She had four, one-dollar bills and just enough change to reach five dollars and two cents. "Mr. Sanders, I've only got five dollars right now. Can I get you the twenty cents when I come back tomorrow?"

He smiled at her. "No need to worry about twenty cents. You show me one of your best drawings and we'll call it even." He rang in her cash and handed her a brown paper sack with her purchases.

She nodded, eyes wide. "Umm, sure, I'll do that." She took the bag. "It may take a while, you know—to learn and all. But I'll be sure to show you a, umm, drawing, someday." She turned and headed toward the door. "Thanks again, Mr. Sanderson," she called out as the bells on the door rang out overhead.

35

Adina stood in front of the Groceteria with her bag of purchases. She wanted Daniel to have the new colored pencils now but had no idea how she would get them to him. She hadn't seen any prisoners around town for days, so having one of them deliver the gift to Daniel was out of the question. Of course, she could always venture across the O'Brien property and take the trail to the back of the camp where she could hide out behind the trees in hopes of seeing Heimee or Freddie again. But she was tired of hiding in the shadows. She felt no shame in being in love with Daniel Christensen. She didn't care who knew. In fact, she was fairly sure word had spread around the entire camp after the night they were caught coming back from the coast. She had been denied access by Major Williams and her father. How was she supposed to have any type of contact with the man she was so deeply in love with if she didn't pursue it herself?

Standing there next to her bicycle, she decided to do something about it. Reaching into the paper sack, she pulled out the notepad and one of the pencils and began to write.

Dearest Daniel,

My heart is aching to see you, but I know that it isn't possible at this time. I remembered you said that your sketches were missing some color. Hopefully these pencils will help you to recreate the beautiful day we shared. I think of you constantly.

My heart belongs to you alone,

Adina

She added one of the black pencils to the colored pencil tin, wrapped the note around it, and placed the gift in the front basket of the bicycle. She then started out toward Camp Windsor.

Private Mike Baxter was standing guard at the front gate. He stepped forward as Adina approached, narrowing his eyes and holding up his hand.

Adina stepped off her bicycle, taking the gift out of the basket. Tentatively, she walked toward Private Baxter. She realized that laying on the charm and flirting with him wasn't going to work anymore, at least not like it did that first night she visited Daniel alone. She had misled the private just enough to get what she wanted. He'd been jilted by her, and for one of the prisoners, nonetheless. The look in his eyes said it all.

"Hello, Mike," she said, sheepishly. "How've you been?"

"You're not allowed to be here, Nurse Robbins. I have direct orders from Major Williams," he said with no smile and no winks.

She took a few steps closer. "I know, Mike. I'm well aware of the major's orders. I wouldn't have come here if it wasn't important." Adina's attention was drawn to some unusual activity going on behind the fence. A gray bus was parked in front of the administration office. Prisoners were lining up, some with rucksacks. Others were milling around as usual.

"You need to turn around, get on your bicycle, and leave immediately," Mike said, his tone sharp.

Adina started at the sound of his voice. She placed her hand on his arm, causing him to step back and place his hand on his side arm. She knew he was serious. "Mike, please. I just need to ask if there is a way to get this gift to prisoner Daniel Christensen?" She handed the wrapped tin to him.

He took it from her, turning it over in his hand. Tipping his cap up, he pursed the side of his cheek. "I guess you don't know then, do you?"

Her stomach lurched. What was that look on his face? "Don't know what?"

He pulled his cap back down just above his eyes and smirked, laughing slightly under his breath. "They're starting to ship these Nazis out of here. As a matter of fact, I believe your favorite PW should be boarding that bus right there behind me. They'll be pulling outta here this afternoon."

Adina's eyes widened, feeling as though she couldn't catch her breath. "What do you mean, shipping them out? Today? Where will they go?" Again, she reached for his arm.

He looked at her hand as though it were a nuisance. "Did you think they were gonna stay here forever?" He shook the tin box near his ear.

Adina felt her chest tighten. "Please tell me. Do you know for sure that Daniel Christensen will get on that bus today?"

He didn't answer her question. He just hemmed and hawed, chuckling through his teeth.

"Please, Mike. I need to speak with Daniel. Are you sure he's leaving on that bus?"

He noticed the tears welling in her eyes. "Yes, I'm sure, Adina. I've seen the lists. It will take weeks to get them all out of here and back on trains to the east, but I'm certain Christensen was on the list for the first group to be bused out of here today." He pulled his arm away from her hand, his eyes softening. "I'm sorry. I have my orders. I can't let you in."

Adina's mouth hung open, and she shook her head. Standing on her toes, she craned her neck, looking past Baxter to get a better idea of what was going on. Was Daniel actually leaving the camp today? Now? This couldn't be happening. She needed to get to him.

Whipping around, she picked up her bicycle and pedaled as fast as she could to the end of the road. She hadn't even realized she'd left her gift for Daniel in Mike Baxter's hands.

Her heart pumped fiercely, and the tears on her cheeks dried from the wind almost as quickly as they rolled down. She arrived at the

O'Brien property and didn't bother with leaving her bicycle at the head of the trail. She rode it all the way through the dirt and ruts, over rocks and tree roots, until she arrived at the back of the camp where she first met Daniel. She could see a movement of men in and out of the last two tents, carrying their rucksacks. Still, there was no sign of Daniel. There was no sign of Heimee or Freddie, either. A hopeless panic set in.

Follow the Bus

Sweat dripped down the back of Adina's neck as she pedaled with all the strength she could muster. She skidded left, back onto the main road. Just as she was approaching the camp road, the gray bus pulled out in front of her, making a slow left turn. She stopped to watch, eyeing each window, her heart racing. *He's gotta be in there*, she thought. And then, she recognized the soft wave of his red hair. Sure it was him, she rode forward toward the bus.

Daniel turned, catching sight of Adina. Eyes wide, he placed his hands on the window and mouthed her name, pounding on the glass as the bus pulled away.

Adina followed behind, legs aching and lungs burning. She kept on, despite the fatigue, staying as close as she could.

Getting up out of his seat, Daniel made his way to the back of the bus. With one hand on the window, he watched her as she pedaled with all her might to keep up. Her mouth moved, crying out his name. He turned toward the driver. "Please, stop the bus, just for a moment," he yelled, yet it was near impossible for his voice to be heard over the chatter of voices and wind rushing through open windows. He looked back out the window. Adina still rode behind as they slowly made their way through town.

The bus came to a stop sign, allowing a mother pushing a baby carriage to cross the road. Adina stopped, drawing in deep breaths. Her eyes, pained and tear-filled, stared at Daniel, and he at her. Daniel

Christenson, the German prisoner and unlikely love who stepped into her life so suddenly and unexpectedly. For a brief moment in time, like a dream, he became her hope, her salvation. She loved him more than she'd ever loved anyone...So much so it hurt.

Daniel retreated from the back window for a moment. When he returned, he held the tin of colored pencils and the letter up against the glass so she could see. His eyes held hers, filled with oceans of blue, and he mouthed the words, "I love you."

She watched him and touched her lips.

A black cloud of exhaust puffed out the tailpipe as the bus accelerated forward, curving onto the main highway.

Again, Adina followed, pumping her tired legs with all her might.

The bus moved faster now, its guttural sounds growing fainter. Exhausted, she grunted and pedaled until her legs gave out. She stopped at the side of the road. No longer could she see Daniel's face, but still, she raised her arm high in a wave, watching until the last bits of exhaust drifted on the breeze and the sound of the motor could no longer be heard.

She got off the bicycle, allowing it to fall into a pile of dirt and weeds, as soup cans and boxed crackers tumbled from the basket. For a moment, she stood staring down at the meaningless items she'd purchased to bring home to her father. Items that weren't needed, nor would he have noticed or even cared. Such a waste.

Sitting down in the dirt next to her bicycle, she picked up one of the cans. She brushed the dirt from it, held it to her chest, and sobbed.

36

Struggle to Get Home

The idea of going straight home didn't make sense to Adina. Nothing made sense. Sitting in the dirt on the side of the road, she looked at the pitiful items lying there and then back down the highway through eyes that burned with tears. She caught sight of her dirty hands and noticed a grease stain on her cotton skirt. She knew she couldn't just sit there, yet she didn't have the heart to move. She hoped maybe this was all some kind of mistake and that if she sat still long enough, staring hard down the highway, just maybe she'd see the gray bus in the distance coming back into town. But she knew her hope was in vain. Daniel was gone.

Adina stood. She picked up the soup and crackers, placing them back into the paper sack in the basket. She brushed the dust and dirt from her skirt and wiped her eyes with the back of her hand. She then began the slow, tedious ride back into town. There was no reason for her to rush. Why would she? She had no place to be. She felt lost and alone.

People and houses sailed by in a blur. Somebody called out a hello, but she didn't respond. She'd ridden this route day in and day out and knew it by heart. She could ride it with her eyes closed if she wanted to, as though riding through a recurring dream.

Before she knew it, she'd ridden back to the O'Brien property. She left her bicycle at the back trail entrance and began walking to the back of Camp Windsor. The shadows from the oaks were lengthening. She wasn't paying attention to the time.

Adina walked to the spot where she and Jeanie first hid and sat, secluding herself in the shadows, under the arms of the leafed-out oak trees. Hugging her knees to her chest, she watched PWs meandering in and out of tents, oblivious, as if nothing had happened to disrupt their day. How could that be when her day had been turned upside down, obliterated. The whole earth should be groaning in agony, just as she was.

Mike Baxter had said that today's bus was only the first of many. Her heart softened at the thought of Mike. He obviously made the effort to get the gift to Daniel before the bus left. Daniel held it to the window so she could see.

"*Baxter, good man...*" That's what Major Williams had said.

She watched as a small group of prisoners in the back field kicked the ball around. Adina couldn't escape the memories it stirred. Daniel's smile, hair tousled and falling in his eyes as he approached the fence. "*Guten Tag, Fräulein.*" The cold, starry night after the Christmas dance. How he held her, kissed her. Every touch, every breath, each laugh, each word... All of it haunting, excruciating, wonderful.

The bell for the evening meal rang out, and she closed her eyes. The sun was setting, bathing the tents in its purple glow. Adina rose from her hiding place and began the walk back, the laughter and voices of the men echoing behind her in the soft rustle of the wind through the trees.

Talk with Mama

The Oldsmobile sat parked in the drive. The clinic was closed up and dark. Adina stood next to Mama's rock and flower garden, noticing a few piles of pulled-up dried weeds. It appeared her father had tried to clean up some of the dead overgrowth. Obviously, he'd given up. "Didn't even throw out the dead weeds," she said.

She knelt in front of a stacked tower of rocks. The one at the base was the largest, smooth and round with a mesa surface. Five other rocks were stacked on top according to size, one on top of the other, to a height of about four feet. She ran her fingers over the cool stone and wondered at its ability to still be standing, perfectly balanced, after all these years. All the rocks in her mother's garden had withstood the test of weather and time. "They're all still here, Mama," she whispered to the rocks. "But you're not."

She waited, listening. "If you were still here, I would've told you all about Daniel. He's wonderful, Mama. I love him so much. He's unlike anyone I've ever known. He's everything I've ever wanted." A gust of wind blew the dead weed piles up against the wall beneath the porch. "I can't talk to Papa about any of this. He's a cold, empty container, living in a life of lies. He's as hard as these rocks, Mama."

Adina stood, narrowing her eyes at the rock tower. "You went away, and Papa's never been the same." Lifting her foot, she placed it on the third rock from the top and pushed. The top two rocks fell into the dirt. The remaining three still stood, unmoved. Pursing her lips, she bent over and wrapped her hands around the top two and pulled. It took more effort than she had anticipated, but they moved, tumbling into the dirt with a thud—all but the large rock at the base. Determined to see her destruction through to completion, she squatted, gripping the large rock with both hands. When it wouldn't budge, she used her fingers to dig out the dirt from around and under the perimeter. Then, with a firm grip on each side, she pulled on the rock, grunting out her frustration, until it released from its dirt encasement and flipped over next to the other rocks. Pill bugs and earthworms scurried about in search of a new hiding place.

Standing up, the lines around her mouth and eyes now more at ease, she turned her back to the garden, grabbed the paper sack from the bicycle basket, and went inside.

37

Letting Go

A burnt aroma wafted throughout the kitchen. Adina set the paper sack down on the counter and walked over to the stove where a pot sat over a low flame. Its hissing contents had bubbled down to a charred, brown paste stuck to the bottom. Assuming it was leftovers or some such thing her father was reheating for their supper, she turned off the flame and moved the pot to a cool burner. She then removed the cans and box of crackers from the sack, wiped away the remaining road dust, and put them in the cupboard. She washed her hands and splashed cool water on her face, drying off with the dishrag. She then mechanically folded the dishrag, laying it on the counter.

The setting sun cast a speckled, orange glow through the lace curtains in the living room. The house was quiet, amplifying the sound of her steps on the creaking wooden floorboards as she walked into the entryway. She hung her medical kit on the coatrack and hooked her beret on top. Running fingers through her tousled hair, she turned to see Papa quietly watching her as he sat in his chair in the living room.

Adina looked at him, curious as to why he didn't say a word when she walked in. He just sat there, looking at her. She felt raw, broken. Like that pot left sitting on the flame with its burnt, bubbling remains, the angst and sorrow of today's events boiled inside her. She had just watched as her last hope for a life of love was carried away on a gray bus in a cloud of black smoke. Yet here her father sat, watching her in silence. Everything inside of her screamed for answers.

"You knew, didn't you?" she blurted, her eyes accusing. She walked toward him, the tension tightening with each step she took.

"Knew what, Adina Luisa? What is it you are referring to?" he asked, sounding genuinely confused by the question and possibly shocked that she was speaking to him after weeks of avoiding him at every turn. He held his empty pipe, turning it in his hand. The circles beneath his red, watering eyes appeared darker.

"The prisoners at Camp Windsor," she said, finding it difficult to discern the look on his face. "They've started sending them away." Her throat tightened.

Papa looked down at the pipe, gently rubbing his thumb over the polished wood on the bowl.

Adina stomped a foot forward to stand directly in front of him, forcing him to look up at her. "Answer me, Papa. Did you know?" She clenched her fists at her sides.

Henry laid his pipe in the dish on the end table and looked up at his daughter. "Yes, Adina. Major Williams let me know that the first group of prisoners would be leaving today."

She steadied herself. "And did you know that Daniel Christensen would be in that first group?"

He took a deep breath. "Yes, I knew this as well."

She squeezed her hands tighter, her fingernails digging into her palms. "You knew?" she asked, hearing the breathy screech in her voice. "You knew he would be leaving today, yet you said nothing to me." She shook her head. "Why, Papa? Why would you keep it from me? I had no time, no chance to see him or talk to him before he left. I could have at least found out where he was being sent." Her eyes begged him for an answer that would make sense.

"You were told to have no contact with that prisoner, Adina Luisa. That is why I said nothing. It was for your own good."

The feelings of betrayal overwhelmed her. For her own good? What possible good could he be talking about? From the time of her mother's death, he'd denied her his own love and attention, and now he was denying her Daniel. Where was the good in having the love of her life taken from her?

Her eyes reddened, filling with tears. "Why, Papa? What have I done that you would despise me in this way? I miss Mama too. Do you blame me that she's gone?" Unable to look at him, she turned away, looking out the window. The sun, now beneath the horizon, darkening the sky in deep blue.

"Adina," Papa responded. "I have never despised you, nor would I ever blame you. I've always taken care of you. How is it that you could believe such lies about me?"

She whipped her head around. "Lies? Who are you to speak of lies? Your entire life is a lie. You are a Jew, Papa. Why do you hide this? Our name isn't Robbins. Isn't that true?"

Papa looked over at the photograph of his wife. He shook his head, his eyes pleading with the ghostly image for help.

"Papa?"

He stood from the chair. "Adina, you must stop this. Please, I am asking you to not become hysterical over the things of which you have no understanding." He walked to the grandfather clock. Opening its cabinet door, he reached in and stopped the pendulum from swinging.

"Rabinovitz," Adina said.

Papa stood silent, brushing the weighted brass chains with the tip of his finger.

"Henrikas R. Rabinovitz. That's your name, isn't it, Papa?" she said. "Did you think I wouldn't find out?" She walked over to him. "You're a Jew. Mama was a Jew. The family name proves it. That makes me a Jew as well. Isn't that right?"

He turned to look at her, the corner of his lip quivering as pain filled his eyes. "Why are you doing this, Adina? You have accused me in this way before, have you not? I believe the exact accusation was 'Fearful Jew,' yes?"

Turning back to the clock, hand over hand, Papa pulled the chain of the first weight. There was the familiar sound of mechanical clicks as the tubular brass weight ascended to its place. "What do you intend to accomplish by bringing this up to me? There is no way you could understand decisions that were made many years ago."

Adina boiled inside, her eyes piercing him from behind. She wanted to break him, as he had broken her. "Understand?" she said, hands shaking. "How could I possibly understand anything of the truth when all you've done is hide and lie?" The tears that fiercely burned behind her eyes now poured down her cheeks. "Ever since Mama died, all you've done is—"

He spun around to face her. "Tyla!" he yelled.

Adina placed her hand to her mouth. The intense volume of her father's voice shocked her. She recognized the Lithuanian word "silence." Letting her hand fall from her parted lips, she pondered her father's eyes, glassy, filled with years of pain, heartache, and anger.

"Papa, I—"

He held up a finger. "Do not ever speak of your mother with anger," he said, his voice choking. Tears pooled in the creases around his eyes. "And do not use her as an excuse for your anger with me, Adina Luisa." He slowly walked past her. Sitting down in his chair, he rested his elbow on his knees and gazed at the photograph of Mama, lamplight bouncing off the waves of gray in his hair.

Adina was afraid to move, afraid to speak a word. Cautiously, she sat down on the sofa next to her father's chair and waited.

"I was very young, Adina, when the pogroms happened in my country. Too young to remember the brutal killings that happened in other villages and towns. What I do remember is the fear that my mother and father lived with. I remember my mother crying at night for her family members who were murdered, the ones she would never see again." He paused, folding his hands tightly in his lap to steady himself. "After the Great War, the difficulties continued. It didn't seem to matter that I bravely served as a medic on the battlefield. I saved the lives of generals and privates alike; I did not discriminate. Yet back home, in Vilna, my medical practice failed to produce what we needed to survive."

He stopped and looked at her. "You must understand, Adina, the Jews were always blamed. Blamed for the war and all the world's problems." He looked again at the photograph. "But your mother, my precious Luisa, she was the only one who mattered to me. She brought me comfort and kept me sane in the middle of it all. She made me so very happy. And when you were born, mallo dukra," he said, looking into Adina's eyes, "my life was complete. You and your mother were all I needed to live."

She watched her father, intently listening to him, feeling as though her emotions were running out of control. He was finally being honest with her, yet she wasn't sure she wanted to know the truth anymore. What difference would it make now? She had given so much and tried so hard to break down the walls before, only to be wounded in the process.

Papa looked at her, a spark of light in his eyes. "Do you remember it, Dukra?" he asked. "You were two years old."

She looked confused. "Remember what, Papa?"

"When we left Lithuania, Adina Luisa. Can you not remember any of those days?"

Adina shook her head. "I have no memory of any of it." She was flabbergasted. How could he think that a two-year-old would have memories? She looked at the picture of her mother. "Even when I see the photographs, there is nothing."

"It was in the winter, 1927. Everyone felt the economic crisis coming. We were struggling but getting by. We had each other, that is what mattered. My mother and father were long gone, but Luisa still had her family nearby. Her mother and father, your grandmother." He lovingly looked at Adina. "Oh, how they treasured you, their only granddaughter. Also, Luisa's brother, Levi, your uncle."

Adina ached to remember. She had grandparents who loved her, yet she had been led to believe she had none. Now they were dead and gone. She looked at Papa in disbelief. "Why, Papa? I don't understand. Why did we leave them?"

He turned his eyes down, looking at his hands. "I was afraid, Adina. Afraid of the hate. It was only getting worse with the financial depression setting in." He looked at her, eyes pleading. "I knew that if I didn't take steps—great steps—to protect my wife and daughter, we would not survive it."

Adina didn't speak. She listened to her father painfully recount his memories. No matter how difficult it was, she knew she needed to hear it.

"Great steps," he continued, "meant letting go of everything: our family, our heritage, our faith. I knew what this would mean for your mother. I didn't ask her, I told her how it would be. We would no longer be Jews. We would leave Lithuania for a new life in the United States. Our name would be changed. Gone would be the only life we'd ever known. Luisa would have to leave her mother, father, and brother." He ran his hand over the back of his neck. "Yet that was not the worst of it," he said, his voice shaking as the sorrow intensified.

"What, Papa? What else is there?" Adina asked.

"Your mother would have no more contact with her family. She would deny her Judaism, and they, in turn, would reckon her as dead. All of us would be dead to them." He covered his face with his hands and wept.

Adina sat paralyzed. The last time she heard her father cry was when she was twelve years old, her birthday, the day her mother died. His words whirled in a tornado of questions in her head. Some of the story was beginning to make sense, while so much remained unanswered. "I don't understand," she said. "There must have been some form of communication after you settled us here in the US. Mama's family couldn't have completely cut her off. Are you telling me she never heard from her parents—my grandparents—ever again?"

Papa pulled a handkerchief from his pocket and wiped his eyes. "Your mother wrote many letters. At least twice a month, she wrote. None were ever answered. Eventually, any letter she wrote was sent back, 'Return to Sender.' Still, she kept writing." He looked at Adina. "That is, until I forbade her from writing anymore."

Adina narrowed her eyes. "Why would you do that?"

Papa straightened his back, folded the handkerchief, and tucked it back into his pocket. With his head held high, he looked again at the picture of Mama. "Because, Adina, we were dead to them. Truly dead. Writing letters would only cause an unrealistic hope to languish." He took a deep breath. "It was done. We had our new lives here in the United States, in this wonderful town where nobody knew who we were. Do you think that was easy? We were foreigners, fresh off the boat. I had a thick accent. My English was atrocious. My medical license came from another country. We were starting all over again. It took patience and determination to achieve a good standing and to earn the trust of this community. Your mother and I opened our medical practice and worked very hard to achieve the respect of the residents in this town. We persevered, and it paid off. The Robbins name is a respected name in our town, Adina Luisa." He stood from his chair, turning toward her. "It remains so to this day. I will do nothing to destroy that." Taking his pipe from the dish, he tapped its bowl twice on the palm of his hand and tucked it into the pocket of his trousers. He then walked toward the kitchen.

Adina stood, her mouth open. Papa's words repeated in her head. Patience, determination, achieving respect, the name Robbins. None of it made sense. Nothing he said answered her one important question. Why the lies? In an instant, she stepped forward, as though her tongue had been loosed, and she spoke. "Then I was right, Papa. You're a coward." Her voice was calm and controlled.

Papa stood with his back to Adina. His shoulders rose and fell with each breath he took. He turned his head, taking one more look at Louisa's photograph, then at his daughter.

Adina wondered at the softening of his facial features. The look was familiar, like a warm childhood memory. His dark blue eyes pooled with tears once again.

"Love has the power to make us do things we never thought we were capable of doing. Wouldn't you agree, Adina Luisa?" He walked into the kitchen. "Come, Adina," he called. "It appears I've ruined our supper."

38

October 2011

The rain stopped, giving way to clusters of white clouds in a crystal blue sky. The sun shone brightly through the SUV windows, bringing its warmth inside.

Talia sat quietly, having just taken in her mother's story. She stared out the window at the moving landscape.

Adina examined her daughter's face and wondered what Tali was thinking. A story such as the one she'd just told on their drive could either be shocking or intriguing, especially since she had never told anyone before—not Jeanie Mae, not even her late husband, Joseph. The only other person who knew about Daniel Christensen was Papa, and he was gone.

"Talia, I need to make something a bit clearer. Your Grandpa Henry… He was a good man. A very good man. After Daniel was gone, he wrote several letters to the war department on my behalf, seeking information as to where Daniel may have ended up. I was writing my own letters, yet I had no idea that my father was doing the same. There came a day, about a year later, when I just happened to see one of his inquiries in a stack of outgoing mail. Of course I questioned him about it."

"What did he say?" Tali asked, not turning her head from the view.

"He informed me that this particular inquiry would be the eighth one he sent over the course of the last year. He had little to no hope that it would bring any different conclusions. He had been receiving the same responses from the war department that I had received. Nobody could tell us where Daniel was."

Tali turned to Adina. "Mama, it was wonderful that he did that. It must have helped you greatly to know that he truly did care."

"I always knew he cared. I knew he loved me. Even my childish angst couldn't take that truth away. And yes, it did help to know he had written all those letters. It helped to know he cared about what I needed. It was definitely a step to break down some of those bricks in the wall. It was like a healing balm on my wounds. I believe it was for him as well." Adina folded her hands and closed her eyes. "Baruch Hashem. He knows I am grateful." She then lit up with yet another memory. "Also, a good piece of news. Jeanie Mae came home a married woman."

Talia's face lit up. "What?"

"In her letter, Jee said she had a surprise. That was it. She fell in love with a British captain in the RAF. Captain Jerald A. Smythe. They were married in London before she came home. She brought him to meet her family, and of course, everybody loved him. They were perfect together."

"You were with the two of them when you met Daddy, right? At that ball in San Francisco. I know I've heard that story before."

Adina smiled. "Yes, they begged me to come to an officers' ball in the city with them. Sort of a last hurrah before they returned to England. That is where I met your father. Truly, I never thought I'd be able to love another man. But then your kind, gentle father stole my heart. Though it didn't happen all at once, you see. Joe—your dad—had to return to Europe to finish his service, but he wrote to me constantly." She paused, gazing out the window. "And in his letters, he taught me what it truly meant to be a Jew and to embrace our culture. Joseph was my stable rock—my guide. It was through those letters that I fell in love with him."

Talia grabbed hold of Adina's hand. "I'm so glad you did," she said, pecking a kiss on her mother's cheek. "And what about my grandfather? Did he ever come back to his faith?"

"Only in secret, Dukra, like that day I walked in on him as a young girl."

Adina barely recognized the town that had once been her home. What she remembered as open fields and farmland had been replaced with shopping centers, industrial buildings, and hotels. So much had changed in almost sixty years. Nothing looked the same.

The driver signaled and took the exit that read "Old Redwood Highway, Central Windsor." He came to a stop at the traffic light.

Adina sat forward, her eyes darting. This was the main road she knew so well. The same road she'd ridden her bicycle up and down every day. Back then, she could do it with her eyes closed. "Excuse me, sir," she said to the driver. "Would you mind taking my daughter and I on a bit of a detour?"

"Mama," Talia said. "We don't have time. It's almost one thirty. We have an appointment with the director of the historical society at two. You must be tired and hungry. You haven't eaten since before our flight."

A spark ignited in Adina's eye, and she patted her daughter's knee. "It'll be just fine, Tali. We have plenty of time. Besides, it's a very small town," she said, eyes glued to the road ahead.

The driver looked back at her in the rearview mirror. "Sure thing. Where would you like to go?"

Adina placed a finger to her lips, turning her head right, and then left. "I think we should turn left."

The driver made the turn, and Adina scouted the sites all around her as they passed under Highway 101 and made their way into town. She tried to visualize the past. Where was the Texaco station and the post office? They were gone. They passed by a set of old brick buildings that seemed familiar.

"I think that used to be Sanderson's Groceteria," she said, pointing to the right. To the left, she saw Ginny Hopper's old house. It was still standing, and other than a different coat of paint, it looked exactly the same. Several of the original homes along the main street, homes she'd visited many times, were still intact. Her excitement rose, drawing her further back in time. Visions of the past combined with the present unfolded before her eyes. Her heart beat with anticipation. They passed the Windsor Grange, and she knew it was just up ahead.

"Just a bit farther," she said to the driver as she held on to the seat in front of her. "It should be just up ahead." She then saw a street sign that read "Old Camp Road." She told the driver to pull over. The car came to a slow stop, parking in a bike lane.

"Is this the spot?" the driver asked.

Adina peered out the window. "Yes, I believe it is." She sat still, staring through the glass at the grassy field where the oak trees grew along the narrow road. In the distance stood a bare flagpole. She reached for the door handle and found it locked. "Would you unlock my door, please?"

"Mother, wait," Talia said. "There's no place to walk here. You might fall."

"Then walk with me, Tali," Adina said as she removed her seatbelt and opened her door.

Talia, running around the back side of the car, came to assist her mother.

Adina grabbed her cane and took hold of her daughter's arm. "I'd just like to walk up the road a piece."

The gravel road was puddling and muddy and dipped down to one side. Talia steadied Adina by holding onto her arm as she took careful and calculated steps toward the road entrance.

"Just up here, Dukra," Adina said, pointing with a shaky finger.

There wasn't much left of Camp Windsor. The flagpole still stood where the entrance once was, a dilapidated shed and a couple cement foundations just beyond. To the far right was the pullup bar, the same one the prisoners had used. Off in the distance, the view of the vineyards and hills was still as beautiful as Adina remembered. Standing there, that's just what she did. She remembered.

Like a flood, the memories came, solidifying all she had just recounted to her daughter on the drive, and so much more. Then the emotions came, more than sixty years' worth of buried sorrow. Tears filled her eyes, and she placed her hand to her chest. Had she truly never grieved her losses? The losses of her mother and Daniel. Leaving the town she loved so dearly, as well as the friendships that touched her life. And not having more precious time with her father. Why bury it, hide it until now? Breathing in the scent of wet earth and listening to the wind as it rustled the leaves of the oak trees, a thought came to her. Maybe she was more like her father than she realized.

"This is where the camp was, isn't it, Mama?" Talia asked.

Adina held tightly to her daughter's arm and swallowed back the tears. There was nothing left here. All that once was would have to be tucked away in the recesses of her memory.

"Yes. This is where the camp once was."

"It sure is lovely out here," Talia said, taking in the view.

Adina smiled. "It is. Still one of the most beautiful places I've ever seen." She squeezed her daughter's arm. "Now let's get going. We don't want to keep the director of the historical society waiting."

The Windsor Historical Society was run out of a 1930s-era home situated across from a majestic row of cypress trees. Adina recognized the house, remembering it as being built by one of the prominent families in Windsor, yet not recalling their name.

Rows and rows of tract homes had been built up around the old Spanish-style house, making it look a bit out of place among its modern surroundings. Still, the neighborhood had a welcoming air, with children playing in manicured yards, an occasional dog walker, and the mailman making his daily deliveries. Not much different from the town Adina knew long ago.

The driver pulled the SUV alongside the walkway in front of the old house and turned off the engine. "I'll be waiting right here," he said. "Take all the time you need."

Talia took hold of Adina's hand. "Are you ready?"

Adina looked out the window with curious yet tired eyes and gently squeezed Talia's hand. "I've come this far." The corner of her mouth curved up on one side. "It wouldn't make much sense not to be." She gave her daughter a wink.

The door to the old house gave way to dark hardwood floors and stained wood archways. Antique furniture and curio cabinets lined walls and filled nooks, laden with vintage heirlooms and articles of the way of life in the town long ago. Framed photographs and paintings depicting town founders and their families hung like ghosts in residence on cream-colored walls. The musty scent of aged fabric and lavender filled the air.

Talia held open the creaking door for her mother. Adina let go of her daughter's arm and walked inside, feeling as though she were walking through a portal, transporting her back in time. She was surrounded by so many artifacts, pictures, and trinkets, she wasn't sure where to begin. The house was quiet, and there didn't seem to be anyone around to direct them.

"I wonder where everyone is," Talia whispered. "We did have a two o'clock appointment, didn't we?"

Adina, much too enthralled with all that surrounded her, didn't respond. With her cane for support, she walked around the main room, allowing her eyes to take in as much as she possibly could. There was so much to explore. She circled around and walked through an archway into another room. In the center of the room was a glass cabinet. The sign above read, "Camp Windsor." Her heart skipped a beat. She thought to get Talia's attention but, glancing back, noticed her daughter was in the other room, deeply engrossed and hovering over a large old book.

Slowly, Adina walked toward the display case. How could it be that after so many years, her steps felt just as they did the first time she walked into Daniel's tent that fall evening so long ago? How her heart raced, just as it was racing now. What did she think she would find? A memory? A photograph of him? "It's not his tomb," she told herself.

She stood at the display, gently placing her fingers on the glass. Above hung photographs of the prisoners. Black and white pictures of the men wearing the uniform with the PW, working in the fields, pruning trees. Another one of the men playing their instruments in the camp band. Looking closer, she thought she recognized someone. "Heimee. It's Heimee," she whispered. There were pictures of the tents and the outbuildings, the Camp Windsor sign, and the gate at the entrance. All of it, just as she remembered. More photographs filled the inside of the glass display, as well as handwritten letters sent from family members of the prisoners. Adina stood on the tips of her toes, carefully poring over every photograph, making sure to read every bit of information she could. But there was nothing of Daniel there. She wondered what she was expecting to see. *Sixty-six years have gone by,* she thought.

"Mama?"

Adina started at the sound of Talia's voice.

"I'm sorry to startle you, Mama. Mr. Lockwood, the historical society director, is waiting for us in his office."

Adina removed a handkerchief from her coat pocket and dabbed the corner of her eye. "Let's not keep him waiting, shall we?" she said and took Talia's arm.

The director's office was furnished much like the rest of the museum, from heirloom framed pictures on the walls to the antique maple desk. The desk's one modern feature was the laptop computer sitting on top of it.

An older gentleman stood from behind the desk. He had thick, wavy gray hair and a mustache to match. Warm, friendly smile lines encircled his eyes. He wore a pair of glasses that rode low on his nose, conjuring memories for Adina of her father.

"Hello, Mrs. Ableman," he said, holding out his hand. "I have been so looking forward to meeting you."

Adina took his hand. "Thank you, Mr...?"

"Lockwood. Please, take a seat." He folded his hands in front of him on top of the desk. "First of all, I must apologize for not giving you more information as to why I wanted you to come." He removed his glasses. "You see, the item we've come upon seems—well, how shall I say this? It's much too sentimental of a piece to not present to you in person."

Adina swallowed down hard the lump that had formed in her throat. "Item?" she asked, searching the man's eyes.

Reaching into the side drawer of the desk, he pulled out a small drawstring pouch. Its fabric was old and worn, and tattered threads sprouted from its bottom side. He handed it to Adina.

With trembling hands, she took the pouch and held it.

"It's really quite amazing how we got it," he said. "Go ahead, take a look."

She carefully loosened the ties of the pouch, her stiff, arthritic fingers giving her grief, and opened it. Reaching inside, she removed a tattered, brown-leather journal. Turning it over in her hands, she knew at once. "It's Daniel's," she said, holding it to her nose, breathing in the scent of the leather.

"We were amazed at its preserved condition," the director said.

She untied the leather straps and opened the book. Though smeared and faded, Daniel's mother's inscription remained. Adina then began to turn the frail pages, as Talia watched over her shoulder. Sketch after sketch, as though time had stopped right on the page. There was Daniel's brother, Max, and the old man. The village with the cobblestone streets from his home in Germany. She came to several sketches of oak trees and squirrels, as well as drawings of the camp with its tents and the broken barbed-wire fence. She paused to look at her daughter and smiled. The turning of the next page took her breath away. She stared at it in wonder.

"Mama, are you all right?" Talia asked.

Adina looked at the picture as though it were a dream. There on the page was a full-color sketch of the coast at Goat Rock. The browns and golds of the sand, the greens of the sea grass and sage brush on the hills.

The deep blues and grays of the ocean and the purple glow of the setting sun. But it was what Daniel had added that took her back, causing her heart to feel as though it would melt away. For there she stood in front of the crashing waves, her face turned as though she were looking directly at him where he stood that day. He had captured her perfectly. Her smile and eyes, so bright with the exact colors of green, gold, and blue. Hazel eyes. Her windswept, auburn hair blowing to the side. How was it possible that he saw her that way? He knew her so well, better than anyone else.

"He used the colored pencils. The ones I bought for him that day,"

"I'm sorry?" Mr. Lockwood replied.

"I had left a gift for Daniel, the day he was shipped out. It was a box of colored pencils. I left it with the private standing guard at the gate. The guard was angry with me then and I didn't think he would give the gift to Daniel, but he did and—" Realizing she was rambling, she smiled, looking up at the director. "How did you get ahold of his journal, Mr. Lockwood?"

The director folded his arms, sitting back in his chair. "Actually, it was your name."

Adina looked at him, confused. "My name?"

"Turn to the last pages," he said.

She flipped to the last pages of the journal, and there, written in beautiful cursive, was her name. First, "Adina Luisa Robbins." Then under that, "Adina, Adina, Adina," over and over. Next page, "Adina Robbins, Windsor, California, USA."

"I tried to send letters," Adina said. "For two years after the war. I contacted the war department here in the United States, trying to get information on where he'd been sent. I was told that most likely he would go to England first, to help with the rebuild. I wrote to the British embassy, but they had no records of a Daniel Christensen. Nobody could help me. It was as though he had just disappeared."

Mr. Lockwood placed his glasses back on his nose and looked over a document on his desk. "Well, he sort of did, as you said, Mrs. Ableman, disappear."

"Please, call me Adina," she said, her curiosity spiked to know the truth.

"You see, Adina, Daniel Christensen *was* shipped over to England after the war ended, just like many of the prisoners were. From there, we think he may have been sent to Germany. We can't be sure. Back then there was such a push to simply get the prisoners out of the United States that many became lost in the process. Many ended up in—how should I say this—less than forgiving hands." His eyes grew serious.

Adina's heart sank. "There were Russians in Germany."

Mr. Lockwood nodded. "The Russians were very much in control of Germany at that time. German soldiers returning home were not treated well, even the ones who had opposed the Nazis." He paused, eyeing Adina with concern. "Let's just say that the Geneva Convention didn't mean much to the Russians."

"Please, tell me what happened to him," she said.

He took a deep breath and continued. "Several of the prisoners from Camp Windsor, including Daniel Christensen, were transported to a work camp—a gulag, if you will—just on the outskirts of Siberia. Once someone, whether a political prisoner or prisoner of war, ended up in one of these camps, they were never heard from again. It was unlikely that any would survive the camp. Most died from disease, the elements, or starvation." Again, Mr. Lockwood paused, raising his eyebrows to look at Adina. When she didn't say a word, he continued, "We know that Daniel was at this particular gulag because the journal you're holding was found nailed shut behind one of the walls in a bunkhouse where the camp was. It was discovered as the old building was being torn down. From there, the journal was sent to one of the local government historical departments. It finally ended up in the hands of a German historic records firm. Then came the process of finding out who Adina Luisa Robbins actually was."

"And how did you manage that?" she asked. "Which name did you use? Robbins, Rabinovitz, or Ableman?"

The director chuckled. "All three, actually. It wasn't an easy task, but we finally found you. And here you are."

She nodded her head. "Yes, Mr. Lockwood, here I am." Looking at him intently, she hesitated at her next question. "Is there any chance he may have survived?"

Mr. Lockwood removed his glasses and laid them on the desk. "From the little bits of information that we have, nobody is known to have survived the camps in that area. I'm sorry, Adina."

Adina nodded, feeling her daughter's hand lightly rest on her shoulder. There was no shock in her eyes, no sinking feeling in the pit of her stomach. Only a gentle acceptance that Daniel Christensen was gone. For a moment in time, he was her beautiful German prisoner. He loved her for who she was, made her feel love in ways she'd never felt before. He ignited a desire within her to be true to herself and to embrace her Jewish heritage. Daniel told her she was mutig...brave. He made her want to be brave. He changed her life for the better.

She closed the leather journal, tied its straps, and carefully placed it back in the tattered fabric pouch. Then with some effort due to her stiff joints and aching hips, she stood from the chair and handed the pouch to the director.

"Oh no, Mrs. Ableman," he said, holding up his hands. "You misunderstand. The journal is for you to keep. It has your name in it. It belongs to you."

She smiled at him, her hazel eyes blazing with the confidence of years gone by. "No, Mr. Lockwood. This journal belongs to the town of Windsor. Put in that glass case in the other room where the town can cherish it and learn from it."

Adina took her cane and extended her arm to her daughter. "Let's go, Dukra. There's so much more I want to show you before we fly home tomorrow."

Photos of Camp Windsor

The Entrance to Camp Windsor circa 1944
Published with permission of Windsor Historical Society

Tents at Camp Windsor circa 1944
Published with permission of Windsor Historical Society

Pruning in the Fields circa 1944
Published with permission of Windsor Historical Society

Prisoner of War Band circa 1944
Published with permission of Windsor Historical Society

Author's Note

More About Camp Windsor

In the small rural community of Windsor, California, the US government established a prisoner of war camp in an unused migrant labor camp and named it Camp Windsor. As one of the satellite camps of Camp Beal, Camp Windsor was situated on seventy acres and housed, on average, 250 German prisoners of war. The camp atmosphere was said to be generally relaxed. Four-foot-high barbed-wire fences outlined the perimeter with only two low-standing guard towers, which sometimes went unmanned. Thirty guards were housed in tents along with the prisoners.

With most local farm workers fighting in the war overseas, the prisoners at Camp Windsor presented a welcome source of labor to local farmers. They harvested hops, grapes, and prunes. There was one successful, yet brief, escape attempt by two prisoners who only wanted a glimpse of the Pacific Ocean. Once recaptured, they were returned to the camp no worse for the wear. For the most part, recorded stories and memories of Camp Windsor were fondly positive. Townsfolk recalled captured Germans who were grateful to not be fighting anymore, as so many were forced to do so against their will. They were happy to be safe, with a bed to sleep in, food to eat, and the ability to provide a hard day's work. Camp Windsor was the first of the satellite prison camps to open in 1944 and the last to close, in 1946.

More about the Volkssturm and Forced Conscription

In 1944, Germany's Volkssturm was the mobilization of German civilians to form a militia to resist the Allies. It was a last-ditch effort to bolster the dying Wehrmacht. An estimated six million men and women between the ages of sixteen and sixty served in the Volkssturm. Out of these, only about one million were armed. The rest were used as labor forces. A general conclusion of the Volkssturm effort is that it was a failure of epic proportions. For the most part, these recruits were poorly led, poorly trained, badly equipped, and comprised those who were physically and chronologically unable to withstand the severity of combat. Though accurate numbers are hard to come by, it is estimated that some 175,000 of these civilian troops were killed.

"While the egalitarian image of the Volkssturm was a facade, millions of men were forced into it."

(Thompson on Yelton "Hitlers Volkssturm; The Nazi Militia and the Fall of Germany, 1944-1945")

(Thierry Etienne Josephy Rotty; Senior Controller at NATO)